D0040945

JUDENSTAAT

JUDENSTAAT

SIMONE ZELITCH

A TOM DOHERTY ASSOCIATES BOOK
NEW YORK

This is a work of fiction. All of the characters, organizations, and events portrayed in this novel are either products of the author's imagination or are used fictitiously.

JUDENSTAAT

Map by Jennifer Hanover

A Tor Book
Published by Tom Doherty Associates, LLC
175 Fifth Avenue
New York, NY 10010

www.tor-forge.com

The Library of Congress Cataloging-in-Publication Data is available upon request.

ISBN 978-0-7653-8296-2 (hardcover)
ISBN 978-1-4668-9000-8 (e-book)

First Edition: June 2016

Printed in the United States of America

0 9 8 7 6 5 4 3 2 1

For Harold Gorvine, *l'shem shamayim*

AUTHOR'S NOTE

One morning, I was lying in bed with my husband, and I said, "What if a Jewish state had been established in Germany after the war?"

The very idea was a provocation. Yet I continued to consider: If Theodor Herzl was right when he wrote *Der Judenstaat* in 1896, and the only answer to what he called "the Jewish Question" was a Jewish state, then what if that state had been established as a kind of national project of reparation and even retribution for the Holocaust? How would that shape its history and a politics and national character? I think I speculated out loud for a while—it's that kind of marriage—and then my husband went to brush his teeth, returned, and said, "What about the Soviet Union?"

What about the Soviet Union? It existed. So did Stalin, who might have had his own plans for a Jewish homeland; he had created one called Birobidjan and slaughtered most of its inhabitants in purges. What about East Germany? It didn't exist, or more precisely, this country would encompass much of its territory, though its borders, I decided, would be those of Saxony, east of Berlin. And yes, there's a wall; it keeps out German fascists. The story begins in 1987. The wall is about to fall.

There is no single model for Judenstaat, though a reader will quickly find some parallels: two nations—Israel and East Germany—founded within a year and a half of each other. Both nations claimed to be a response to fascism, a way to move beyond tragedy and to rebuild ruined lives. Judenstaat borrows freely from the trajectory of both countries, with periods of postwar renewal, isolation, suppression, upheaval, and liberalization. A rough timeline appears at the end of this book. As a fortieth anniversary of my country approached, surely it would be time for a historical reckoning.

In constructing what follows, I couldn't help but consider the nature of counterhistories, like Philip K. Dick's *The Man in the High Castle,* a novel that considers what would have happened had Germany and Japan won the Second World War and goes beyond the thought-experiment to look at the fragile nature of history itself. Then I was led, inevitably, to Orwell's *Nineteen Eighty-Four,* a vision of a future where the past can shift depending on who writes the story.

There is no answer to the Holocaust—or as they say in Yiddish, the Churban. There is no single answer to the Jewish Question. We keep on asking question after question. Perhaps the question that most shaped what you're about to read is not national, but personal: What happens when you lose everything, but have to go on living? Who do you become?

We all know suffering is real. But in the end, all countries are imaginary.

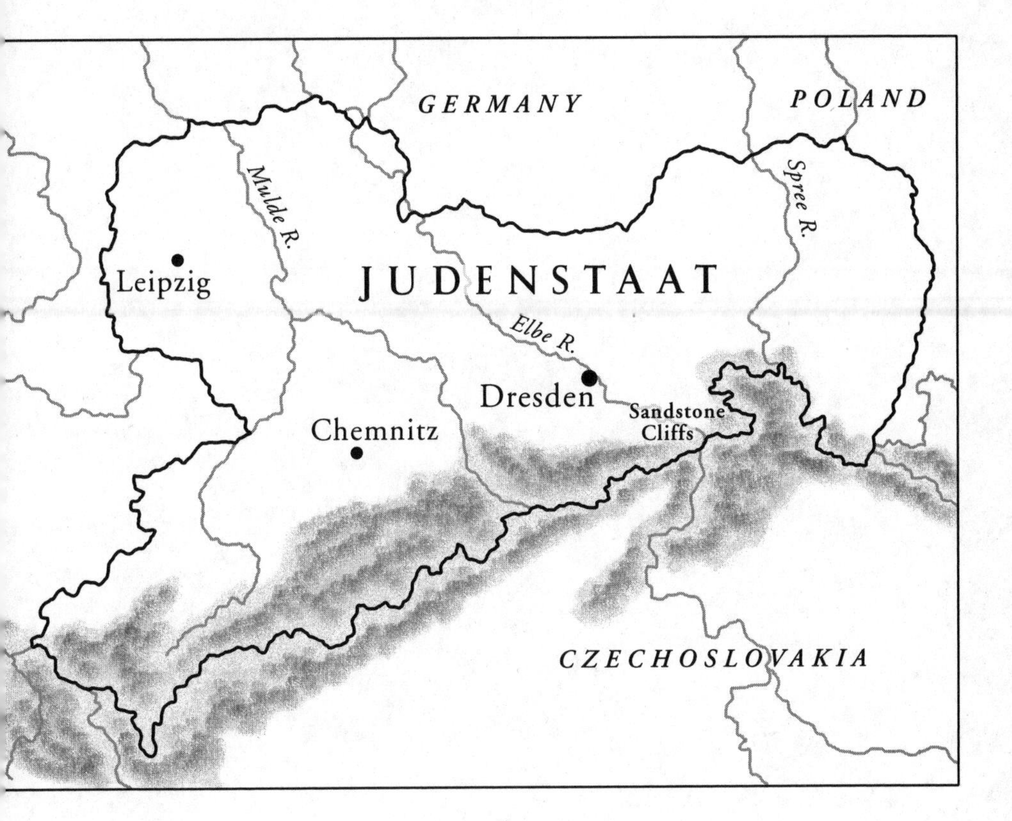
GERMANY
POLAND
Mulde R.
Spree R.
Leipzig
JUDENSTAAT
Elbe R.
Dresden
Sandstone
Cliffs
Chemnitz
CZECHOSLOVAKIA

Out of this universal feast of death, out of this extremity of fever, kindling the rain washed evening sky to a fiery glow, may it be that Love one day shall mount?

—Thomas Mann, *The Magic Mountain*

When you leave a graveside, you mustn't look back.

—S. Ansky, *The Dybbuk*

A Specter Is Haunting Judit

1

GERMANY was the birthplace of Jewish culture. A thousand years ago, we planted roots in Ashkenaz that flowered and brought forth the fruit of the Enlightenment embodied by the fabled Moses Mendelssohn and the Age of Reason.

THE CATASTROPHE—the great CHURBAN—which recently befell the Jews of Europe has demonstrated with new urgency that THE RIGHT OF THE JEWISH PEOPLE TO A HOME IN GERMANY IS IRREVOCABLE.

WE DECLARE that from this moment, the 14th of May 1948, under the establishment of Allied Forces, that the German territory once designated Saxony will henceforth be JUDENSTAAT.

PLACING OUR TRUST in the future, we affix our signatures to this proclamation, and commence with our national project. The very place we faced our death is where we'll build our lives.

Thus, the ghosts of 1948 surface on the editing machine in black and white montage: washed out faces of survivors, signatures on a declaration, flat-bed trucks, a lot of rubble. No audio. Given all the footage Judit had to edit for the Fortieth Anniversary Project, it was easy to roll through the film and make her cuts. And somehow, she was supposed to find something explosively prophetic, something worth keeping. Not this old stuff. The heavy feeder cut and spliced, and the cells floated somewhere else.

But those cells weren't the specter haunting Judit. It was her husband's ghost. That specter stretched its long legs on a work bench, and leaned in to watch her. Its gray eyes were assessing.

Judit said, "I know what I'm doing." There had been a time when she'd been too self-conscious to address the ghost, but Hans had been haunting her for three years.

The ghost of Hans Klemmer never spoke, but its presence worked on her as sharply as her living husband's. It engaged her in a phantom conversation. It didn't like those cuts; it took a hard line against editing. It noticed things she didn't, like cells littering the floor, and it took stock of those cells as though she were an executioner. Every time she cut a frame, she slit a throat.

"It isn't what they're after," Judit said. "Everyone's seen the footage of the signing back in secondary school." How could silence not feel like rebuke? She could only say, "I don't have time for this. I'm on a deadline."

But Hans was dead. Maybe she could shake off Hans Klemmer's specter like a sinus headache. She kept a box of aspirin in a drawer and took two now. That helped sometimes.

And sometimes not. Why did Hans haunt her in the archive? She never saw the ghost anywhere else. The specter should have haunted the Opera House, where he'd been murdered. It would create a public spectacle. Isn't that what specters are supposed to do? To the extent that one could be rational about a ghost, she found its presence difficult to fathom.

Worse, it kept staring, judging. The living Hans had loved her, and this ghost had her husband's form, but it never touched her. It just stared. Did she want it to go away? It made things difficult. She said, "How can I work when you look at me like that?"

That was Judit's question to answer. After all, she was the archivist. Hans was just history. At least he was now.

They were still naming things after him, the Klemmer Regional Concert Hall, Klemmer Memorial Park, and so on. Because Hans died on Liberation Day, every May 14th he was remembered. Then there was the statue of him by the Opera House, with the wavy hair, the baton, and the flying coattails. The first time Judit saw the ghost, she'd thought it was another statue that someone put in the archive as a joke, but who would hate her that much? Then the statue moved its head and yawned. She'd dropped her coffee.

That was the trouble. There was what some clever historian might call cognitive dissonance between Hans and Hans, between the noble statue and the ghost. And there would always be the statue because of how he'd died, three months after he'd been appointed Judenstaat's first Saxon conductor.

The occasion was momentous. To have this ethnic German—orphaned in '46—raise his baton before the premiere orchestra of the Jewish state in celebration of its liberation by the Soviets, how could it help but feel like one of those ruptures that draws a line between one age and another?

The national anthem sounded new again:

"Risen from ruins and turned towards the future
Let us serve you for the good—"

Then Hans froze. He slumped forward, crumbled into the podium, and fell down with it.

* * *

Germans killed him—angry unrepentant Saxon Nazis who marked him for assassination as a collaborator with the Jewish state. Of course a lot of people hated Hans. Judit hadn't been there that night, but she knew hundreds of survivors of the camps had picketed the Opera House when Hans had been appointed. Before the murder, there'd been those phone calls, late at night, with thick, strange silence on the other end. After a while, Judit and Hans had let the phone go on ringing, or Hans would pick up and leave it off the hook under a pillow. Could she remember dates and times? Could she remember if there'd been static on the other end? Or other voices in the background? Why hadn't she and Hans reported those calls to the State Security Police?

Those were the kinds of questions she had to answer during the weeks when she was a public widow, escorted from place to place by a polite Stasi agent who also stood by her bed at night. She was pumped full of so much Valium that there wasn't a clear distinction between days of interrogation, and nights when she would find herself in a nightgown that she didn't recognize, and she told them everything she knew and cursed her own precise and nimble memory for detail that persisted even when she was sedated.

Once they found the men who did it, she was left alone. She took to wearing Hans's old duffle coat. It served as camouflage. Still, she was sometimes invited to memorials, especially on Liberation Day. Judit's mother, Leonora, took an interest in such things. Last May, she'd dragged Judit to a performance given in Hans's memory at the Opera House, a choral recital by Saxon children, and she kept whispering to Judit how wonderful it was to see that not all of them hated us, and how important it was to teach them young, before their minds were poisoned by their culture.

"I wouldn't know, Mom," Judit said. Why had she agreed to come?

"Well, maybe you and Hans never had children of your own, but these are your children, honestly, Judi, and that's what matters. Don't you agree? Aren't they your children?"

What could Judit do then but stare at the program with its silhouette of Dresden's restored castle and the Opera House's dome? Below, in flowing script: "The Fire Returns: A Dresden Season to Remember."

What was the point of memory? Nothing surprised her. Even now, with the lights switched off, her touch was automatic—drawer open, film into the feeder, and before she even looked down, she knew just what she'd see, the long-shot of workers climbing the scaffolding of that same opera house. It was the first structure rebuilt in '49. Old news, and worthless.

If she remembered everything, then how could she find—what did it say in that press release about the documentary—explosive footage? She ought to experiment and fumble for a change, move her hand a little to the left. There was an unmarked case.

She slipped the film into the feeder. And what was this? A Soviet production, surely. Hand-held camera, by the look of it. Rubble and ruins, and another one of those eternal flat-bed trucks of camp survivors, and Leopold Stein again. He stood before a crater that was once the site of Dresden's Great Synagogue. Stein's mouth was moving, obscured by the beard that gave the footage a date: pre-'47. She knew what he was saying, what they'd written in that declaration, that Germany was Jewish at the root, that if the Jews needed a home it was right under their feet. This was their monument. This was their prayer-house.

Old news. But there was something about those enormous hands of Stein's, big as boxing gloves, tracing a circle in the air and resting in a bridge below that beard. Old beard. Old bombed-out crater, blurry Soviet liberators with their rifles. She switched off the machine.

"Why stop?"

Judit froze. Her eyes stayed on the empty screen.

"So you don't like that story?"

It wasn't Hans's voice. It wasn't her intern, Sammy Gluck. It had to be a Stasi agent, but not the one who made regular courtesy visits.

Something creaked, then creaked again deliberately. Judit turned. It was so dark that she could make out no more than something darker. Then, that high, coarse voice again.

"You better like it. You know what I risked to get into this fucking fortress?"

Not Stasi. Without warning, the sharply living presence backed her into the work bench, and he slammed something onto the table and a pile of footage toppled over. So did Judit, nearly. Then he was gone.

He'd left a note. She switched on the viewer. The bulb was dim but steady. The text itself was written in the neat copybook handwriting of a child.

They lied about the murder.

2

AFTER liberation, most refugees pass through Germany and move on, but Jews remain. Some live in Displaced Persons camps near Munich but the greatest number concentrate in the Soviet sector. The German state of Saxony is home to close to a million Jews who survived the concentration camps or sought a temporary home in the Soviet Union through the war and crossed the Czechoslovak and Polish borders. They occupy crude barracks built on the grounds of Saxon spas, or castles expropriated from their German owners.

Although the refugees are under U.N. auspices, the true administrators are the Bundists, the Jewish Socialists and trade unionists who'd spread through Eastern Europe in the years before the war. Most survivors are not interested in politics, but they know where their bread is buttered, and who serves the strongest coffee.

Above a coffee urn, a banner: WE ARE HERE. The credo of the Bund: a refrain taken from the Ghetto Partisans.

The coffee that the Bundists serve is, as Leopold Stein says, "as strong as an ox, as rich as a Rothschild, and as black as the soul of man." Not that Stein believes in souls, but if history dictates that souls are black, then who is he to argue? Stein lived out the war underground with the Free French in the Rhineland and has emerged with his shirtsleeves rolled up his hairy arms to build a Jewish state in Germany.

Stein has a cloud of ill-kept hair. He is never quite clean-shaven. He'd grown a beard in hiding and it came in gray. In some surviving images, he peers out through all that hair into the camera, embarrassed at his resemblance to a rabbi.

Yet famously, Stein says, "Why pray at all?" He always adds that Moses Mendelssohn was drawn to enter Germany two hundred years ago through the gate reserved for Jews and cattle, and when the guard asked him his trade, he replied, "Reason." In these unreasonable times, that's what Jews bring—intolerance of nonsense, pragmatism, deep generosity, and vision.

Stein came of age after the Great War when Jews from Poland flocked to his hometown of Munich. Although it used the Hebrew alphabet, their Yiddish was almost completely German. German burned inside their Yiddish like light refracted in a lantern. Surely, Germany lived inside those Eastern Jews, ancient Ashkenaz where Emperor Charlemagne invited Jews a thousand years ago and where they'd brought their gifts from East and West and flourished until driven into exile.

Those Jews returned. And all the while, the Germany Stein knew, the Social Democratic Germany, receded. He felt a persistent urgency, a wild compulsion that made him travel through the country to form alliances and hone his argument, and even all the way to Vilna for an international conference of Yiddishists and Bundists in 1929. He urged them with all the passion of a man with a fixed idea to build a Jewish state in Germany.

They laughed at him. They listened, but they laughed, those poets and linguists who had no use for states at all, or Socialists who'd walked out of the Third International or who stayed and then regretted it and who had weathered years of fixed ideas. "*Young man,*" said one delegate in stately Litvak Yiddish, "*If I were you, I'd take a walk around the park and calm down. For what do we need a country?*"

Stein had an answer, but it wasn't one they would be ready to accept. Not yet. He would quote Comrade Stalin on the National Question. Here were a people with a common culture. All that was missing was a land.

"*Then go to Moscow,*" someone countered. "*I hear they treat Jews well there if they stay on their leashes.*"

"I'm not a Russian," Stein said in his insistent German, a language any Yiddish speaker understands. "I'm a German. So are you. Come join me there."

That started a back-and-forth so fierce and hostile that Leopold Stein felt battered and invigorated. Afterwards, a few delegates came up to him and asked if he'd written a position paper laying out his platform. They went to a café and kept on talking until the place closed down. By 1945, all of those people would be dead.

Now 1947, in Schmilka Camp, Stein fills a coffee urn at a water pump. In a camp outside of Gorlitz by the Polish border, Stein at a long plank desk below a banner: WE ARE HERE. The credo of the Bund. The very place we faced our death is where we build our lives. That's what it means, to live in Judenstaat.

Stein in a work shirt and dungarees, holding a spade over his shoulder. In Munich, his hometown, Stein filmed with a hand-held camera by American occupation troops as he walks none-too-steadily through the milling crowd, overwhelmed by the force of his own logic, and the camera lingers on two men who share the Bundist newspaper, *A Home.* "No Hope for U.S. Visa in Bavaria. President Truman Urges Surviving Remnant: Go to Saxony!"

Beside Stein, Stephen Weiss, Auschwitz survivor, bird-of-prey demeanor. Weiss is not a Bundist. Weiss is not a brawler. Few images of Weiss survive, though his early prominence is not disputed. Where there is a Stein, there is a Weiss. History demands it. Weiss is the editor of *A Home.* Yiddish and German are two of his eight languages, and he shares with Stein the common language of a fixed idea. He was born in Vilna. Talent and ambition led him to Berlin. Then, following what he thought were sound instincts, he crossed the border to Vienna, then to Budapest, and at the prospect of induction in a labor battalion, he chose to stay with distant relatives who promised him a job at their printing press in Warsaw. This was in 1939.

Stein knew Weiss before the war when their paths crossed briefly in Berlin. Weiss had been a different man then, a kind of aesthete, always with a cigarette in a holder, babbling and posing. Now, the cigarette is gone. He looks like an emaciated owl. No one can match Weiss's single-minded energy, nor can they understand what drives him.

Stein, Weiss, a crowd of adolescents, and row after row of boots. The film stock, rare and near decay, is not officially catalogued. The boots are laid out on a long table. Stein's people have stuffed each boot with a note. The young men remove the notes in a hurry, papering the raw dirt as they measure the soles against their feet, and swap them with their neighbors. All the notes are printed in bold German typescript: WE ARE HERE. The credo of the Bund. You have your boots. Now, don't go anywhere.

Yes, all of this is well documented, the continuity of Ashkenaz, the people and the nation, through generations of development and then expulsion and renewal, and the stirring of a revolutionary Age of Reason, and finally the Churban. What monument will mark what they have lost and have survived? Their lives themselves will be that monument. Is Stein naïve to open negotiations with Soviets and Americans and keep the country nonaligned? That is the work of Stephen Weiss, who arranges meeting after meeting.

What would become of the Jewish Autonomous Region of Birobidjan on the Manchurian border, or of England's failed experiments in Palestine and Uganda? Their failure is fresh proof that the Jewish state is right under their feet, and fascists fear Jews for that very reason. Yes, Leopold Stein can be very persuasive. Surely he emphasizes humiliation of the enemy. Truman may not be drawn in that direction. Stalin is another story.

There will be opposition from some quarters, opposition that can only be overcome if they act quickly, before forgetting starts. Forgetfulness will be the enemy. A promise is revoked and then renewed and then revoked so many times that when they approach the checkpoint, Stein and Weiss cannot be sure that the guards who meet them there will follow orders.

The orders are to raise a flag. Now, speculation: the night before, Stephen Weiss laid out the materials, and by the light of a Primus stove, he patched together the design. He knows the cloth; he knows the thread. He unfolds the flag that afternoon; in spite of careful preservation, it is in danger of unraveling.

Weiss does not believe in flags as a rule. He has lived under too many of them: the crest and crown of the Hapsburgs, the double-headed eagle of the Russian Empire, the optimistic flags of four republics, the Soviet flag, and, of course, the flag that brought him close to death. But this flag, he believes in.

Of course, a man who's lived under so many flags can never claim a country. Such is the nature of a Cosmopolitan, opportunistic, cynical, and ultimately loyal to no one but himself. Weiss's role is a cautionary tale. But here is documented fact. That day, at an army checkpoint in 1948, Stein and Weiss meet at an arranged time with the Soviet officers who have a quiet conversation with the guards and lower the red flag of liberation. Then, they raise the new flag, constructed from the uniform Weiss wore in Auschwitz.

Blue and white prison stripes; in the center, a yellow star. The flag of Judenstaat.

3

YOU'LL hate this," Oscar Kornfeld said to Judit, "but it's just not what they're after."

Judit said, "It's what I've got."

"What can I say? I'm not the one who makes decisions," Kornfeld said.

Who makes them? Judit didn't say that, but she thought it all the time since she'd started working under Kornfeld, a nebbish who seemed to be paid to warm his desk. He'd been promoted on the strength of a series of taped interviews with camp survivors. He had a way with old people, probably because he was born old. The series had languished since his promotion. He seemed to miss it.

"Sweetheart," Kornfeld said, "you know we won't be showing this movie to schoolkids. We're talking worldwide distribution, dubbing in English, Italian, who-knows-what. No one cares about those men in Vilna. Can't you find something more original?"

Of course, there was Stephen Weiss. Weiss had been airbrushed out of photographs, and his image had not appeared in any film produced by the museum. Kornfeld might have asked her where she'd found that footage, but he didn't mention Weiss at all. Case closed. No need to raise more questions.

Kornfeld could tell that she was agitated. "Don't worry. You'll come through fine. Maybe another field trip, dig through some regional collections. Isn't that where you found those photographs of Prime Minister Sokolov in Birobidjan for the coffee table book? We broke out that bottle of brandy."

"I didn't drink any of it, Oscar." Judit only used Kornfeld's first name when she'd reached her limit and he knew it. "That book was a rush job, and I'm still not sure those pictures were authentic."

"You think the prime minister wouldn't recognize her own hometown? What more proof do you need?" Kornfeld appeared to smile as Judit stood to go. "Take care of yourself. You're all flushed. I hope you're not coming down with something. This would be a terrible time."

It was a terrible time. That note was in the pocket of her duffle coat, the flap secured by a single khaki button. What was she supposed to do with it? Throw it away? She hadn't been present at the trial. Everyone understood, even if she herself did not quite understand what made her avoid reading anything about the case. Why would anyone bother to break in and leave a note like that? It was as though she'd been mistaken for someone else.

After Hans died, she could have had Kornfeld's job. She'd been up for a promotion that would have put her in line for the directorship. She turned it down. Nothing was more revolting than being the public face of any institution. At the same time, it was clear that she was not just another museum employee. For one thing, she was left alone. For months now, there'd been pressure to transfer the entire film archive to video and move her work upstairs. It never happened. Judit just said no.

She had been working in the archive since she had moved back to Dresden with Hans years ago, compiling material for the permanent exhibit on the early history of Judenstaat. Her film montages were projected on screens between glass cases of artifacts, and she made a practice of searching through bins at flea markets or asking pensioners if they had family photographs or reels of film stored in the attic. She had no use for stock footage. Her methods were considered controversial. Moving images in exhibits were something new, and this was the sort of institution where the gatekeeper was the same man Judit knew as a girl. When she signed in that first morning, there was ageless, friendly Mr. Rosenblatt with his full head of white hair under the official sky-blue cap. They hadn't been surprised to see each other. The National Museum was an old-fashioned place.

Still, that was changing. Last year, Judit had attended a trade show where sleek young people in turtleneck sweaters filled screens with fuzzy images that they manipulated into other images with even worse contrast and resolution. Something called Avid, weird dots called pixels. The very language was repulsive. Her intern Sammy Gluck was there too. He nodded a lot.

Whenever Sammy came down to her film archive, he'd knock like he'd made a mistake. Judit ignored it. Then he'd get more forceful, and she'd have to surface from whatever she was doing and let him in. He was studying computer science at Dresden Polytechnic, and until the trade show, Judit didn't know what his work had to do with hers. Once she knew, she had even less use for him. He spent most of his time three flights up, in something called the Media Room, working on footage that had been transferred to cassettes. When he did look in on Judit, he'd keep hovering and nodding, and blinking at her through his aviator glasses. She used to think he had a crush on her, but he brought his girlfriend once, a very pretty chemistry student. She nodded a lot too.

Sammy once said to Judit, "You know, I saw him."

"Who?" Judit asked, not very nicely.

"Your husband," Sammy said.

For a moment, Judit thought he'd seen the ghost. She couldn't decide if she felt relieved or violated. But Sammy had been in that archive countless times and looked right through the ghost of Hans. That wasn't what he'd meant at all.

"My parents took me to hear him conduct. It was still controversial, I mean his appointment. I couldn't believe it when it happened." Sammy meant the murder; that was clear. Then he added, "Everyone still remembers you. In New York, they'd send us any new equipment we wanted. State of the art. All you'd have to do is sign off on it." This was his way of telling her that she had authority, and she could claim it any time she chose.

Judit's mother Leonora never understood why she had turned down the promotion. If Judit had real connections, she could have found her a desk job in the National Museum and she wouldn't have to take the forty-minute bus ride to her desk job at the nursing home. Leonora lived in the Altstadt and could see the museum from her balcony.

The apartment had been reclaimed by her husband after the war. His family had lived in Dresden for generations, mostly in that apartment. The place was too big, room after room, light bulbs that always needed replacing, furniture under dull plastic slipcovers. Aside from the kitchen and the parlor, it looked like no one lived there anymore, but if she gave it up, Leonora said, who knows where they would put her? Probably across the street from the nursing home. When Judit pointed out that this would eliminate a long commute, her mother shook her head.

"You don't know what it's like out there. Those black-hat parasites spreading out from Loschwitz. You can't look at the wall without seeing a dozen of their *pashkevils* telling me to cover my hair and not to show my elbows in the summer." She switched to Yiddish. "*Imagine if I turned on the light on Shabbos, they'd burn the place down. I'd be a prisoner in my own home.*"

Leonora had no use for black-hats, but it didn't keep her from lapsing into their jargon when she got the chance. Like everyone else she knew, she flew the Stripes and Star from her balcony on May 14th and hung on every word of Prime Minister Sokolov's speeches, but there was still something of the Polish girl remaining, and the Yiddish remained with it. So did some superstitions. Every October, Lenora made a heavy New Year's dinner of brisket and honey-cake. October was also the anniversary of Rudolph Ginsberg's death, and Leonora—who believed that only backward Jews went to synagogue—paid a black-hat to say Kaddish for him, purchased a memorial candle at the Chabad House, and visited his grave.

They met a year after the war. In their wedding picture, Leonora wears a silky dress that had made do for several brides at their Displaced Persons camp in Gorlitz. She had asked Rudolph to find her a German name and he'd chosen a heroine from a Beethoven opera, which she then asked him to spell for her—both "Leonora" and "Beethoven." In that photograph, she's skinny and intent—all eyes—clinging to the arm of her abstracted-looking husband like a lemur to a tree.

Rudolph Ginsberg had never completed his degree in biology before he was shipped off to a labor camp in Riga. By the time Judit was born, he worked in Dresden's Hygiene Museum constructing displays on the human body, and writing instructive labels on jars of brains and livers preserved in formaldehyde. One of Judit's earliest memories was of that museum where she opened drawers labeled "Foreign Objects," filled with oxidized coins and bobby pins, misshapen marbles, most of them well over a century old. They had all been removed from the stomachs of children. As Judit opened drawer after drawer, her father had said, "Isn't it strange, Judi? Here are all these things the children swallowed, but all of the children are dead." Nobody else's father talked like that. Leonora would say, "You'll scare the child." But Judit was never scared. She was bewildered. Even then, she knew the difference.

Rudolph died when Judit was in college. Leonora still kept his chair turned to the window. Neither sat in it.

"So I take it you're too busy to visit Daddy this year," Leonora said.

"I don't see the point," Judit said. "It's not like he notices."

"I like to make sure his grave isn't overgrown," said Leonora, "and the little bush I paid for, nobody watered it. I had to see the caretaker and get it replaced. Those things don't just take care of themselves." She wrapped a hunk of brisket in heavy foil and loaded a striped plastic tote bag with honey-cake, stewed carrots, and a dozen other things that Judit hadn't asked for.

"Mom, where am I supposed to put all this? My fridge isn't big enough to hold it."

"Then get a bigger one. Really, I don't see why you stay in a dormitory at your age. You could move back here. It would make a world of sense. You're getting so thin, a strong wind would blow you away."

"I was always this size," Judit said.

"It's an observation, not a criticism. Maybe it's the coat. It swallows you, Judi. I know why you won't give it up, but take a look at yourself in the mirror and you'll admit. It's a man's coat. And an old one too."

"I know it's old," said Judit. "And I know it's a man's coat."

"You take everything I say the wrong way today. What's the matter? You're so pale. Have a banana. You know they used to be impossible to get, and just today they were on sale. It's just a little bruised."

Judit told her mother that nothing was the matter, but in the end, of course, she took the banana, along with the striped bag full of food she knew she wouldn't eat, and once she was outside, she put her free hand into the enormous pocket of the duffle coat that had belonged to Hans and put the banana there. Next to the note.

4

They lied about the murder.

What she should really do is give the note to the Stasi agent who visited her dormitory once a month. That agent was unfailingly polite, so tactful and insistent that he was there for her protection that he would probably just take that note and pursue the matter without further questions. After what happened in the archive, how could she doubt that she needed protection?

Yet she remembered the form that protection took, the constant presence of that agent by her bed, the oppression of that tact, the way she felt all of the air pumped out of her and something else pumped in. No—it had been more than three years since the murder and not once had she asked a thing of that man. She would be vulnerable. So what?

Her silence didn't make her complicit in a crime. No matter what lie they told her, Hans was just as dead. He might as well be murdered by the Saxon fascist with his forty-year-old gun. He might as well be on a list of Saxons who collaborated with the Jewish state. The case was closed. She'd throw the note away. She did not throw the note away.

* * *

The bus took Judit from Altstadt, where she worked and where her mother lived, to Neustadt, gray with concrete, glass, and steel. There was a new bridge across the Elbe: the Bridge Between East and West. That bridge had been called Augustus Bridge before the war, and then Mendelssohn Bridge, and its most recent incarnation was white and sleek, with a translucent crest of cables. Judit used to see swallows dipping and soaring below. She never saw them now. Somebody must have cleared their nests away.

What happened to the fabric store with the embroidered butterflies in the window, or the coffee shop where she and Hans used to get pancakes on Sunday mornings before rehearsals? Once there had been electric trams that took you everywhere. There used to be a little steam train in the park run by children dressed as conductors and engineers. Like every child in Judenstaat, Judit had longed to be an engineer on that train. The chosen few asked for tickets solemnly and pulled levers in signal boxes even in the rain. Those trains were gone.

As recently as last year, Judit liked to get herself ice cream at a little stand on Joseph Roth Square, and the last time she'd tried to find it, the stand had been torn down and replaced by a glass door stenciled with some acronym: DonReDox or RonDexDo, maybe a Danish corporation or one of those upstart companies financed by Soviet Jews who'd started emigrating in the past few years. That was Sokolov's doing—some trade agreement. It was easy to get past the checkpoints now.

Since Prime Minister Sokolov had taken office, the homely, hopeful Dresden that had been rebuilt after the war had disappeared. They were still tearing up the trolley tracks, and half of the streets were disemboweled and crosshatched with orange safety fencing. Lanes were widened, cables buried, thoroughfares constructed over the rubble of what Judit still remembered.

Because of the construction, Judit had to get off her bus early and walk the last half-mile to her dormitory, through an underpass, around the engineering building of the Polytechnic, and across a complicated intersection where cars waited five minutes for a signal change. She liked passing all those cars on foot. Her mother always wanted her to take a taxi home. That was out of the question. Why put herself at some driver's mercy? She could cross against the light, walk against traffic on a one-way street, and if she wore herself out, that was nobody's business but her own.

Judit's dormitory was built in the '50s when everything was painted the same Judenstaat yellow. There was an old-fashioned coffee bar and canteen in the lobby, and the only available telephone was in a booth outside. Even the porter, a snarling lady in a hairnet, had been on the job since the building opened.

"Hello, Mrs. Cohen," Judit said as she arrived. She feigned a brightness she didn't feel.

Mrs. Cohen responded by flipping a page of a movie magazine. Richard Gere was on the cover. Even the magazine was coated with dust. Her cousin in America had sent it over, and although she probably couldn't read English, she always had it in front of her so she would look occupied.

Judit asked her, "Would you like some brisket?"

"Don't keep food in your room. It'll spoil," said Mrs. Cohen, and she took the brisket for herself, and left Judit a few jars of stewed carrots and prunes and the honey-cake. That dormitory couldn't last. It was bound to be demolished. Judit was amazed it had been overlooked this long.

5

JUDIT had lived in just such a dormitory fifteen years ago at the University of Leipzig, but back then, the porter was a crone who liked spy novels. She'd never look up from that book when Judit slipped past her after a night with Hans.

Hans couldn't live in a dormitory. He was distinctly unofficial. Some colleges did admit Saxons, but it was understood that the few spots in elite institutions had to go to Jews. Yet there he was, sitting next to Judit in the middle of a lecture on the Jewish revolutionary Rosa Luxemburg. He didn't look so very different from the other students, though there was nothing on his desk but his elbows. He leaned forward with a distant smile.

As ever, Judit was taking notes like a madwoman, and her hair kept falling in her eyes. She pushed it away compulsively. Then someone pushed it for her. She stopped short and blushed. There was Hans, looking right at her. She couldn't decide if his eyes were gray or blue. She couldn't take any more notes after that.

Later, he said, "I'm glad you're not one of those girls who uses hairspray."

"I should," said Judit. "Or I should get it cut short."

"It's like lamb's wool. The golden fleece. Or not golden. Soft, though."

She gathered that fleecy hair in one hand and twisted it up in a way she'd seen other girls do. It stayed in place.

With that same grace and ease, they walked together. Hans had a loping, unapologetic tall man's walk. He didn't carry any books. He took her own substantial knapsack, slung it on one shoulder, and said, "What's in here, anyhow?"

"Three dictionaries," Judit said. "A compilation of Aramaic translations from Hebrew. And of course my notebooks."

"Of course," said Hans.

They had coffee in a shop Judit had never noticed, a wood-paneled alcove with three round tables, bottles stacked behind the counter, and a weathered Righteous Gentile Certificate that must have dated from the early 1950s. It was a place where Saxons drank. That much was clear, just as it was clear now, in case Judit had doubts, that Hans was Saxon. The men at the bar wore overalls and probably worked as janitors on campus. Hans ordered two coffees with cognac.

The proprietor set those coffees down, and that was when Hans told her that he'd talked his way into the conservatory and had been studying music theory and teaching violin, but he remained distinctly off-the-books.

"So you don't have to sit for examinations?" Judit asked him. "Not at all?"

"Not at all," Hans said.

"So you go to lectures just because?" Judit shook her head. "You don't take them seriously, though. You were smiling the whole time."

"Some lectures are a pleasure. I take pleasure seriously. Don't you?"

"I don't know," Judit said. "I've never had a conversation like this before." She finished the coffee and cognac, and hurried to her three o'clock linguistics seminar, and some of the grace and strangeness of the encounter carried on. No one knew that she was a little drunk. She heard herself decipher a particularly tangled bit of Aramaic in a way that made Professor Romarowsky say, in a startled voice, "Well, that's a way to look at it, Judit, if one were trying to be original."

Afterwards, as planned, they met in the library stacks. Hans showed her the libretto of an opera from the '60s based on the life of Rosa Luxemburg, and he confessed why he had smiled as the professor detailed the specifics of her assassination. "I was thinking about the music."

"Is it the sort of music that makes you smile?" Judit asked. "It shouldn't be. Not if it's telling the truth."

"I'll play it for you. There's a listening booth downstairs. I'll bet you never even knew the library had one."

But Judit persisted. "You need to know this about me. I believe in facts. I believe in documentary history, in things that really happen. And I believe there's such a thing as justice."

Hans didn't answer for a moment. His face was very close to hers. His shaggy, light blond hair was pushed back from his forehead. It was a long face, in every sense. The face was more serious than he was, really, or than he had seemed to Judit. Yes, his eyes were gray and narrow. They held her own. He said, "You need to know this about me. I believe in facts too. But I'm not sure I believe in history. And I know I don't believe in justice." Then, he kissed her.

The kiss didn't come suddenly. After all, their cheeks had been touching as they paged through the libretto, and ever since that morning, she had felt the touch of his fingers in her hair. She had met him in the stacks, knowing that this would happen. Yet to have his mouth on hers just after he'd said he didn't believe in justice made her light-headed. She pulled back to catch her breath.

6

UNTIL the day Hans Klemmer kissed her, Judit had few distractions. She was a few years into a graduate degree in library science and had just curated her first exhibition on postwar Leipzig. She loved choosing the images, laying them side by side on a long, clean table. Should the picture of the concrete mixer by the ruins of the Cathedral go next to the picture of a paint-spattered worker listening to a phonograph?

The exhibition had come off well, and now she was at loose ends, keen to find another project. There was nothing she liked more than sitting in the library all day with a bunch of documents no one had bothered to touch in twenty years. With her pencil between her teeth, she'd decode chicken-scratch until a little bell announced the library was closing. Then she'd find her way back to her dorm with a head full of the past.

But now, Leipzig was about the present. In 1972, Judenstaat had just started getting exports from the West, French and American films, translation of poems by Allen Ginsberg, and of course the kind of music that throbbed through the floor. Everyone smoked marijuana. Young border guards bragged about gathering hallucinogenic mushrooms in the woods by the Protective Rampart. They'd make tea out of them, get sick, and brag about that too.

Of course, there were courtyard parties every night, but after a while, girls stopped inviting Judit. They wrote her off as a prig, the sort of girl who'd belonged to the Junior Bundist League until she was old enough to be a Youth Leader, and kept all her badges and trophies. They would be right. One of those trophies was from Archeology Camp. It was a small brass spade in a block of sandstone: "Junior Excavator: First Class." She brought it to college.

She'd earned her Junior Bundist history badge by following the path of Elsa Neuman, a martyr from the Churban. The path began at Elsa's home on Budapester Street. Each Junior Bundist had a different address and picture of a martyr, and some of the more ambitious girls brought cameras and handed over their photographs to Mr. Rosenblatt, the guard, who took those pictures with great ceremony and promised to make sure they'd find their way into the Churban wing of the National Museum.

Judit loved the museum: exhibits on the Golden Age of Ashkenaz, and the portraits of Moses Mendelssohn and the Age of Reason, and then, through a passageway of glass, there'd be the Hall of the Churban, stuffed floor-to-ceiling with mementos, photographs of martyrs, accounts from the concentration camps and death camps, all lit by candle-stubs in cheap tin boxes. It was only by climbing out of that hall, and crossing an outdoor terrace, that they could reach the third wing and the final exhibition on the founding of the Jewish state. That moment on the terrace, where they shook away the horror and gazed across Stein Square to the clean, familiar Dresden skyline was like coming back to life.

Elsa Neuman had been forced from her home to a Jew-house just south of the park and soon after, she'd been deported by train from Dresden to Thereisenstadt, where she was murdered. It was weird and moving how Judit and the other girls engaged in following the paths of different martyrs converged on the Dresden train station. Old Saxon ladies sold violets for the girls to leave on the tracks.

Afterwards, there was a final ceremony at the Great Synagogue, an empty lot that—according to the photograph from a book held up by Youth Leader Charlotte Kreutzberger—had once been a magnificent nineteenth-century structure with a hexagonal dome and Moorish interior. The synagogue was burnt by fascists in 1938 on Kristallnacht, and then—Charlotte closed the book for emphasis—when British and American airplanes rained incendiary bombs on Dresden in 1945, the fire returned.

Charlotte was a tall, stern girl with straight black hair and a sonorous alto voice that managed to carry even in the open, in front of the rectangle of grass where the synagogue once stood. She asked the group: "Why wasn't the synagogue rebuilt?"

Few of those girls had been inside a synagogue. They were for old people and black-hats. The question was obviously rhetorical, but Charlotte had the answer.

She swept her arm across that empty rectangle and said, "This is our prayer-house. This is our monument."

When Judit found treasures buried in odd places, when she reproduced the past without amendment, it was as though she raised the dead. Back then, she kicked a little of that synagogue grass and wondered what the dirt contained.

Summers in Archeology Camp had been the high point of Judit's life. To scrape away coarse sand and clean a fragment of blue tile engraved with oriental patterns common to Jews who traveled with Charlemagne, to fit it seamlessly into a fragment someone found two years ago, nothing could match it. The Jewish settlements were buried under Saxon barns and pigsties and even fascist bunkers. They had been waiting for her for a thousand years.

At night, the campers would toast bread over an open fire, and eat it with honey that would scorch their lips and tongues. Nothing could match the sensation of burnt honey mixed with sand that got into their bread and even into their knapsacks, and the August moon doing crazy things to the black and yellow cliffs of Saxon Switzerland as they sat at the mouth of a pit they'd spent the summer excavating.

So yes, she brought the Junior Excavator trophy to college. She also brought her sewing machine, a graduation gift from Leonora. It fit into its own suitcase. She sewed her own clothes. She would have mended other people's clothes if they'd bothered to ask her. No one asked her. That was the sort of girl she was, at least until Hans Klemmer kissed her.

In 1984, Judit would be using that same machine in the apartment she and Hans had purchased after they'd moved to Dresden. The place was new, and still felt raw and strange, not fully furnished, not their own. When Hans conducted, she liked to stay in her little sewing room, the one they'd hoped to make into a nursery. That's where she was, in her robe, at nine o'clock when the doorbell rang.

It couldn't have been Hans. She sat at the machine for a moment, running a seam down the edge of Hans's new dress shirt. Then she got up and pulled her robe a little tighter. She walked to the door. It was already open. The agent stood there, in his brown hat, with his mild face. He just looked at her. That's when she knew.

Judit had always suspected that the Stasi agent had been Hans's bodyguard and he'd been delegated to her case as a perverse demotion. She could never see him again without reliving that night. Thus, when Mrs. Cohen said, "That man's in the sitting room," they exchanged a look of resigned complicity that made Judit grateful, yet again, that she lived in the dormitory, particularly when

Mrs. Cohen added, "Don't let him go too long. It's common space, after all. The other girls don't like it."

The sitting room was another artifact. It was supposed to be for gentleman callers. Its big glass partition faced the hallway, and it contained a square modernist chair and two uncomfortable couches. The Stasi agent sat on one of those couches. At some point in the past three years, he'd stopped wearing the hat. Rising, he began, as ever, "Just a courtesy visit." Then he said, "How are you, Mrs. Klemmer? You look tired."

"It's the lighting in here," Judit said. "It makes everyone look tired."

The agent motioned for her to sit in the chair. She kept on standing. She looked at her watch. She'd found that if she stood and looked at her watch, he'd usually leave sooner, but sometimes he would just say, as he did that day, "Please sit down."

Then she would have no choice. She'd sit down as he went through his litany of questions about her schedule, her route home, and any changes in her routine.

The agent shook his head. "It's not just the lighting. You're worn out. I believe you're under pressure at work and it's interfering with your health."

There was a probing quality to this conversation. "I always look like this," Judit said. "You sound like my mother."

The agent allowed himself a small, wry smile. "I'm flattered."

"She'd love a visit from you," Judit said. "It would impress the neighbors."

He laughed. "I'm sure the neighbors are already impressed with Mrs. Ginsberg. Returning to the point at hand, if you're running into trouble in the archive, we could help. I've said all along, we have access to resources that would make your job far easier." The agent did say that. All the time. The fact that his laughter was rueful and disarming did not make Judit like him any better.

She said, "I work best independently."

"You've made that clear," the agent said. "But you should understand that your mother and I are alike in putting your welfare first." Now he did something so quickly that she didn't have time to stop him. He took her hand, turned it over, and checked her pulse. "When is the last time you saw a doctor?"

"Surely you have access to that information," Judit said.

"We've told you many times that we don't interfere, or pursue trivial questions. Yet there is a question that isn't trivial. In fact, it's a very interesting question."

He gave Judit a look, half-tender, half-diagnostic, and he hadn't yet released her hand. His fingers pressed in gently. Then, without warning, his gaze hardened and focused in a way that cut through to the bone. Judit had been under that particular microscope before, and the degree of intensity never ceased to startle her. She said, "What question?"

"The question of why you won't let us help you. Is there any other question, Mrs. Klemmer? Is there something else you want to tell me?" And this whole time, the note was on her. Why hadn't she destroyed it? He could smell it. There was nothing about her that this agent didn't know. He didn't pursue it, though. He was no fool. That was the trouble.

He released her wrist and handed her his card. It was the same card that he gave her every month. She had a stack of them in her room. Somehow, they never made it to the wastebasket. There were times when she wondered if, by keeping those cards, she compromised herself. The fact was, she was used to those visits, and if she was going to be honest, had grown to depend on them. Leaving aside that ghost, the agent had become the only man in her life.

"Get some sleep," he said. "And don't hesitate to contact me. For any reason. We can help you get a new room. You know, this dormitory is slated for demolition next year."

7

THE Ministry of State Security knew everything. Judit had grown up hearing stories of heroic Stasi agents who neutralized Nazi bandits in the '50s through a network of informers and helped secure the borders in the years before the Protective Rampart. When Leonora learned the Stasi would look in on Judit, she'd been so relieved, she cried. Still, if the Stasi were so all-knowing and all-powerful, Hans would still be alive.

Judit's dormitory room had a narrow bed and a pressed-wood desk and chair, and she sat at that desk for a while with the note spread out in front of her. The print was faint and growing fainter by the hour. She switched on the desk lamp, but the glare made things worse.

Maybe she wasn't at the trial, but she couldn't help hearing about the spectacle. Arno Durmersheimer was arrested with half a dozen others—all men in their sixties. They were members of some ridiculous Saxon folk-dancing club. Durmersheimer played the accordion. With his overalls and close-cropped red hair, he was the kind of Saxon you see everywhere and never see at all.

Durmersheimer had been one of those Rathen snipers who'd terrorized Judenstaat until he'd been deported to the West. He had been unapologetic. "I have nothing against Jews unless they're Reds or Cosmopolitans. I wish I'd gotten more of them. Now, I guess, Jews hunt me."

How did he re-cross the border? It was a question that must have been answered at the trial. The bullet had come from Durmersheimer's gun. Hans Klemmer's name was on a list of so-called collaborators found on Durmersheimer's person. Durmersheimer seemed bewildered by the trial itself, never denied the charges. He kept repeating: "What's a Saxon to you? Just shoot him in the head if he gets in the way, or let the Reds do your shooting for you."

There was more—she was sure—about the other suspects, the folk-dancing, the list of collaborators. There must be a transcript somewhere. She could certainly request files to be transferred to the archive. Yet if she took that step, it would raise questions that felt—against all logic—private. This was not state business. Whoever broke into her archive had risked something to get to her.

No, she couldn't pursue this openly. She had other sources: what Kornfeld called her "regional field trips." Loschwitz was worth a try.

The Stasi had no jurisdiction in Loschwitz. Those people had their own laws and their own courts. There were no street signs, only Yiddish *pashkevils* in Hebrew script reporting births, deaths, and feuds between rabbis. Sometimes there'd be a *pashkevil* in German to address outsiders: "Women: Be Modest" or more jarringly, in some shop window: "Bundists are not Jews." Tucked between synagogues were shops that sold black-market goods or exchanged Judenmarks for foreign currency. Rumor had it that a girl who got into trouble could bypass the state clinic for an abortion in a room above a kosher butcher shop.

When Judit went to Loschwitz, she took care to cover her head with a beret and wear a calf-length skirt and stockings. The disguise was worth the trouble because it was in Loschwitz that Judit found a junk shop, never in the same place twice, but always carrying the same inventory: plastic bowls and tarnished flatware, magazines from Judenstaat's deep past, some in yellowed slipcases, and others half-chewed and unreadable.

The owner had a long, thin beard and wore a skull-cap, and he never met Judit's eyes, but he took care to push a certain bin in her direction. The film canisters and photographs in that bin had all been marked DISCARD in red, and when she sorted through it, they proved to be from Judenstaat's earliest years.

She asked, "How much?"

He answered in the high-pitched Yiddish of the black-hats. "*Three zloty.*"

She gave the man ten Judenmarks, which he did not reject. The next time she managed to find the shop, he asked for fifteen dollars, and the third and fourth time, twenty Deutsche marks. In every case, he took what Judit offered. In every case, she went straight back to her archive and spent the night viewing and sorting until her eyes gave out and her legs gave way.

She'd never been sure why some footage was discarded. The images of Stephen Weiss were hot stuff, sure, but then there were other reels that seemed harmless enough, though certainly unfiltered: American- or Soviet-made. She kept the Loschwitz footage in a separate drawer and never included it in her formal catalogue; she kept its contents in her head:

A newsreel from 1950: six young Ghetto Fighters waving across an airfield. Leather jackets slung over their shoulders. The propeller hums, and a Soviet pilot urges them on board. They're headed for Moscow, where they will become the officer corps of Judenstaat's defense force.

Grainy footage of three slender Americans in well-tailored raincoats, walking beside Leopold Stein as they survey the sandstone foundation of Judenstaat's new Parliament. 1949. One of the Americans whispers something to Stein, who turns his head away.

A carnival in a Displaced Persons camp in '47, Churban survivors pitching pennies next to girlfriends who are dolled up for the evening, looking proud in their high heels. Why was this one discarded? Were they too happy? How vulnerable they seem, as they flick American pennies into those bowls, neat as sharpshooters.

Stein and Weiss and the flag. Weiss at Yalta, half-buried in a fur coat with his glasses flashing. Weiss standing by the ruins where the Great Synagogue of Dresden once stood, obscured by smoke. No, the film she'd screened a few days ago was not Stephen Weiss at the ruins of the Great Synagogue. It was Stein, pre-1947.

That's what she'd been watching the day that man broke in. Stein with his mouth moving through that full beard, his hands making that round, half-shrugging gesture. So you don't like that story? Then she knew: she'd never seen that film before.

They lied about the murder.

That stranger—she could just make out the shape of him. He was not the black-hat from the junk shop. He wasn't lean and frail. He'd shouted in coarse German and he'd slammed that note down with a force that shook the table.

Judit held that note in her hand, and then that hand began to shake as she inferred another meaning. What if Hans was still alive?

8

From Helena Sokolov's Inaugural Address: January 1986. Released in special video edition from the National Museum, November 1987.

[Sokolov enters the Grand Hall. Standing ovation as she walks down the center aisle and shakes hands with representatives. She moves forward before turning back to wave at Anton Steinsaltz, on whom the camera lingers. She is at least a head shorter than everybody else, and once behind the podium, only her face and trademark ink-black pageboy are visible. She adjusts the microphone and waits for the applause to end, waving and gesturing happily, then raising her hand for silence.]

> I come to you as a true outsider. You knew this when you chose me, and I make no secret of my past. I am young, not much older than this country. I come from a foreign land, Birobidjan, that region on the border of Manchuria that has become a desolate wilderness. And I am a woman. How many women have ever sat in Parliament? I say to you

that when a girl like me can stand before this body and tell the truth, everything is possible.

Moreover, I am the leader of a party that breaks with tradition by its very nature, the Neustadt Party, that group of young upstarts from the Polytechnic's School of Economics which itself was only created ten years ago. There was once a rule that no member of the Neustadt Party could be over forty. Then, two of us turned forty. [Some laughter.] Once, Anton Steinsaltz said that we would never be taken seriously until at least one of us had gray hair. I told him that if he joined, he would have enough gray hair for all of us. [More laughter. Camera briefly cuts to Steinsaltz, who isn't looking at it. Scattered applause.]

And why did you choose me? I know there are some among us who say that tradition is the very foundation of the Jewish state. I also know that there are some who fear that to break with tradition is to break a sacred covenant that binds us as a people and a land. What I will carry forward as we begin our work together is perhaps the greatest of our traditions. I speak now of the need to let go of fear, to embrace possibility, to chance an opportunity. I declare to the world: Judenstaat is a nation of opportunists.

Have Jews not, in our long history, embraced opportunity? Did we not embrace it when we planted deep roots in this land so long ago? And have we not taken this greatest of opportunities, a return to our own land? Here at last, we can live out our destiny, we can be safe, we can be free. [Applause.]

Who are we, citizens of Judenstaat? We are Jews. We are Saxons. We are united under one flag. [Scattered applause.]

As I stand here before the Stripes and Star, I think of my first glimpse of the flag many years ago, when we crossed three borders with the help of Czechs and Poles, and, of course, Germans. Many are times I've praised these Righteous Gentiles—[From the floor: "The fascists have their own damned flag! That's why we build the wall!" This is followed by silence, and a moment when Sokolov lets the echo disperse before continuing.]

My family were opportunists. After we came to Judenstaat, my mother got her diploma from a Dresden secondary school at the age of forty-five. We took the opportunity to work. My father made use of what he'd learned in a Soviet forced labor camp and joined the Saxons in the local gravel pit. My mother scrubbed floors in a Chabad House. We had no family here. But the more opportunities we took, the more it bound us to our neighbors. The more we felt invested in this country. The more we felt at home.

Let us look to the future. The world is changing. New technologies, new methods of communication, new faces on the television at night. In Washington, an unpretentious president speaks the plain truth about world affairs. In Moscow, his counterpart acknowledges the very crimes that cost my grandparents in Birobidjan their lives in 1938. If we want to be true to our best selves, we need to make the most of this historic opportunity. We must take our place as part of the world community. We must step forward, with a daring pragmatism that is the trademark of our national genius.

But, some may say, if we are opportunists, what of our principles? What of our founders and what of their ideals? How can we help but think of Leopold Stein at this moment, who stood where I am standing nearly forty years ago? He was not much older than myself. And he looked at the world around him, a very different world, and he held out his hands to that world. He reached for opportunity, and at the same time, reached beyond our borders. In his own words, "We shall build a bridge between East and West."

Prime Minister Stein poses the challenge. We must hear it as an opportunity. We must reach for this opportunity and know the challenge of this generation will be for Judenstaat to join the family of nations, fully and enthusiastically. And know that in doing so, we are fulfilling our historic destiny. [Sustained applause.]

The Saxon Question

1

Journal of Historical Inquiry: March 1973

On the eve of our country's twenty-fifth anniversary, the nature of the ever-present Saxon Question has changed both in form and substance. As was once said by the most venerable of historians, Bruno Webber, "Everyone knows a German, but nobody knows a Saxon." In short, both the individual identity of Saxons and thus the German State of Saxony was dismissed as—at best—myth, and at worst, sabotage intended to undermine our historic claim to our land.

What is Saxony? Is there, or at the very least, was there, a Saxon tribe? Are there Saxon traditions that constitute a separate identity with commensurate forms of ethics and cultural norms and historical memories? A close examination of the documentary evidence opens this question further, and ultimately leads scholars to more existential questions about the nature of claims, or memory itself.

The article gave Judit a headache. Still, she was willing to wade through this pretentious nonsense if it held a key to the man whose bed she had been sharing, and who made her see the world all over again. She tried to concentrate and failed. The library's reading room smelled like him. She walked across the lawn and every blade of grass gave a sweet crunch. Back at her desk, she recopied her notes, and her hand wouldn't cooperate; it crept up through her hair and raked through strands until the curls stood straight up. She had to keep things secret.

Judit had been in love before, with boys in school, always older and smarter, who told her their troubles and never kissed her; with her counselor at Archeology Camp, who was about to be inducted into the army and on his last night of freedom did kiss her and do some other things to her in the back of a van; with her physics teacher, who made quiet jokes about gravity and time, and who treated all his students with such tenderness that any of them would have followed him home. This was different. Somehow, the secret made it different.

Judit was a vessel for that secret. She carried it around, fearing and hoping or even daring it to tip and swell. She slept only fitfully. Something precious and dangerous was inside her. Later, she would learn that all lovers accumulate secrets, the ones they share, the ones they keep, and the ones that spill into bed. With great luck, those secrets never stop feeling powerfully dangerous.

What did she know about Hans? He had no memory of his mother and father. He'd spent his first few years with an uncle who owned a tavern and who had crossed the border into Brandenburg, leaving Hans at the Chemmitz Home for Unclaimed Children.

Judit did the math in her head. So he'd been born just after Liberation. And if he'd never known his parents, they must have fled just after Judenstaat was established. Were they musicians too? "I haven't a clue," said Hans. And they just left him with an uncle in a tavern? "It was a very nice tavern," Hans said. "Sawdust on the floor. Clean curtains. Three solid meals a day."

"So your parents couldn't feed you? That's why they abandoned you?"

"What makes you think they abandoned me? I tell you, I have no idea. And I couldn't care less, frankly. As far as I'm concerned, I just sprang up like a weed and kept on growing."

There was a dizzying and rootless quality to Hans, with his big apartment two kilometers from campus in a shabby neighborhood where he piled stacks of sheet music as tall as Judit, and kept a bin of soapy water on the coal-fed heater to wash dishes. He had a sink, but most of the time, laundry soaked there. The first time Judit spent the night, they cooked canned stew on his hotplate, and she was amazed that he could anticipate such terrible food with such enthusiasm.

"You'll have to introduce me to home cooking," he'd said. "All musicians are citizens of the world."

Judit laughed. Hans was nearly thirty, but he sounded like an earnest schoolboy. "If you weren't a Saxon, I'd accuse you of being a Cosmopolitan."

Hans let the comment pass. But Judit wished she could have taken it back. It had felt sophisticated to use that word, but everyone knew professors who had lost their jobs in 1968.

Still, back then, Judit was an unreconstructed Bundist. What if Hans really was a Cosmopolitan, loyal to nothing but himself? What if he didn't believe in a state with a Jewish character? Or worse yet, what if he was one of those Saxons who rewrote history and denied any Jewish claim to the land? Where were his parents during the war? Did they play a role in the Churban? Judit couldn't bring herself to ask these questions. Instead, she watched the hotplate glow as he searched for his can opener and cooked that stew right in the can. He had two spoons.

2

THE textbooks Judit read in school all marked the years after Liberation with arrows bending across eastern territory into Judenstaat. Each arrow was marked with a number: three thousand, sixty thousand, eighty thousand Jews streaming into the country. Then, there were arrows that pointed outward from Judenstaat, west, to Germany: ninety thousand so-called Saxons.

Well, some of them stayed. No doubt, Hans's uncle had one of those Righteous Gentile certificates displayed in that tavern. They weren't hard to get, back then. It just took a single Jewish witness. Even now, you can still find them framed in some old Saxon-owned cafés. Borders always shift after a war. Half of the population is on the road. One might speak of justice—a rough justice—for the Muslims who choose a destiny in Pakistan or the Japanese who pull up shallow roots and leave the nations that they'd occupied, or the East Prussians who may or may not lay claim to disputed territory. Those who remain should have few expectations.

Saxons were just a footnote to heroic years of rebuilding: American-funded reconstruction of the Opera House, the new Parliament that rose like a white wave on a field of rubble, artful and modern Bauhaus apartment blocks, all blue and yellow like the flag, and thanks to Soviet engineering, somehow and suddenly those trolleys that would take you just about everywhere.

The night the electricity started working, everyone stayed up and filled the streets, pushing their baby carriages—everyone had babies—or in the case of Rudolph or Leonora, just strolling because Judit was not yet born. The cafés were open too. Back then, there were forty newspapers in Dresden alone, half in German, a dozen in Yiddish, the rest in languages that ranged from Russian to English to Hungarian. The Bundist Party organ, *A Home,* was still published in Yiddish in those days.

Judit read about all of this in Bruno Webber's classic book *The Battle of the Languages,* where he described debates between Leopold Stein and the Yiddishists. In 1950, all of the state-run newspapers switched to German, and mobs overturned printing presses until Soviet soldiers had to fire in the air to maintain order. After that, the other Yiddish newspapers were shut down.

Years later, who knows how, a story came out. Joseph Stalin had said to Stein during their historic Yalta meeting, "Don't give me another country full of Yiddish speakers. They're not to be trusted. Birobidjan was a disaster. We had to get rid of most of those Jews in '38."

More widely known was Stephen Weiss's reaction when he was asked to weigh in on the matter. "Well, we could always speak Esperanto."

The role of Stephen Weiss would soon be clear, as laid out in his secret manifesto. The foreigners hired to build roads, the supplies trucked from Berlin, the open borders, they were all the first step to a full invasion bankrolled by America, and there would be brutal consequences. After the espionage crisis, Leopold Stein's legendary vigor faded, month by month, and when it became clear just how deeply the Cosmopolitans had infiltrated, it would only be so long before Stein himself would be held accountable.

Judit was just two years old when Stein suffered his stroke in 1953. Her parents, like everyone in Judenstaat, could remember the moment when they heard the news, in Rudolph's case from a neighbor who stood in the courtyard, staring at the gray sunlight as though he couldn't believe the day was still a day. As for Leonora, some instinct made her turn on the radio. The two of them put Judit in a baby carriage that she was too big for, and went to the square that would be named after Stein that same year. They stood there with five thousand others, waiting for something to happen.

Stein had been attending Stalin's funeral, along with dignitaries from around the world. Afterwards, he'd been found unconscious on the floor of his hotel room. He was flown to a special hospital, accompanied by a male nurse from Odessa. Jews packed into the square between the Opera House and the smooth sandstone edifice of Parliament where a black banner draped the columns, and they watched snow drift down, big flakes that didn't melt right away.

Judit was certain she remembered snow. She also remembered that there were smears of lamplight or candlelight everywhere. She tried to catch those smears of light, but they melted on her mittens. She kept on trying. She got wet through, but neither of her parents noticed, and she didn't cry.

1954: Dresden suburb raided for provisions, a kindergarten burning. Fragments of newsreels document the aftermath of raids by Nazi bandits across a barren landscape. Fire boiling up in black and white. Fire spreads and turns the Elbe into a stream of dirty milk. Sandstone cliffs glow in the distance, steep, the surreal formations of the region once called Saxon Switzerland with its hidden tunnels and countless caves.

1955: Newsreel. Soviet troops stand at the ready, in persistent rain. Their fur hats are wet, and around them, black sandstone dissolves into brown streams that foam and boil into eroded crevices like brewing cauldrons. Out of the cavern creep three ghastly Saxons, raising their arms in surrender as they bow their heads. The cache of arms, glinting as the camera is thrust into the cave: explosive devices, German Lugers and assault rifles, bazookas shipped from America. The next year, Judenstaat sealed the border and began work on the Protective Rampart.

And they told Judit that one of those Saxons crossed that border and killed Hans Klemmer. Or they lied about who killed him. Or they lied about his death. The footage at the reel's end flapped with a kind of recklessness.

3

KORNFELD pushed the footage back at Judit. "What can I say?"

Judit tried to keep her tone civil. "I thought you asked for a historical overview."

"Actually, no," said Kornfeld. "What we want is a historical reckoning."

"What the hell does that mean?"

"It means, what do we add up to, Judit? We can't show the face of forty years ago. We need to show where we'll be forty years from now."

"Sorry, Oscar. That I can't tell you," Judit said.

Kornfeld cleared his throat. Then he leaned across his desk and said in a lower voice, "They're thinking of bringing in someone. A director."

"To direct what?"

"Interviews. Maybe work with a script." So it was going to be another parade of Kornfeld's camp survivors speaking against a backdrop of stock footage while a ponderous voice read out the numbers on their tattoos.

But that was not the specter haunting Judit. It was the footage she'd been screening when the stranger left that note—that unmarked reel. The canister looked like a hundred other canisters.

Kornfeld misread what Judit's face was doing. "The director isn't my idea. Believe me. She's from across the border. From Germany." Kornfeld's voice hardened. "You know this couldn't come from me."

It wasn't like Judit to let films go uncatalogued. Yet she'd been thrown off balance then, and she might well have left it anywhere. That voice—that note—it was all bound up with the grainy images that looked so much like all the other Soviet footage from 1947 back when Leopold Stein had his beard and nothing had been reconstructed. But no—she had not seen that film before and couldn't find it now.

"You're not even listening," said Kornfeld. "I told you, we're on a deadline and this feels more and more like it's out of my hands." He shook his head. "I just wish you'd reconsider about video transfer. If we could work faster, they might lay off. A program like Paint Box—Sammy's work is really something. Look at this still."

He pulled out a blurry frame from a folder and laid it down: Anton Steinsaltz and Khrushchev on a beach somewhere. She hadn't seen the original, but she could tell that cracks and white space had been smoothed away. Both men were in formal dress and sat on folding chairs, facing the ocean. Someone lurked behind them, obscured by sunlight, a shaggy figure in bathing trunks.

"Who's that?" Judit asked. "A lifeguard?"

"That, darling, is John Fitzgerald Kennedy," said Kornfeld. He formed the words one at a time, all the while looking at her. "Do you know what that means?"

"Not really," Judit said.

"It makes us look at Anton Steinsaltz all over again," Kornfeld said. "That's what I mean. We think of him as a hack—or maybe some old ghetto fighter with a knife behind his back. We think of Judenstaat as closed off to the world, and here Steinsaltz is in 1961 with Kennedy. *Kennedy!* This is just the sort of thing that would make them leave us alone to do our goddamned work! And if we have the tools to polish those old images it's like—" He struggled to find the right words. "—like polishing a precious stone. In the Media Room, with those computers—"

"I get it," Judit said. "The image looks like crap. You can tell it's been doctored. The sunlight's coming from the wrong direction. I will not fabricate. It will not happen."

Kornfeld sat back and took his aluminum worry-balls from their mounted shelf. He rolled them between his hands. "Thank God for the Protective Rampart at least. I'll tell you, Judit, I'm all for free trade, minority rights, all that stuff, believe me. Sokolov's the only reason we have a future at all. But a German. From Berlin. Hell. Why would anyone in their right mind choose a German to direct a film about the future of the Jewish state?"

Judit knew Kornfeld would dismiss material about the Saxon Question. Even her mother—who had once told her not to take candy from the Saxon lady who cleaned the hallways—even Leonora said a while ago, "You know, Judi, I have to say that the Saxons show a lot more sense than a lot of Jews when it comes to voting. If it wasn't for them, Prime Minister Sokolov would never have won, what with the parasites in the provinces"—she meant the black-hats—"and now we'd be so isolated from the world, I wouldn't even be able to get a television signal."

Leonora certainly hadn't felt that way the first time Judit had brought Hans home. Granted, that had happened far too soon, only because Hans had gotten tickets for a concert in Dresden and Leonora had called the dormitory several times and didn't believe her when she said she'd been out with friends. What friends? Evasion never worked with Leonora. Judit warned Hans that her mother was a handful, but even she was shaken when the first thing Leonora said to Hans was, "What did your parents do in the war?"

Hans replied, "I don't know, Mrs. Ginsberg."

"Mom, he never knew his parents," Judit said. "He's an orphan."

"I thought you said he didn't know if his parents were alive or dead. If he's an orphan, then they're dead. So are they dead or alive?" Leonora asked, pursuing the question in a way that amazed Hans to the point of speechlessness. Since he didn't speak, she went on. "Understand, I have a number on my arm. My husband—may he rest in peace—grew up right here in Dresden, but your people shipped him to a concentration camp in Riga. I have the right to ask anything I want, Judit. Don't make that face."

Hans did speak then. "I was told they died."

"How?" Leonora asked.

Hans said, "I don't know. And I don't want to know."

"What's wrong with you that you don't want to know what happened to your own mother and father?"

Hans paused. Then he said, "I think there are some things I don't have to know. I think, sometimes, when you don't know, you're free."

Now Leonora addressed Judit in Yiddish. "*Never trust a man who talks about freedom. They're the ones who trap you and get you into trouble.*"

"*Mom, I'm not in trouble,*" Judit said. Then, "*You know he can understand Yiddish.*"

"*I can't speak it, though,*" Hans said, in terrible Yiddish.

This disarmed Leonora somewhat, and she offered Hans a glass of cranberry juice and a slice of cake. She said she'd heard he was a musician. The only people more musical than Germans were Jews, and her own husband, Rudolph, being both German and Jewish, had an unusually good ear and sang in the Community Choir. She still had all of his old sheet music. Maybe Hans could take a look and see if there was anything he wanted to bring back to Leipzig.

Later, when Judit and Hans emerged with two shopping bags full of yellowing choral sheet music, Hans said, "Lamb, what else do I expect? You're Junior Excavator, First Class, and she's Senior Excavator, First Class."

What had become of that persistence? She'd lost it when she lost her husband. She'd never seen his body. A month after the murder, his ashes had been scattered over the Opera House. She had not attended. Everyone understood. She was the widow and got to make those choices. Yet would Hans understand what kept her from questioning the circumstances of his death?

She walked out of Kornfeld's office. She would get no more work done that day, and she left the museum without a real sense of direction. It was late afternoon. A keen, late-autumn wind came up from the Elbe and blew her coat flat against her chest. Her hair was in her face, and she blinked until her eyes teared. The faux-baroque façade of the National Museum threw a dense shadow on Stein Square. Why had they tried to replicate what had been blown to pieces? What were they trying to prove? She suddenly found her whole life repulsive, inauthentic.

Once, revisiting closed cases had been her nature. Since Hans had died, her own life had become like one of the archeological parks where she could revisit old ruins and unearth them a millimeter at a time. Did anyone still go to those parks? They were out of fashion. Now everything moved relentlessly forward, and when all of those roads in Neustadt were widened, no one bothered to sift through all the rubble. No one cared. It was just her. And maybe that stranger who had left the note.

When you dig, you can't help but work in the dark; that is, if you climb into what you dig, or rather, if you're stupid and determined and brave enough to climb into what you dig. You climb into dark places. And then, Judit was aware that she'd been walking in circles.

The ghost of Hans Klemmer never spoke. If Hans were still alive, what would he ask of her? What would he say?

Judit pulled her baggy coat a little tighter. She knew where she had to go.

4

THE bus to Loschwitz didn't have a number. It left the northeast corner of the garment district a few blocks from Stein Square at five-fifteen precisely. Judit had boarded without going home to change, and so she waited in her duffle coat and trousers amongst the black-hats milling at that corner. They stared past her with a hostility so clean and direct that she almost turned back. When she did not, they stubbed out their cigarettes and boarded the bus. The motor was running.

What did the Yiddish on the side of that bus signify? There was a lot of it, in Hebrew characters, a regular list of blessings, curses, and restrictions, like their *pashkevils.* Judit had read plenty of Yiddish documents in graduate school, but black-hat Yiddish always eluded her. It was deliberately elusive. What if the bus were going to one of their neighborhoods in another district, or the village near Zeitz they'd named after one of their rabbis? The center door opened. One of their women—stone-faced, hair covered in a turban—got on board. So did Judit.

When Judit was a little girl, she'd sometimes see them around the garment district. Her father always said, "Don't be afraid. They're just ghosts. They can't hurt people who are still alive."

Nobody else's father talked like that. She hadn't been afraid, though. If Rudolph had let go of her hand, she would have followed those angry-looking men in their long black coats and high black hats across Stein Square to see where they were going.

Now, the bus pulled away from the center of Dresden. It filled with black-hats like a net fills with fish: jewelers carrying heavy cases, caftan-wearing men with low-crowned hats and broad, aggressive shoulders. There must have been one of their girls' schools not far from Parliament because the middle doors swung open and girls poured on—at least a dozen of them—bundled up in sweaters, with their legs encased in thick brown stockings, all carrying identical cheap knapsacks and angling for seats next to their friends. They whispered girl-secrets in Yiddish. So they had taken over that neighborhood too.

Of course, Chabad was different. They had always been in cities. Their headquarters was the Yenidze, an ostentatious mosque-shaped former cigarette factory in Dresden, and they made it their mission to get all Jews to perform mitzvot and speed the coming of the Messiah. Judit herself was often accosted by a woman in a wig who tried to get her into a white Mitzvah Tank. The woman spoke good German and promised her an audience with Rabbi Schneerson, who would receive her like his own child and give her a dollar—a real American dollar from the United States. Frankly, Judit was allergic to Chabad. The people who fell in with them always looked like they'd been hit on the head too many times and started to like it. Chabad were the friendly black-hats.

The men and women on the bus were not Chabad. They looked through her as confidently as Sammy Gluck had looked through the ghost of Hans Klemmer. They believed in ghosts, the spirit world: demons, angels, the raising of the dead. They did not believe in Judit.

* * *

Judit wasn't sure where to get off the bus. The first time she found the junk shop, it had been below street level, down a short metal stairway. Then, when she'd returned a few months later, it had moved, and she wandered for hours until the same old man appeared two blocks away, pulling a heavy grate across his door to lock up for the night. It seemed to move less by design than by necessity.

Was the junk shop a going concern? Had it simply appeared when she appeared? More and more now, she suspected that all the discarded footage hadn't found its way to her by chance. The shopkeeper never seemed surprised to see her. Still, if he had an opinion about Judit or her work, he didn't show it. He took her Judenmarks and passed the merchandise without meeting her eyes.

Every time Judit went to a black-hat neighborhood, she crossed into another country. The note in her pocket felt like an imperfect road map. Like any map, it looked different every time she traveled in a new direction. It might lead her astray. But one thing was certain: if someone wanted to disappear, to be erased from public record, there was no better place than Loschwitz. A room above a junk shop, say, a bed in one of their rooming houses, and no one could trace you.

Could she even allow herself to attach Hans's name to these speculations? To do so felt too dangerous, like stripping herself naked. But someone might disappear. Then years would pass. He'd send an emissary.

Or, at the very least, someone had sent the stranger with the note. She hadn't seen a face—just a shape that pushed her into that table in a way no black-hat would have done. But the film had come from Loschwitz.

As the bus progressed through Dresden, it passed by the nursing home where Leonora worked. The neighborhood had taken on an aggressive theological ugliness. All those cheap concrete houses, the fat women with their baby carriages, gawky beardless boys in white shirts, hurrying somewhere. *Pashkevils* plastered everything, marking territory. No street signs were necessary. Judit couldn't help but wonder how she'd found that junk shop in the past, and that was in the daytime. It was getting dark.

Someone tugged at Judit's coat. At first, she thought she'd imagined it, but the tug was insistent. She turned and craned her neck. A girl sitting behind her had attached a hand to Judit's sleeve. She addressed Judit in careful German.

"Are you lost?"

"*Shaindel, Shaa!*" That must have been her mother who was standing in the aisle holding a bag of groceries, and when she turned to reprimand her, the babies in her double-stroller started bawling, and she tried to find a way to balance the groceries and somehow pick up one of the babies. Every seat on the bus was occupied except the one next to Judit.

Shaindel's hair was pulled back severely, and her sweater was buttoned to the neck, but she had a sly expression. A little boy sat next to her—probably her younger brother—and he sucked his hand. She pulled the hand out of his mouth and addressed him in German too. "That's dirty!"

The boy snatched his hand away and said in Yiddish, "*Stop showing off.*"

Shaindel cheerfully replied, "*You're the big show-off. Hashem knows every filthy thing you do. That lady paints her fingernails when she meets a man. She isn't modest. But at least she doesn't stick her fingers in her mouth. She has more sense than you.*"

Judit hesitated. Then she leaned over and whispered, "Excuse me. How well do you know this neighborhood?"

The girl peered up at her. "I know everything."

"There's a shop. It's got a lot of junk. Old movies."

"Oh, I can take you right there," Shaindel whispered. "I know where it is. Just get off when we do, but walk a little behind, okay?"

At Shaindel's signal, Judit pushed her way through the center doors. She should have gone home and changed. In her trousers and duffle coat and her loose hair, she couldn't have been more conspicuous, and she felt all the more on display as she waited for Shaindel's family to disembark. They took a while: the girl, her brother, the mother with the double-stroller, two more toddlers. They headed down an alley in ragged formation, and Shaindel made a great show of pausing to tie her shoe. Then she looked up, and motioned Judit over.

Shaindel said, "You're Stasi."

Judit said, "I'm afraid not. Nothing that important."

"Then why do you want to find that shop? The owner's a bad man. You should arrest him."

"Your German's very good," Judit said, by way of changing the subject.

"I'm the best girl in my class," Shaindel said. She led Judit up a steep passageway. "The boys don't even study it in school. They just learn Talmud Torah. I'm glad I'm a girl even though I can't clean and I hate babies. We have so many babies that I'm not home half the time and no one misses me. They'd miss a boy."

Judit knew that they were heading in the wrong direction. She was in a different part of Loschwitz altogether, residential, dull-yellow blocks of flats. They climbed yet deeper into a labyrinth of housing blocks, criss-crossed by hanging laundry, littered with overturned wagons and tricycles. Judit almost tripped on half-embedded stairs, and actually had to pick her way along like a mountaineer.

Shaindel looked down and laughed. "You're out of breath. I'm not. I don't even feel it. We're used to climbing because you people won't fix the elevators. You must be my mother's age. Why don't you cover your head? Aren't you married? Why are you wearing a man's coat? Are you a man? No? Follow me through the playground."

Judit wouldn't have called it a playground. There was a rusty metal frame from which hung two lengths of chain and a single precarious swing. Shaindel planted herself right on the swing and rocked a little.

"The man you want to see, he has a little room in back."

"A room in back?" Judit struggled to keep her composure but she switched to Yiddish to make sure the girl understood. "*Is there someone living there, a tall man around my age? He has blond hair.*"

The girl gave her a ruthless look and answered in German. "What are you talking about?"

Judit paused to collect herself. Then she tried again. "What's in the room in back?"

Shaindel let herself be sidetracked. "A screen. It's a place to watch"—she struggled for the word in German—"the sexy." Then she blushed. "Is that what you want? Those kinds of movies?"

Judit hesitated. The sun had set an hour ago. The lights in the blocks of flats winked on behind closed shades, and she was pretty sure she'd never find her way back to the bus stop. They were nowhere near the street where she had always found that junk shop. Maybe it no longer existed. During her old forays into Loschwitz, the prospect of a store selling forbidden films that was supplemented with a screening room would have made her heart beat faster. It beat fast now. She felt it, almost heard it knocking in her chest.

Finally, Judit said, "I do want to see that shop, Shaindel. And I do want to see the room where people watch those movies."

Then, Shaindel stopped the swing. She stared right at Judit, looking both comical and daunting. Her sweater had come unfastened over her modest white blouse, and her ponytail was askew. She said, "What will I get if I take you there?"

Judit thought for a minute. Then she said, "You can watch the movies with me."

That was the right response. Shaindel smiled. She said, "He won't like that. I'll have to sneak in. I'm a good *gummie.* Is that the word in German?"

"That means sneaker," Judit said. "Like a tennis shoe." They continued up the hill together.

Judit had no idea where Shaindel led her. They might not even be in Loschwitz anymore. Identical five-story concrete apartment blocks reproduced themselves in tiered rows, painted in shades of pastel that were all muddied in the darkness. Shaindel had led her to a dull-pink concrete block. The side was plastered with the usual assortment of *pashkevils,* and a hand-printed sign in German:

Prosecute Bundist Assassins

Shaindel gave it a glance. "Oh, that's for outsiders. We already know that."

Judit had to keep herself from taking the note out of her pocket for a direct comparison. She said, carefully, "Do you learn to write in German at school?"

"Of course," Shaindel said. This line of reasoning seemed to try her patience. She urged Judit forward. "You have to go first, or he won't open the door."

Then they were in the dark, climbing flight after flight of stairs, and each landing was punctuated by activity, a child shrieking, someone hammering a nail into the wall, the rhythmic throbbing of a washing machine on spin-cycle. Somewhere in there, Shaindel produced a plastic flashlight.

"I got it for my birthday," Shaindel said. "I always keep it for emergencies. Like in a thunderstorm, or when I go into the sewer."

"Sewer?" The conversation felt as improbable as the circumstances.

"You find money there," she said. She kept the faint light just ahead of them as she directed Judit to a battered door with a card wedged into the nameplate. In Latin characters, badly formed, too careful:

Moses Kravitz, Importer

Same lettering. She didn't even have to check it against the note. She heard herself say, "This isn't the right place," all the while fighting back whatever was rising in her. Hans could be behind that door. But what if he were someone she couldn't even recognize?

"Knock," Shaindel said.

Before Judit could turn around or lift her hand, the door was opened by a short man in a skull-cap with a wild red beard. He wore a caftan that looked as though he'd slept in it. In Yiddish: "*You've got the wrong apartment.*"

He wasn't the man who left the note. The voice was an octave lower and the shape was all wrong. He looked like an angry dwarf. It was hard for Judit to justify remaining now, but Shaindel made escape more complicated, so she asked, "*Do you sell films here?*"

"*You speak Yiddish like a German,*" he said, and like the man in the junk shop, he kept his eyes averted, but he opened the door a little wider. Then he caught sight of Shaindel. "*Up to your mischief again?*"

Shaindel said, "*Uncle Moishe, would it hurt this lady to take a look? She came all the way here. And she's not going to be all sexy.*"

"*Who taught you to talk like that, Shaindel?*" Moses Kravitz said. He gazed at some middle distance, and with a small wave, motioned them inside. He closed and latched the door. "*I'm overloaded, lady. Every day new shipments. You want, you take.*"

The kitchen table was littered with bright slipcases of videos, some German, some French, most American. Judit knew just enough English to decipher a few titles: *Top Gun, An Officer and a Gentleman.* Some of the cases still held videos, and some were empty and propped up to display their lurid, shabby covers. Through the door, Judit could see a bathroom stacked floor-to-ceiling with loose, black tapes, tapes in the bathtub, tapes piled on the toilet and leaning against the wall.

Now that the door was closed, Kravitz seemed more inclined to engage Judit in conversation, and his tiny eyes flashed up like needles. "*I get plenty of men here but never ladies. Maybe you want a little something for your husband. Maybe he sent you. Or maybe,*" he said, "*you have your own little collection.*"

Shaindel said, "She wants to see the room where that man was."

Judit was speechless. Moses Kravitz frowned and shook his head. Judit could tell that he was reassessing her. She wasn't Stasi. He'd met those types before. She wasn't a prostitute. No prostitute would wear that coat. What was she then? Judit watched him flick through those limited categories and wondered if he'd come to a conclusion that would make him take out a gun. He probably owned one.

Shaindel tugged at Judit's sleeve, and said, in clear German: "Isn't that what you want? To see the room? He's gone now."

"*Good riddance,*" Kravitz said. "*He drove away my other customers.*"

"*Was he a bad man?*" Shaindel asked.

"*He was like all men,*" Kravitz said. "*He wasn't good, he wasn't bad. When he first came here, he was scared of his own shadow. An outsider.*"

Shaindel added, "He would watch movies all the time. That's all he did. The sexy movies."

Judit asked, carefully, "Where is he now?"

Kravitz shrugged and answered in Yiddish. "*What's he to you? He owes me money. You want to pay his bills?*"

Now she felt she had little choice, and hadn't come prepared. In her wallet she had maybe thirty Judenmarks, a twenty and assorted singles. She took the money out. She knew that Kravitz wouldn't touch her hand, so she laid it on a pile of videotapes. He twisted his mouth into that full red beard, and put the money in his pocket.

Shaindel watched this exchange with fascination and horror, and she broke in: "*Uncle Moishe, can't you tell she's a pauper? Look at the way she's dressed. No one with money wears clothes like that.*"

Kravitz ignored her, and said to Judit, "*I can show you his whole collection. It's right here.*" He pointed to a box in plain sight, an overwhelming assortment of reels and videos, some in cases, some loose and clearly broken, and because she wasn't sure what else to do, Judit sorted through the pile. Old habit overcame her, and by examining even the loose material she could estimate the age and country of origin: French, Soviet, American, and a few Bundist standards.

Then she pulled out a canister that was clearly marked. She held it in her hand for a little too long.

Shaindel peered at the label. "What's that?"

"*Shaindel, that's not for you!*" Kravitz said. "*You shouldn't see that kind of movie.*"

"*Is it dirty?*" Shaindel asked.

"*The gentleman in question, well, let's just say it must have been his favorite. He looked at it all the time.*" Then, to Judit, "*You want me to set up the projector?*"

"I can run the film myself," Judit said. She'd spoken German, but Kravitz had no trouble understanding her. He backed off, and studied her again.

"*Experienced at this, lady? What's your business, anyhow?*"

The film was *Monument.* Judit had conducted the interview and edited the footage in 1980, four years before Hans died. It was a documentary about the Churban.

5

[Firebombing of Dresden by British and American forces as seen from the air. White flame pouring from collapsed dome of the Cathedral, ash and fire and blackened stone, then empty roads, strewn with rubble. A woman's voice:]

> You begin with nothing. When I saw the bombs fall from the sky, it was like looking at the face of God.

[A woman appears, standing underneath an awning, as rain falls on either side of her. She is past middle age, well dressed, with animated features and a nervous smile, a lot of gray in her curly brown hair.]

> No. It was more like looking at myself, like I was flattened. All that confusion behind us, during those days when we were marched, half-naked, starving, marched for miles through the snow in Poland, with liberation at our backs—the Soviet gunfire we heard everywhere—and then packed into that railroad car that took me, took me, of all places, took me back home.

[Speaker identified. Caption: "Leahla Abramowitz." She gestures towards the door.]

> This was my house in Dresden. My parents came here from Lodz after the Great War, and my father had a little optical business in the center of the Altstadt. I knew this neighborhood.

[Photograph of a young girl holding a parasol in front of that same entrance, her face almost crazed with that same enthusiastic animation. Cut to the same old woman, holding an umbrella as she leads us down that same street where rain continues to fall.]

> This was the way I walked to school. It was just around the corner.

[Building appears, blurred by rain, not in good condition, ramps extending from both sides, the windows dark. She approaches, and hesitantly opens the door. There's a little wan sunlight spreading across the black and white tiles.]

> I think it's a hospital or a nursing home now, but it was a Jewish school back in the '20s and '30s. I remember everything. And back across the railroad tracks—

[Abramowitz makes a sweeping gesture.]

> That's where we had our club. The Bundist club, where we met every afternoon.

[Amateur footage with a hand-held camera, children banging pots and pans and wearing paper hats, as a young man, wearing a sandwich board with Yiddish writing, steps forward and recites something forcefully. A series of still photographs of exteriors, in grainy black and white, identifying structures as Abramowitz speaks.]

> Of course there were dozens of those clubs. The sports club, the craftsmen's club, a nursing home, a burial society, and the Mendelssohn club too. That one they wouldn't let us in, because we were Easterners. They also had no use for us at the fancy synagogue by the Cathedral. No, my father would pray in a little room in somebody's basement.

[Abramowitz continues to walk down a busy street, umbrella furled now, and pauses before a gate flecked with rain and obscured by passing pedestrians. She makes an effort to clear space, assisted by a visible cameraman, and points to a grille in the shape of a Star of David.]

> There's what they used to call the New Jewish Cemetery. It was already full by the time we came to Dresden. So was the old Jewish Cemetery. My dead, they're buried somewhere else. The Germans deported all the Polish Jews in 1938.

[Slow montage of images, exhumed pits from the Chelmno death camp, with the earth still clinging to the dead, pit after pit, and lingering on a tangle of bones and half-decomposed flesh. During this sequence, Leahla Abramowitz's voice continues:]

> I remember the restaurant in the Neustadt where we had to wait before they took us by train back to Poland, across the border. You can still eat in that restaurant. We waited there for the truck to take us to the station.

Maybe even then, my father, my mother, my two brothers, maybe we knew where we were really going.

[Back to Abramowitz, who stands beside the tracks at the Neustadt station, staring right at the camera.]

But we didn't know how it would end. See, I know now. After the ghetto, the camp, after I marched in rags, in broken shoes, to a train that was supposed to take me to another camp so the Russians wouldn't find us, I found myself back where I started. In my Dresden. I found myself there the day God rained down fire. What could I do?

[She smiles.]

I stayed.

[Contemporary footage of Dolzchen forest on Dresden's outskirts, villas, evergreens, a sandy path covered with pinecones. Abramowitz walks away from the camera, gesturing towards a clearing.]

In the confusion, in the chaos after the bombs fell, many girls escaped from the factories where we did forced labor, where we made fuses. There were four of us who found each other.

We knew pretty quickly that we'd have to get out of the city center. We'd steal clothing from laundry lines and potatoes from gardens, and the first month—in the cold—when we couldn't find any other shelter, we dug ourselves a trench and tried to keep a fire going. We hung on to each other—a Polish girl named Maria and two Jews like me, Beryl, Gitel.

And then one morning—it was April, yes, maybe late April. We were in that trench, the fire was long out, and we were all of us in a tangle, dressed in what clothing we could steal, and that was the first time I heard it. Russian. And they were taking photographs.

[Photographs]: barely clad women, naked legs across each other's backs, focus on a hand around a shoulder, a filthy cheek, a bare buttock. Then the camera pans to show the tangle of them.]

Then I just kept still. My heart jumped inside me because I couldn't believe they were here. And they were standing right over us taking those photographs as evidence because they thought that we were dead.

[Abramowitz speaks to the camera, still surrounded by shadowy pines.]

Now I couldn't speak Russian, but somehow I knew—I knew what they were saying and I was the first to stir and get myself to my feet. My God—I was so ashamed and weak—and I told them not to take my picture, and I was speaking German, and the soldiers looked at me in such a way—I was afraid. But something made me say: "We're Jews." And then, their officer—

[Photograph of Soviet officer, full face, cocked cap, crisp uniform.]

He speaks and says, yes—he speaks in Yiddish to me—"*All of you, Jews?*" And when I hear that Yiddish, I know this officer—he's one of us. And what could I say? I spoke in

Yiddish also and I told a little lie because I loved Maria. "*We are all of us Jews.*"

[Photograph of Leahla wearing officer's coat, standing in the forest. She looks at the camera with terrified, wide eyes. The coat comes down to her knees.]

And then he said, he was still speaking Yiddish, "*You are free, all of you. Go where your hearts desire.*" How can I describe? This man, this officer, a fellow Jew, he was riding, no joke, a white horse. And I said to him, "I came from here, from Dresden. I can show you—I remember everything."

[Wedding photograph. That officer still in uniform, and a plump, fully recovered Leahla in a dark suit, with both her arms around his waist. Caption: "Leahla and Dmitri Abramowitz, 1948."]

Well, it took a while. I had typhus, of course, and around five other things as it turns out, but Dmitri kept saying, I want that tour of Dresden, you promised to show me Dresden, and what could I do? Of course, we had to go where he was stationed. Here we are, in Rathen. That's after our two sons were born.

[Photograph of the family on a picnic by the Elbe, sandstone cliffs in the distance. Dmitri Abramowitz frankly stout now, in a porkpie hat and shirtsleeves, holding the hand of a dark-eyed toddler, as Leahla's head bows over a child in her arms.

Cut to Leahla Abramowitz holding that same photograph.]

That's the last picture I have of him. He was on duty, and a fascist shot him. A sharpshooter. That was in 1954. I want to show my grandson his stone.

[Leahla Abramowitz stands at a cemetery with a young child, and together they pass black and white markers, each at the head of a rectangle of grass, ivy, or flowers. In the distance is the Elbe, and beyond it, those same white and black and yellow sandstone cliffs.

She pauses at last before a marker with Dmitri Abramowitz's name engraved in German and Cyrillic, and above it, a red star. Then she whispers something to her grandson, who turns his face towards the camera, fleetingly and with impatience. He picks up a stone. She guides his hand to place that stone on top of his grandfather's marker.]

> I always like our tradition, to put a stone on top. I don't know why. He doesn't know we've been here. But someone will know.

[She faces the camera.]

> Honestly, can I tell you what it means, living here? In this country? It means facing it all over again, every day. It means swallowing my own *kishkas*. But I can tell you, it always means really, really knowing–

[Off camera: Unidentified woman's voice:]

> Knowing what?

[Abramowitz looks right at the camera.]

> That I'm alive.

6

KRAVITZ turned off the projector. He addressed Judit in German. "Well?"

It was clear that Kravitz knew that Judit was familiar with what she had seen. He'd watched her watch it. Through the moss and rust of his beard and tangled side locks, his face was undeniably expressive.

Brusquely, Judit replied in Yiddish, "*I'll pass. Not what I'm looking for.*"

Now there was no doubt. It was the same voice Kravitz had heard off-camera at the end of the film. He clearly struggled to find a way to turn this information to his own advantage, and persisted in his awful German. "So maybe you still want to make a business. The man who watched, you want to know a little more about him. A real character. Watch out. He took a special interest, I think, in the lady who made that movie."

She didn't say a word.

"Interest in you," Kravitz said, "and your husband."

Judit's hand was in her pocket now. Her fingers closed around the note. She said, "My husband is dead."

She wanted Kravitz to deny it. She tried to will his mouth into forming the words and telling her that Hans had sat in that same screening room just where she had been sitting, and that for a price, she could know where he'd gone. Instead, Kravitz reverted to Yiddish. "*This country is built on a cemetery. When the dead rise, they'll want their bones back. You need to put that in the film you're making now. I think you already got some very interesting material. Am I right?*"

The screening room was cramped and sticky with the residue of who-knows-what. What had possessed her, to come here? What stupid hope? Nobody sent a messenger. The messenger had sent himself, and fueled with pornographic movies, he had found her alone in the dark.

She finally asked, "*Does he have a name—the one who takes a special interest?*"

"*You think I ask those questions of outsiders? I wouldn't ask him any more than I'd ask you,*" Kravitz said. "*But he's a jailbird. That much I can tell you. I've got an eye for it.*" He removed the film from the projector and put it back in its case. Then his gaze rose from below those red eyebrows like oil rising through dirty water. "*Don't take chances. Look what they did to your husband. You want protection, I make arrangements.*"

Judit said, "*You don't have anything I want.*"

Kravitz said, "*Suit yourself.*"

7

EVEN before she'd reached the bottom of the stairs, Shaindel had asked what film Judit was making and interrogated her to the point where she was forced to admit that she worked for the museum that had been the source of what they'd seen upstairs. To Shaindel, this was as exotic as working for the Stasi.

"Then did you see all those bodies?" Shaindel asked.

"Somebody took those pictures a long time ago," Judit said. "As evidence." Then she had to explain about the archive and the photographs and footage that she catalogued and sometimes edited and spliced into the films approved for public distribution. Shaindel had never heard of the National Museum. As the two walked back to the center of Loschwitz, where Judit hoped to catch a bus back to her dormitory, she addressed question after question and described the rooms devoted to the Golden Age of Ashkenaz, the Hall of Bundist Heroes, and the exhibit on Judenstaat's early history.

Shaindel had heard of Leopold Stein. "Oh, Stein the butcher," she said, with a throwaway authority that Judit couldn't counter. Then: "It doesn't matter where Jews live. When the Messiah comes, there won't be any countries."

"This is your country," Judit said in German, which Shaindel had continued speaking. "You need to know our history."

"It's not real history," said Shaindel.

"What's not?"

"That movie. All those dead people naked."

"It know it's hard to see," Judit said. "But it's all true."

There'd been debate about incorporating those photographs. The National Museum had a strict policy about Churban artifacts: they must originate with the survivors. Purists considered images like the ones they'd used sheer voyeurism. Judit had argued at the time that the Soviets who took the photographs weren't pornographers. They were documenting genocide. If the pictures made people feel violated, that was the whole point.

Judit thought all this, but what she said to Shaindel was: "My mother survived Auschwitz."

Shaindel asked, "What's that?"

Judit stopped walking. They'd come to the center of Loschwitz. Most of the shops were closed, though a few basement enterprises were open for business. What light there was filtered through their grated windows, and turned the dark street gray. How many of those shopkeepers came from Hungary or Poland and had family who died in Auschwitz or Treblinka? Then Judit remembered. The black-hats believed that the slaughter was a consequence of Jews like Judit who had turned their backs on God. Maybe Shaindel's ignorance was better than what someone might have taught her.

Finally, Judit said, "Auschwitz was a camp."

"Oh," Shaindel said. She must have known that Judit had left something out of the story, but she didn't pursue it. "Like an army camp. Where they train people."

Now, the public bus passed by. Judit flagged it down and boarded before she had to say what people were trained to do.

* * *

Judit hadn't seen the last of Shaindel. The next day, the girl appeared in the archive. Judit had been trying to concentrate on the Anniversary Project, and began by sorting through her earliest material, a 1922 Ernst Lubitsch spectacle about the life of Moses Mendelssohn, and faded Dresden footage that included incidental glimpses of the Great Synagogue before its destruction. No historical reckoning. Nothing explosive. She knew that Kornfeld would reject it all, and the futility was a great comfort to her.

Maybe Judit would be fired. Then she would melt away somewhere untraceable, and she could stop looking over her shoulder every time she turned a corner or walked through that isolated underpass by her dormitory. She was edgy, rattled, and at the same time stubborn about interruptions. Thus, it was no surprise that Shaindel had been knocking insistently for at least five minutes before Judit—who'd assumed it was Sammy Gluck—opened the door.

"Shouldn't you be at school?" Judit asked.

Shaindel shook her head emphatically. She thrust a bulging plastic bag at Judit and said, "For your movie."

Judit had no choice but to put the bag down on the worktable and remove what was in it: twenty videotapes, including *Rambo II, Nine to Five,* and *The Breakfast Club.* Most of them had no slipcovers at all.

"He watched these too," Shaindel said. "Can you use them? Are you mad at him? Why is it so dark in here?" Then, "Who's that?" She'd seen the ghost.

The ghost saw her too. It stared back with detachment. Judit fully expected it to sweep the tapes to the floor, but it just receded in its smooth, uncanny way and assessed the titles Shaindel had deposited. Judit watched Shaindel watch the ghost and fought her own sense of utter violation.

The girl's eyes followed the specter with curiosity, and she repeated her question. "Who's that, Judit?"

"My husband," Judit answered.

"Do you work here too?" Shaindel asked the ghost. Judit was so sure the ghost would answer, or do something worse, that she broke in.

"He's not alive."

"Oh," Shaindel said. Her mouth tightened. "So he's a dybbuk. I've heard of them." She turned back to the ghost and started to say something else, but Judit interrupted.

"He doesn't talk. He's just here."

"Why?" Shaindel asked.

"He just lives here," Judit said savagely.

Shaindel didn't look convinced. "When a dybbuk comes back, it's because it forgot something. Or because it wants something. Unless you visited the grave and looked back. You should never look back. Did you call out to the Evil One?" she asked as though it were an ordinary question.

Maybe it was an ordinary question for those people. After all, they believed the dead would rise from their graves and want their bones back. They considered Judenstaat a massive cemetery, so it was only natural that Shaindel would see the ghost and speculate about its motives, but Judit didn't care. "He's just here," she said. "He lives here. And you'd better leave before he hurts you."

Shaindel departed with reluctance. She said, "You'd better find out what he wants or he'll end up inside you. That's what dybbuks do, if you're not careful."

When the Stasi agent appeared for his November visit, before he rose from his couch in the sitting room, Judit said to him, "So I guess you know I was in Loschwitz."

He was on his feet now, courteous as ever. "I know. Good afternoon."

It was impossible to throw that man off-balance. Deflated, Judit sat down in the couch without his invitation. If that struck the agent as unusual, he gave no sign. He asked the usual questions about the bus line to the dormitory and her detour through the underpass.

"You realize," he said, "we'd sooner you didn't risk it. It's an enclosed area and not as secure as we'd like."

"What? You think someone's going to shoot me down there? Who? The old Saxon lady who sells violets?"

"Not her," said the Stasi agent. He smiled a little, or at least the edges of his mouth turned up. He had on his winter coat. Over the past three and a half years, Judit had seen the man so often that she could mark the changes of season by the brown corduroy, the black wool, the tan worsted, the beige trench coat. He went on. "In reference to the earlier matter, I must remind you that when you leave our jurisdiction, it makes our work very difficult."

"Surely you could have followed me," Judit said. "You'd just need the right kind of hat."

"Mrs. Klemmer, if you want to make a joke at my expense, I certainly won't stop you. But I'm sure you're aware that the residents of Loschwitz are not like us."

"I'd say they're a lot like you," Judit said. "Dead certain. Except when they're not, if you know what I mean."

He shifted in his seat. Why was she playing with him? She had no proof that he'd been Hans's bodyguard, but his very discomfort fueled her own suspicions. He had not protected Hans. What made her think he could protect anyone else? She could just hand him that note, and his reaction would tell her more than she knew now.

The agent had run through his list of required questions and had to get on with the rest of his miserable day. Where did he go after these monthly interviews? Did he walk to the phone booth on the corner and file a report? Did he take a taxi to an office full of surveillance equipment and watch somebody else? No, improbably, she sensed she was his only case, and he was stuck with her.

Still, he certainly seemed unusually anxious to move on, and finally, he got up, and for the first time in three and a half years, he was the one to end the interview.

"So any time I need you? Is that what you're going to say?"

"Any time you'll let us help you," the agent said.

"Well, I needed you that night," Judit said. She didn't elaborate, but she looked right at him.

He bowed his head and buttoned his coat. "It's cold out, Mrs. Klemmer. I hope you don't have any great plans. If you don't mind my saying so, get some rest. Your health hasn't improved since my last visit. You may not realize you're sweating. Do you own a thermometer?"

"I don't," Judit said. She took his card, and held it in her hand as she watched him go.

If she ran, she could catch him. The wind swept across the windows, and the hallway was so bitter cold that Mrs. Cohen the porter wore her coat indoors. As Judit walked past her, she looked up and said, "You'd better put on something warmer if you're braving what's out there."

"I don't have anything warmer," Judit said.

She looked surprised. "What do they pay you where you work? I've seen Saxons who dress better than you do."

The statement had no answer. Judit was suddenly aware of how she looked to Mrs. Cohen: the cotton trousers from college, the sweater that had belonged to Hans, the duffle coat that had belonged to Hans. She looked deliberately vagrant, homeless. How long had it been since she'd just sat down and made herself something nice on her sewing machine? It was as though she wasn't worth the trouble.

She walked up to her room and switched on the light. That evening, it felt too small. She sat and laid the agent's card on the middle of her desk.

Joseph Bondi
Lieutenant Colonel
Central Organization for the Protection of Secrecy
Ministry of State Security
ARtur 5-3112

And on that card, the sword crossed behind the shield with its blue stripes and yellow star.

On the right-hand corner of the desk, beside her pencils and her sharpener, were a stack of those cards from the past three and a half years, the ones she had accumulated as a way to mark that time had passed at all. They were the physical evidence that she was three and a half years older, three and a half years alone. Her hand on the desk looked alien to her, with its short nails, skin hardened with the cold, the wedding ring.

She picked up a card and turned it over. On its back, in Yiddish:

I love you.

Judit flipped the card back over and laid her hand on top of it. She sat there for a while. Her first thought flew by too quickly to name. Then: it's an agent's trick. Then she thought: Yiddish, in Hebrew characters, how did he learn to do that?

Finally, and fully, it was clear: he was somebody else. It was all too confusing. She could never call him now.

The Battle of the Languages

1

EVERYONE understood spoken Yiddish. Reading and writing were another story. Aside from black-hats and a few scholars like Judit, young people couldn't do much more than slowly sound out the letters of the Hebrew alphabet. The assumption was that Yiddish would die a natural death, and by the time Judit was old enough to go to school, that seemed to be the case.

Back in those days, Leonora used to pick up a Yiddish magazine called *The Book Peddler* that published fiction and poetry, but when the corner store stopped carrying it, she didn't complain. "It was nonsense—fairytales about goblins and loose women, rabbis making deals with the devil. Better we should forget those stories." A scholarly periodical called *Studies in the Mother Tongue* hung on until the mid-'60s, when it got into trouble for a piece attributed to no single author: "*A Stylistic Analysis of the Manifesto of Stephen Weiss.*"

The article contained no more than a few passages from the manifesto, the same ones that the prosecution read into the transcript of Weiss's trial-in-absentia. In a public statement, the editors insisted, "We quote the passages for one reason alone, to analyze their Yiddish, the syntax, the absence of Hebraisms, the choice of Slavic rather than Germanic synonyms, and most of all the impossibility of accurate translation into any language other than Yiddish."

Maybe that's when it began: the rumors. Had the magazine taken it upon itself to translate the entire manifesto into French, German, and English just to prove that it couldn't be done? Was the full document still in circulation? It got around that if you held *Studies in the Mother Tongue* to a pane of glass, you'd see the whole of the manifesto written in flowing Yiddish script. Copies disappeared from public libraries, maybe taken by the authorities or maybe taken by someone else and duplicated.

And some say Weiss himself had never died in exile. No, a dummy had been sent to the morgue in Buenos Aires, or one of his notorious apprentices was buried in his place after allowing his face to be reconstructed by a plastic surgeon. Or Weiss had died but not before he had arranged for his successors to disseminate his manifesto and carry on his treachery worldwide. Under the guise of so-called neutrality, they would sell Judenstaat to the highest bidder, sabotage the Protective Rampart, and put the country in German hands again.

Judit's father Rudolph would say of Weiss, "He should have found a different line of work." Then he would smile in his abstracted way. Nobody else's father talked like that. Leonora said, "You'll scare the girl." But Judit wasn't scared. She was disgusted.

There was no story too wild in 1967. Maybe it was because of stirring in the east, across the Polish and Czechoslovak borders. Judit was a young girl then, impatient and judgmental. She sang the Bundist songs and knew the story of her country. She thought her ideological education was long over. The chaos forming around her seemed absurd, and she had every reason to believe she could wear her certainty like a magic cloak and stride forward in good Bundist fashion. How would she know that in six years, she would meet Hans, and nothing would make sense again?

2

AFTER she'd introduced Hans to her mother, Judit had looked forward to giving him a tour of Dresden. She'd dragged him all over town, to her old school, to the site of martyred Elsa Neuman's house on Budapester Street, to the neighborhood community center where the Bundist Youth Group met, a former church with fabulous acoustics for their concerts. They took the little steam-train that ran through the park, and Hans managed to stifle his amusement as a grim little boy in a uniform and visor told them that their tickets were invalid and they'd have to get off at the zoo. Then they visited the Hygiene Museum, and she showed him the drawers full of foreign objects children swallowed.

"And there's a slice of a person under glass, a real slice, head to toe, so you can see everything, the brain, the bones, the bowels, the organ systems," Judit said. "But it's not here. It must be closed for renovations."

Hans said, "What are they renovating? I hope they don't want volunteers."

"I used to dare myself to look at it," Judit said. She blushed without knowing why. She couldn't explain why it felt so important for

Hans to see everything, and for her to look at those places through his eyes.

Finally, she led him to the site of the Great Synagogue, that lush green rectangle not far from Parliament, and she said, “This is our monument. This is our prayer-house.”

Hans gave her a strange look. “I know this place.”

“I should hope so,” Judit said pedantically. “Fascists burned it down in ’38. But the fire returned.” Then she felt foolish. “So when you were at the orphanage, they talked about it?”

“Sometimes,” Hans said. “They said it was a graveyard.”

“Who said?”

“I can’t remember,” Hans replied. “Lamb, let’s move on.”

Of course, Hans insisted that they go to a concert at the Opera House. He had made an extravagant gesture: two box seats for a program of Liszt and Schumann with Vladimir Ashkenazy, a guest conductor. He’d bought the tickets well in advance, and took along a copy of Schumann’s First Symphony so he could follow along as they played. He was too tall for that little box, and he folded himself in half and propped the score on his knees, making notations with a pencil.

Judit felt visible and vulnerable. She knew she ought to be enjoying the performance, but the box creaked every time Hans moved, and she was afraid they’d fall into the orchestra. She was relieved when intermission came and Hans whispered, “We don’t have to stay for the Liszt. I really wanted to know how Ashkenazy would handle ‘Spring.’ ”

“So how did he handle ‘Spring’?” Judit asked when they were safely outside once again, walking across Mendelssohn Bridge with their arms around each other. The train for Leipzig left at ten, and of course, they had to be on it. They couldn’t very well stay with Judit’s mother.

Hans said, “He’s just finding his way as a conductor. You can tell. But it’s moving to see him up there. He knows Schumann inside and out. He's a master pianist, and in ten years, he'll be a master conductor."

"And will it take you that long?"

"Probably," said Hans. Then he whistled something that Judit didn't recognize, and he had to tell her that it was the theme of what they had just heard. He said, "You know, he wrote that right after he finally married Clara. Over her father's objections. Clara's father was very protective of her. She was a virtuoso pianist and a pretty good composer too. They lived in Leipzig when Schumann wrote his best work. Their house is a museum now. I'll take you there."

When Hans talked about music, he walked quickly, and Judit had to trot to keep up with him. They should probably catch the trolley to the station, but the night air was gentle and seductive. Maybe they could just sleep on a park bench in each other's arms. Judit liked the idea just enough to thread her fingers through Hans's hand and slow him down a little. She asked, "Why don't you write music?"

Hans said, "Me? I'm not built for it."

"But you know so much and hear so much, I know you could compose."

"Why are you so set on my being a composer?" Hans asked, and he laughed and pulled Judit down on a bench by the bridge. He opened the score. "Look at all this. You realize what it takes? All those notes, and Robert Schumann had to choose between them."

"You know I can't read a thing," said Judit.

"Come on. You read the Hebrew alphabet. Music's not so hard. But that's beside the point," Hans said. "I want everything—all the notes and what's underneath the notes, their history, who's played them, how well or badly—"

"But we all choose," Judit said. She had turned serious. It was unbearably wonderful that she could have this kind of conversation in her hometown, and with a man she'd share a bed with that night. That didn't make her any less determined to press her point.

"I mean, when I curate an exhibit like the one on Leipzig, I have all these documents and photographs, whole boxes of them, all that film footage to sort through, but most of the work I do isn't looking at it. Looking's the easy part. It's about figuring out what I can use. That's what film editors do. Nothing would get done if you kept everything."

Hans said something unexpected. "Every time you cut a frame, you slit a throat."

Judit said, "That's not fair."

"It's true though," Hans said. "What do you leave out of the story?"

It was a pointed question, one Judit knew she couldn't answer. It was all of a piece with all the questions she couldn't answer. It struck her like a hammer then. She had spent all day dragging Hans to the sacred places of her childhood, and logically, he ought to do the same. Only, Hans had no childhood. He had the orphan home, before that, his uncle's tavern, and before that, nothing. None of those places were sacred to Hans. Maybe enough time had passed to let Hans know that Judit couldn't answer his question, or maybe she had found a way to turn that question back at him. She said, at last, "This Clara, once Schumann married her, were they happy?"

"Very," Hans said. "At least in Leipzig. They had eight children. Then it gets complicated. There's a younger man in the picture, a certain Mr. Brahms. But that's much later, after Schumann went mad."

"I'm glad you're not a composer," Judit said.

"Me too," Hans said.

After that, they really did have to run for the train. The whole time, Judit thought about the parts of Hans's life she'd never really know, the names of his parents and their fates, the place where they were buried. For Hans, every rectangle of green would be a graveyard, every cornerstone a tombstone, and for that reason alone, he would have no country. After they'd boarded the train and were in their seats and out of breath, Judit asked Hans, “When is your birthday?”

Hans didn’t seem surprised at the question. “I don’t know, Lamb. Maybe the year. My uncle told me ’44, but there’s not even proof of that.”

“Well, don’t you have a birth certificate?”

Hans shrugged. Then he said, “Why don’t you choose a birthday for me?”

Without hesitation, Judit said, “September fifteenth.” She waited for Hans to ask her why she’d chosen that date, and when he didn’t, she added of her own accord, “It’s when I always wished I had my birthday. No one’s on vacation, so your friends are all in town, and the weather’s wonderful. Plus, it’s an easy date to remember—right in the middle of the month.”

“Then that’s my birthday,” Hans said. He pulled her close to him, and she leaned her head against his shoulder as the Leipzig Express took them home.

3

MAYBE Shaindel was right. Hans haunted Judit because he wanted something from her. Even as he hectored her about her little executions, he wanted to be organized. He demanded his own coherence. If somebody lied about the murder, she must fill in the missing pieces. Hans demanded the truth, a full historical reckoning. Or did he? What could a ghost demand?

Everything. That was the trouble. If Hans had been alive somewhere in Loschwitz, she could have asked him what he wanted, but now there was no limit and no warmth to humanize those harsh demands. Let her take all the facts and organize them, pornographic images that documented genocide, canisters marked "Discard," and even ordinary footage that no one would find explosive:

February 1949: Leopold Stein and Harry Truman. They walk together at a brisk pace by the Elbe, and Truman stops and points across the moonscape of rubble still in evidence along the banks where American bombs had leveled Dresden not so long ago. According to the German voiceover, Truman has once again repeated his offer of interest-free loans.

September 1951: A riveter is obscured by his overalls. His hard-hat fits badly. He turns off the machine, smiles at the camera, and rolls up his sleeve to show his tattooed number from the camps. His neighbor does the same. Before the not-so-steady camera, worker after worker reveals his number, and they're held up in a line. The camera pulls in so close that the numbers dissolve into an abstraction. What was the point of that unfocused close-up? Probably there was no point. But she won't leave it on the cutting-room floor.

November 1950: The first car to be manufactured in the country, the homely Yekke, rolls out of the factory in Zwickau with great fanfare. It is compact, and its body is made of a special lightweight compound developed in Sweden. Leopold Stein climbs inside; he's too big for the cabin, and his knees are visible over the steering column. He turns the ignition and drives it out of the factory. It is only with effort that the car manages to break the ribbon draped across the door of the garage.

June 1948: A filmed performance of the National Anthem written by Hanns Eisler, the cynical composer who had come to Judenstaat to write a vicious song cycle about the funny little Jewish state. He never left.

> "May fortune and peace be granted
> to Judenstaat our monument.
> All the world is yearning for peace.
> Give the nations your hand."

The choir performs outdoors, with scaffolding and half-constructed landmarks all over a packed square on the fifth anniversary of Liberation Day. They sing below the Stripes and Star, dressed, as was the fashion of the time, in concentration camp uniforms with red neckerchiefs to honor Soviet liberators.

Much later—1960: More amateur footage, eight-millimeter,

surely taken by the father of one of the children in a Youth Group choir as they sing the "Hymn of the Ghetto Partisans," one of the few Yiddish songs that Bundist children learned by rote:

> "*Never say that you have reached the final road*
> *Though the lead-gray clouds conceal blue skies above.*
> *The hour that we've longed for now draws near.*
> *Our steps proclaim like drum-beats: We are here!*"

WE ARE HERE: The Credo of the Bund. We aren't going anywhere. We turn death into life. That's what it means, to live in Judenstaat.

Judit herself had sung that hymn with far more vigor than she'd ever sung the National Anthem. She'd even taught it to Hans. She'd hoped to teach it to her children, just as she'd assumed Hans would teach them to play instruments. She had imagined songs for each of the three girls with distinctly pitched voices: a flute, a clarinet, an oboe.

Judit had been pregnant when she'd edited *Monument.* Maybe her determination to include the images had been driven by sheer happiness, a generosity verging on arrogance that made her certain that the Russians took those pictures with the best intentions. She'd fought hard to include them, those excruciating Chelmno corpses, the girls in the Dresden trench. A few weeks later, the midwife couldn't find a heartbeat. She'd sent her for a sonogram, which estimated that the baby had stopped growing at week sixteen. Judit had counted backwards and had landed on the date she'd finished *Monument.*

Did Shaindel sing the song of the Ghetto Partisans? Certainly not. Loschwitz girls never sang at all because their voices would carry through walls and seduce the men who pored over their volumes of the Talmud. Shaindel was maybe eight years old, just the age that their first daughter would have been.

4

BEFORE Judit could even get past Mr. Rosenblatt at the front gate, he told her to go straight to Kornfeld's office. She found him waiting in the hall, and he threw his arms around her and laughed, "Judit, why didn't you tell me?"

She wriggled out of his embrace. "Tell you what?"

"That's she's on the project. This is going to save us! When I heard the news last night, I thought, Judit's behind it. I should have known you had a card up your sleeve, sweetheart."

Kornfeld was so effusive and looked so diminished and vulnerable away from his desk that Judit felt more embarrassed than confused. She did need to admit that she had no idea what he was talking about.

"Anna Lehmann. Your own Anna Lehmann has signed on as historical consultant," Kornfeld said. "You're telling me you didn't know?"

"I'm telling you I didn't know," Judit said.

"But you're in touch with her. She recommended you for this job, didn't she?"

"Ten years ago," said Judit, but Kornfeld still insisted that she had to be responsible. Now that Lehmann was a player, things would really start moving, and there'd be no more talk about involvement from across the border. He walked Judit back to his office, all the while chattering about what Lehmann would bring to the project, her air of authority, her wide-ranging connections.

"I didn't speak with her personally," Kornfeld said. "Not yet. She's over in Moscow right this minute, meeting with important people. They're releasing all kinds of information there, and we might even have something to show the public by the end of December. You know—a preview."

Judit felt dizzy. She did suspect that she might have something to do with Professor Lehmann's involvement. It was certainly on the strength of Lehmann's recommendation that the National Museum had hired her at all, and when Hans died, she'd gotten a note from Lehmann, a very affectionate and sympathetic letter written in Yiddish with an invitation to "*visit an old woman in Leipzig who remembers fondly the little girl with the big eyes who never turned down a cup of tea from her professor.*"

She hadn't kept track of Anna Lehmann's career. She hadn't kept track of anyone's career. She'd just kept working. Yet it didn't surprise her that Lehmann had kept track of that work and found a way to interfere—"interfere" was the only word she could think of. That interference angered and flattered her in equal measure.

Judit had met Anna Lehmann a year after Hans, and the encounter had made her reconsider the direction of her career. When Judit enrolled at the university, she'd assumed she'd be an archeologist, but the National Parks had become controversial. Some professors dismissed the digs as "state-sponsored boosterism," and an angry minority asked pointed questions during lectures that challenged the patriotism of the instructors. The history department was even worse. The best professors lost their jobs in 1968, and the only ones left gave dry lectures on the Golden Age of Ashkenaz or Bundist ideology and its relation to the Churban, and it was always assumed that there was a Stasi plant in the auditorium.

In short, the academic world was in upheaval. Times were changing, and no one knew what direction things would take. Judit entered the graduate program in library science, hoping to stay out of that disgusting conversation. Still, when she was accepted into Lehmann's famous seminar on historical analysis, she was so surprised, and the seat was so coveted, she couldn't turn it down.

Anna Lehmann had seemed very old back then. She must have been sixty, maybe. Everyone called her Grandmother Professor. The seminar was held in her home in the center of Leipzig, a pretty house with flower boxes in the windows. She had once lived with another lady, a specialist in old instruments who was the only one permitted to touch the organ in the community hall that used to be Saint Thomas's Church, the instrument that had been played by Bach. Her portrait was on the mantle, and her tuning fork was on a piano no one played.

Lehmann was fluent in most European languages, but specialized in Russian, and also a strange form of Hebrew that was developed at the turn of the century in the Rothschild colony in Palestine. Her three-volume study of the failed experiment had taken fifteen years to write. Back in the '50s, she'd published articles on the Soviet Autonomous Region of Birobidjan and had gotten into trouble with the censors, and the very fact that she had been kept on after '68 spoke to both the importance of her work, and also her enduring reputation.

The other students in the seminar dismissed Judit as "the librarian," but for reasons no one understood, Lehmann cultivated her and even allowed her access to her Palestine materials, which were kept not in the campus library, but in a steamer trunk in her own study.

It was while poring over the photographs and documents in Lehmann's trunk that Judit learned that history, like archeology, was something she could rub between her fingers. The photographs from the years before the Great War were yellow, cracked, and exceedingly immediate: bearded men wearing weird knickers, girls in knickers too, and knotted head-scarves. They looked sun-struck and terrified. They carried spades in their hands. Judit leafed through diaries in Cyrillic, bound in leather stained with rain or even blood for all she knew. Exotic flowers were pressed between their pages.

There were a hundred reasons why the Rothschild colony disappeared: the war, the climate, T.E. Lawrence and the promises the British made to Syria and Jordan, even the Russian Revolution. Yet Anna Lehmann's own argument—one that gained currency—was that the messianic element doomed the project from the start. "Messianic" wasn't even her name for it. It was their own. Palestine Jews believed that in returning to the land mentioned in the scriptures, they would become the agents of their own salvation.

"Are you the agents of your own salvation? Are you Biblical prophets?" Lehmann addressed the eight students who sat on plush little stools and a big couch in her living room sipping tea from Meissen china. She was a big woman who wore a housedress like a length of wallpaper. Her steel-gray hair was cut in the shape of a bowl. Really, there was nothing grandmotherly about her.

"No, Grandmother Professor," they all replied.

"Good," she said. "Don't be. Biblical prophets make terrible historians. They never bother with the past, and they always mistake the present for the future. Now sharpen your swords, boys and girls. Beat them into plowshares. Harvest what we've sown and bring it back to Grandmother Professor." That meant they should write papers, and read them out loud in the seminar.

Judit volunteered to present her paper first. It had been based on public records she had found in Leipzig's town hall, and she'd spent long hours writing out requests and waiting for documents and missed a chance to hear Hans perform in a string quartet. He said he understood, but she could tell it mattered to him. All that work had to be worth the sacrifice.

She'd transcribed columns of names and figures into her notebook, and the resulting five-page paper was so dense with information that Professor Lehmann stopped her after half a page and said, "Again, Ginsberg. Slowly this time." She did her best to slow down. Then Professor Lehmann said to her, "That won't do."

"What won't do?" Judit was startled. She'd been expecting praise. In fact, the other seven students were no less surprised.

"This reading of the facts. It won't do. The information," Lehmann said, "is certainly correct. The names of the contractors, are, no doubt, accurate, as are the figures. Nor do I doubt that the contracts were given to those with American connections, as you imply."

"She doesn't come right out and claim it," said the student who had volunteered to read his paper next.

"As you imply," Lehmann continued, addressing Judit. "And it's very likely that people surrounding Stephen Weiss were hardly choirboys, as we all know."

The mention of Weiss changed the temperature of the room. This was 1974, after all, and times had changed to the point where one might talk about Americans in a way that showed sophistication, but never Stephen Weiss. Never like that.

Now, Anna Lehmann turned to the other students. She said, "What Miss Ginsberg has written is an excellent example of the difference between ideology and history. Deductive reasoning begins with a principle and marshals evidence to justify that principle. In this case, the principle would be Bundist orthodoxy."

Judit bristled. The hair on her arms and head literally spiked out like porcupine quills.

"You seem insulted," said Professor Lehmann. "Yet of course, five years ago, that would have been the highest praise." She smiled a little with her sour, badly lipsticked mouth, but that smile didn't touch the rest of her face. "Never begin with a principle, boys and girls. Or you'll end up being the agents of your own salvation, and we all know where that leads. Clear your heads of all that nonsense."

How could it be nonsense? Judit had grown up with principles. She had been taught that corrupt motives lead to corrupt results. Judit's research had confirmed that contracts given by the Cultural Ministry in 1949 had benefited a handful of stockholders in New York. That wasn't ideology. It was just true.

Lehmann, in her uncanny way, addressed what Judit left unspoken. "Why do we seek the truth? Not to pass judgment, surely. We can no more pass judgment on a fact than we can pass judgment on the weather. When we pass judgment on the weather, we call that 'small talk.' I suspect, Ginsberg, that you don't think much of small talk."

Judit was silent, but her thoughts were grim. Also, her heart was pounding.

"Now, it's far more interesting to take those speculators on their own terms. Were they doing something wrong? They lived in an age of speculation. They lived in their own ideological atmosphere with their own set of principles, and it is far more interesting to define those principles. Name them."

"Alright," said Judit. "They're called greed."

Lehmann turned to the other students. "Surely you children haven't lost your imaginations entirely. Surely you haven't smoked so much marijuana"—Lehmann's great joke was that her students all smoked too much marijuana—"that you're incapable of fixing one thought to another."

But if you let go of ideology, then what is history but a lot of random information, informed by nothing? Judit let the other students make that case, and some of them did. Meanwhile, she sank into herself and thought about the summers when she learned how each layer of sandstone corresponds to an age. With her spade, she had dislodged real things. Those artifacts were just as real as Lehmann's room, with its upright piano and the photograph of the stern-looking lady who had played it once, the china cups and matching teapot, the nine small spoons. Let years do their work and bury that room, and then let Lehmann claim her life was only random bits and pieces. Judit knew better.

Judit felt a fierce ownership of Anna Lehmann even as she felt dismissed by much of what she said. Of course, even then, Judit knew the two emotions were entangled.

5

WHAT Judit said to Hans was, "I wanted to take that teapot and crack it over her head. I mean, what the hell does she expect of me?"

"Why don't you ask her?" Hans said mildly. They had just made love, and the very ease and warmth of lying next to Hans made Judit talk and talk. He usually didn't mind. This time, he felt compelled to say, "You could always drop the class."

"It's not even in my field," said Judit. "I just thought maybe I'd learn something, but all I'm learning is that I don't know anything. Plus that picture of her old girlfriend keeps staring at me."

"She's jealous," Hans said.

Judit buried her face in the mattress. "Right. Of a library science student. I mean, I'm sure she's really threatened by me. I bet she'll steal all my material and write a Bundist exposé."

"I mean the girlfriend's jealous," Hans said. Judit rolled back over and couldn't help but laugh and squirm as Hans held her down. "Watch your step, Lamb. That woman's got such a reputation, even I've heard of her. Don't get too dazzled or I'll think you've fallen in love with her."

"I'm not in love with her," Judit insisted. "She's too old!" All the while, Hans pinned her to the bed, and they both hoped it wouldn't collapse from the activity. It was an awful bed.

"So who are you in love with then?"

"You, you, you!" Judit cried, until he fell on top of her and knocked out her breath, which was a good thing because that shut her up. They didn't want the neighbors to complain.

Judit had been spending more and more time in that apartment. On mornings when she'd slip back to her dormitory, what she did and who she was felt palpably apparent. Yes, she was full of sex, and also full of wild anxiety about her circumstances. Would the neighbors complain? Would they report her to the dean who would arrange for Hans to be evicted and expel her from the college? For what? For sleeping with the enemy? Did anybody say that anymore?

When Judit was in Archeology Camp, she was warned to stay close to the group. The implication was that there were Saxons in the area. Charlotte Kreutzberger reported that she'd seen one swimming in a gorge, and when Judit asked her how she knew he was a Saxon, she'd blushed from the neck and whispered, in her ponderous way, "His thing—it wasn't cut." Until Judit met Hans, she had no idea what Charlotte was talking about.

There were plenty of rumors about Jewish men with Saxon mistresses who would do things that a good Jewish girl would never dream of doing. That was the usual line. Again, until Judit met Hans, she had no idea what that meant either, and then he both told her and showed her how to do it. Then she said, "I guess I'm not so good."

"I'm glad," Hans said.

"They'll have to put me in the Hygiene Museum," Judit said, and when Hans looked baffled, she added, "Because I swallow foreign objects."

Then Hans said, "Why don't you move in with me?"

Judit had a thousand objections. The apartment was too small, the bed was terrible, they'd never be able to stop talking and making love and therefore he would get no chance to practice violin and she would get no chance to study.

Hans said, "I'll buy you a desk."

"And I'll buy you a bed."

"Us a bed," said Hans. Neither stated the obvious, that Judit couldn't leave the dormitory without making their relationship public, and that was why Hans wanted her to move into the apartment. He tried to prove that he was capable of practicing the violin while she re-copied notes on index cards. He played half an hour's worth of scales and intervals and trills, and she bore this patiently, until he kept moving closer and giving her comical looks over the bow, and then it all dissolved into its natural element and there was nothing to prove at all.

Of course, everyone knew about the two of them already. In the eyes of certain students, it made Judit a much more interesting person. Some girls from the dormitory asked her, shyly, if she'd like to have a drink with them sometime. One of them said, "We're going to a little place by the train station. They make their own wine from a local vineyard. It's Saxon-owned." Another added, "Is it true they don't use pesticides? That's so authentic." They were earnest, and in no way mocking. When she begged off, they looked sad, and wandered away, talking about how indigenous cultures can't really be revived, only replicated, stealing a glance at her over their shoulders as though they'd hoped she'd overhear the conversation.

Others were less sympathetic. One boy planted himself in front of her as she was crossing campus: "So I hear you like to be punished."

"Excuse me?" Judit said.

She tried to sidestep him, but he wouldn't let her pass and

shouted in a voice that carried: "You like your men with swastikas and pistols. You like to be pistol-whipped. Let me give you a history lesson, baby."

"Let me give you one!" She'd raised her voice to match his own and pushed her way forward. "It's 1974. I can do whatever the hell I want!"

He hadn't expected her to shout like that, and he let her pass but called out after her: "They shaved the heads of girls like you in Paris—shaved their heads and paraded them down the fucking street!"

He stood there all alone, looking crazy and stupid in his tight T-shirt and blue jeans, an artifact of another time, and as she walked quickly towards her linguistics tutorial, warmth flooded through her body, half-relief and half-gratitude. She was living in the present, and she was free.

Maybe it was that same impulse that made her consider changing her major to history. Old things were only interesting if she could figure out how they led to who she was and who the awful boy was, and who Hans was too. Hans may insist he had no history, and she would just laugh and let him keep insisting. In the end, she knew that her life's work would be getting to the bottom of Hans Klemmer.

Not that she said this when she went to Anna Lehmann's office. Lehmann had told her students that she had an office—"a dreadful place, no reason for you to go there"—as she did have official business such as writing course waivers and requisitions from the library and so on. When Judit arrived, the door was open. The professor hadn't lied. Her office was, in fact, dismal, small and overstuffed with books that were clearly of no importance. The light was so poor that it took Judit a while to make out Lehmann herself, who appeared to be writing something at her desk.

Judit stood in the doorway. Then Lehmann noticed her and said, "Oh. Yes. Come in, Ginsberg. Sit down if you can manage to remove what's on the chair."

This, Judit did, not carefully enough, as half a page of something stuck to the varnish. "I ruined it," Judit said. She was afraid she'd start to cry.

"Ruined what? Child, that's just some bureaucratic nonsense that's been on that chair since August and stuck to it. Some travel fund application. No one will miss it. You're overwrought, dear."

"No, I'm fine," said Judit. "I just wanted to ask you about that paper I presented. Should I rewrite it? Keeping in mind what you said about ideology and principles?"

Lehmann asked, "What paper?"

Judit tried not to show that she was hurt. "The one about the 1949 construction contracts."

"Oh yes, carefully researched," Lehmann said. "Very fine work." Judit began to protest, but then Lehmann interrupted. "I've been meaning to tell you, last spring I saw your exhibit on a similar subject. Those photographs. Very well done. Particularly the arrangement. Very little context."

"I'd meant to do more," Judit said quickly. "I could have written something up."

"*Pft. Words on a wall.*" Lehmann's Yiddish took Judit so much by surprise that she answered in that same language.

"*So you like pictures. Why? Because they can mean anything. But isn't that just lazy, Professor?*"

"Rather the opposite," said Anna Lehmann. Her German was deliberately distancing, and Judit felt embarrassed by both the initial intimacy and the shift back to formal discourse. Lehmann went on. "You have a talent in that direction. Make people work. Create mysteries. Let others solve them. Never solve the mysteries for them. Which is of course . . ."

She was going to say that of course that was the problem with the seminar paper, but instead, she sank deeper into the chair, and Judit realized it wasn't a desk chair at all, but an elaborate velveteen armchair that almost matched the pattern on Professor Lehmann's dress. She disappeared into that chair, and something sparked. She'd lit a cigarette.

Then she said, "Which is of course the beauty of archival work. Its power is insidious. Its hand is light. You have a light hand, Ginsberg."

Not sure how to respond, Judit said, "Thank you."

"Keep it nimble and precise. And keep it off his *putz,* young lady."

Judit thought she'd heard wrong. She hadn't. Lehmann stared out from the depths of that armchair, smiling lasciviously and pulling on that cigarette. It looked—was this possible?—as though she'd winked. Judit watched all of this as from a distance, her own cheeks burning, Lehmann's cigarette held between two fingers as she blew a trail of smoke in her direction. Judit finally said, "Professor Lehmann, I don't know what to say."

"Then don't say anything at all," said Lehmann.

"I don't want to get in trouble. I don't want to get expelled."

"Nonsense," Lehmann said. "Who gets expelled for that these days? It's practically a degree requirement. And a pretty girl like you, I'm surprised the wolves have kept away for this long."

"He's not a wolf. He's a musician." Then, "And he's a Saxon, Professor, but you know that already."

"Do I?" Lehmann stubbed out her cigarette. "I can hardly keep track of everything I know. The Saxon Question. Fascinating. There's a dreadful piece in last year's *Journal of Historical Inquiry.* No one has really done justice to the Saxon Question. Perhaps you will, my dear."

Judit retreated from that office, angered, flattered, belittled, and fascinated. She felt dirty. She also felt like rushing back to the apartment and telling Hans that Anna Lehmann had seen her exhibition, and that was probably the reason why she'd been admitted to her seminar. Also, on a level she couldn't quite acknowledge, Lehmann had given the two of them her blessing, but that, she wouldn't tell him.

Lehmann's own story was half a rumor. Yet that rumor was what led students to vie for a place in her seminar and was probably the reason why she'd been kept on through any controversy. She and Leopold Stein were lovers long ago.

6

WHAT Anna Lehmann actually said was, "Oh, Leopold Stein." After a dreamy pause, "Leo and I were lovers." Judit never actually heard her say it, but of course, stories like that do get around. In spite of all the physical evidence, or maybe because of the physical evidence, the story was believed to be true.

Photographs of young Lehmann were awfully arresting. She was a model for some of the great Berlin photographers of her day, not a conventional beauty, but with what some called "the head of a lioness," a strong jaw, Tartar cheekbones, and thickly lashed eyes. Her hair was black, and she wore it loose across magnificent shoulders. She'd been a student at Heidelberg, liberated by the security of her position as the only daughter of a judge and a woman with a generous allowance from her own wealthy family. She was a child of Weimar when there were no restrictions on education for Jews and few for women, born at precisely the right time. She wore her privilege like a fur coat, unapologetically. She had friends everywhere.

As a child, she had a weak chest, so her parents sent her to a sanitarium in Switzerland with a nanny who taught her French. She'd mix with other patients who came from France or England or Romania or Italy, and she would charm them with her precocious questions. Afterwards, she'd spend summers at one country house or another, collecting languages the way another girl might collect butterflies. She'd pin those specimens down and examine them with a good-natured vigor that was a little frightening to those who didn't know her.

In Heidelberg, a casual circle gathered in her room for rolls and coffee, and young Lehmann would question them each in turn about—for example—his opinion of Baptized Jews. At least half of those present fit that description, and it was both a relevant and a tactless subject. She'd blink her little black eyes and classify the topic into its spiritual and intellectual components, and it was around that time when someone would say something like, "Well, it's just easier, Anna." She'd reply, "In fact, you have a point. Maybe I should try it. Do I have to take my clothing off? Will you come with me and watch?"

That was Lehmann, both clinical and playful. Her father, when he noticed her at all, felt that his girl needed to settle down. Her mother, who was a good deal sharper than her husband, replied, "Don't worry about Anna. She likes her life too much to threaten it in any way." Certainly, aside from her originality, there was no cause for scandal. Or not yet. In 1929, when Lehmann completed her degree, her mother asked only two things of her: that she not run through her allowance and that she not get pregnant.

Finances were simple. Young Lehmann's needs were few. She took a room in an unfashionable boardinghouse and supplemented her income by translating lightweight novels and dry scientific monographs from French to German for a local agency. As for pregnancy, that was hardly a danger. Her inclinations ran in less conventional directions. In short, her mother was correct. She liked her little room that looked out over a courtyard where shabby women hung their wash. She liked the Prussian Archive, where they would always save her a desk with very good light. If her friends considered her eccentric, that never stopped them from submitting themselves to her interrogations, and if any of the men tried to make love to her, she'd blink at them and say, "It's a strange impulse, this need to copulate." She was twenty-six years old.

She didn't even try to find a teaching post. She preferred to be an independent scholar, and the subject she pursued with both passion and emotional detachment was the Jewish Question. She'd chosen that subject not because she herself was, as her mother delicately put it, a German of Israelite Descent, but because it seemed to make the best use of her strengths as a scholar. When she was a girl convalescing in Swiss sanitariums, she'd overhear conversations about the Dreyfus Affair, and the very agitation of all parties made her know it was a question worth pursuing. In a junk shop in Vienna, she'd come across a novel by a Hungarian reporter named Theodore Herzl called *The Old-New Land* about a settlement of German-speaking Jews who built a productive nation in Uganda. On the whole, her exploration of the Jewish Question was her favorite sort of project, open-ended, with no chance of resolution.

Then one day, a friend said, "I have an answer to your Jewish Question."

"Are you proposing we move to Uganda?" Anna Lehmann smiled. "Maybe, if you ask me nicely."

Instead, he introduced Lehmann to a young man with wild black hair and a stained and rumpled suit-coat. This wasn't the Leopold Stein of the iconic photographs, not Stein postwar. This was Stein just back from the Vilna Yiddish Conference, in Berlin en route to Munich, with his suitcase in his hand. He was two years younger than Lehmann, and he hadn't slept more than a few hours in the past week. This friend arranged a meeting in a café, and Stein was so full of what he'd seen and what he had discussed in Vilna that, without hesitation, he began to talk and talk.

"Those men have a romantic attachment to exile that's just plain superstition, but in practice the best of them think like Germans.

It's remarkable to see the thread, the consistency of logic woven right into them, a kind of Ashkenaz blood-memory."

Lehmann had ordered all three of them coffee, but the friend soon peeled away; he had heard all of this before. Stein kept on talking, his voice too loud, his hands expressive, his big-ness taking up the table. Lehmann made a few mild attempts to get a word in, but it was no use, and she ordered them both cognac in the hope that Stein would just run out, like a Victrola.

Of course, Stein was saying what he'd been saying for five years, but it was new to Lehmann. "There's a German inside of every Jew in Europe, and if we can only wake that German up—"

"In fact—" Lehmann began, in a fruitless attempt to insert a thought of her own.

"—Indeed. Look at this coffee shop. Look at the dozens of newspapers on the wooden racks. This is our prayer-house, Anna. This is our country. The Germany we made here is a culmination of a thousand years of—"

"—In fact," Lehmann said, "the Jews in France felt the same way until Dreyfus was framed."

"Listen," Stein said. His big, wet eyes looked into hers with such conviction that her own actually widened. "Facts can be lined up. Facts can be knocked down. What matters, Anna, are deeds. What matters is what we do with our bodies."

"Oh," Anna Lehmann said. She leaned back in her chair and realized there was no more liquor left in her glass. He was still staring at her, so she said, "I will admit, Leo, that I have no idea what you're talking about."

He kept the conversation going, though it was punctuated by disconcerting, liquid stares. Later, she'd learn that he would only do that when he was exhausted, but the erotic charge of those stares worked on Lehmann, and after the lights in that café began to flicker, he asked, "What time is it?"

"Past time for bed," Lehmann replied. And then she said, "Indeed."

That same year, Lehmann moved back to Heidelberg, where she assumed a professorship that wouldn't last for long. Lehmann and Stein wrote each other frequently and at length. Most of his letters were lost when she fled the country, but she'd kept a few, including one that laid to rest the rumor that it was Stalin who had ordered Yiddish banned from Judenstaat's public discourse.

Stein had written, "Those men in Vilna have their own reasons for speaking and writing in jargon. They're internationalists, anarchists at heart, and have no use for states or borders. We both know that Yiddish by its very nature cannot be a national language. It's all about crossing borders, not creating borders, and we must have a border, Anna. We must have protection. The Bund itself must be restructured along pragmatic national lines. How can anyone deny that now?" This was in 1935.

Later: "I am afraid, sometimes, that I wear my nerves on the outside. I envy your equilibrium. You are stronger than me."

Lehmann remembered her reply to that one. "Thus, you've recanted, Leo. Facts matter more than deeds. Then, she had signed, "In fact, your Anna," just as he always signed his name, "Indeed, L. Stein."

That exchange dated from 1938, just before Stein went underground. It was cited as proof that his health was more fragile than it had appeared. The stroke he'd suffered on return from Moscow was no sudden thing. He'd finally wound down and stopped. Lehmann kept going. As she might say, the facts speak for themselves.

7

THE last time Judit saw Professor Lehmann was not long before she graduated. She had been summoned to catalogue the material in her steamer trunk. When Judit arrived, she found the trunk itself emptied and pushed against a wall, and its contents piled on a rug in the parlor, some of the old photographs, letters, and diaries still bound with twine, some loose and spread like playing cards. Judit stood, mystified, even angry at the disrespect the scene implied.

"I don't know what's expected of me here," Judit said to Lehmann, who sat in her big chair, watching with her tiny lioness eyes. "Can't you at least let me know where this is going?"

"Would Dresden want it? Probably not," said Lehmann. "Perhaps we should send it to London, or even Jordan. There used to be a museum in Jerusalem before the war. I don't suppose it's been kept up."

The diaries with half their pages missing, the faint, cracked photographs, and on the back of the photographs, Cyrillic or Hebrew script faded to brown, when they were in the trunk they'd looked like treasures. Now they just looked like an impossible mountain of junk.

Lehmann stared at some middle distance, and then glanced down at the piles of documents strewn on the floor. "Of course, if that experiment hadn't failed and we were in Palestine, these papers would be much in demand. Why, they'd be precious. And digs everywhere, dear. Artifacts to catalogue. You'd be a very busy girl indeed. By now, I'm sure, we would have dropped incendiary bombs on whatever didn't interest us and rebuilt the Holy Temple." She lit another cigarette. "It's high time to move on, wouldn't you say? All paradigms have their seasons, and one needs to look ahead, to begin now to find a past that illuminates the future. In fact, I must begin to fill this trunk again. Where will we be in ten years' time?"

She paused. Then, she looked right at Judit. That was when Judit realized Anna Lehmann expected her to answer the question. Judit said, "Professor, I don't know."

"Yes you do," said Lehmann. "You're always in the vanguard. That's your gift, whether you know it or not. Perhaps it's unconscious."

The nature of that statement flustered Judit to the point where she didn't say a word the rest of that afternoon. She did manage to make lists of all the documents and photographs and put in a call to the university library, which accepted them on a temporary basis. As Judit took her leave, Lehmann was standing—one of the few times Judit had ever seen her stand—at the threshold of the house itself, as Judit marked some information on the sides of five cardboard boxes. Upright, Lehmann was not imposing. The doorway didn't frame her to best advantage. If seen a certain way, she might be an ordinary old woman, overweight and unattractive. The library van kept its motor running, and Judit couldn't help but know that she was passing a sentence on those documents about the Rothschild Colony in Palestine. They would be in a kind of permanent internal exile. No one would see them again.

* * *

Judit could have contacted Lehmann in 1982, when she'd booked a room for two nights in a hotel in Leipzig, but she was nowhere near the university. She'd gone there to get a full evaluation at the Teaching Hospital and stayed in a hotel across from a new highway. The hotel was intended for hospital patients and their families, and had been built so recently that there were still squares of dirt where they had yet to plant shrubs around the entrance. Judit's room had two double beds, a color television, and something she'd never seen before, a minibar. She opened that minibar with trepidation and found it contained quite ordinary Hungarian sunflower seeds, a German candy bar, and two Czech beers. There was a pedestrian bridge across the highway to the hospital entrance, marked with arrows to direct disoriented patients. After a night in one of those big, cold beds, Judit felt disoriented enough to be grateful for the arrows, and even the black and white hospital tiles that urged her to put one foot in front of the other.

In the waiting room, a young man behind the desk handed her a sheaf of questionnaires about her eating habits, her sexual history, and the most recent results of examinations by her other doctors. Judit had come prepared with a blue binder that contained records of every visit with the midwife and her own physician, copies of her sonograms, the report from the first stillborn delivery where fetal growth had stopped at week sixteen, and the analysis of fetal matter from the second pregnancy, which had followed the same pattern and, in spite of weeks of bed rest, had died inside her and been expelled at a Dresden clinic. The binder also contained Leonora's records, including her mammograms and recent bloodwork, and a copy of the results of Hans's physical, which Judit had made him get before she came. The binder was so thick that Judit had to hold it in both hands.

Somehow, Judit had expected everyone to be impressed by the binder. The technician didn't even look at it. She also didn't look at the questionnaires. She was a small, thin woman with a distinctive dome of gray hair, and she wore a gray smock and asked question after question with enormous tact and patience. Did Judit take an aspirin a day during the first pregnancy? During the second? Had the midwife prescribed heparin? Was she intolerant to heparin? Was there a history of stillbirth or miscarriage in other members of her family on her mother's side beyond her mother? When Judit replied that every woman other than her mother had been murdered in the camps, the technician informed her that it was possible to find records of stillbirths in village rolls in Poland. Had she pursued this avenue? Somewhere in there, Judit said, "When do I get to see the doctor?" The doctor appeared, with five medical students, and he seemed to have read Judit's whole binder while she was talking to the technician because he summarized pretty much everything in it to those students, while Judit sat there listening to three years of her life passing, and when he was finished, he made some observations about how this pattern reoccurred at week sixteen, and in both cases, the fetus was female. Then he suggested a full body scan, heparin injections, and weekly blood-work, not to her, but seemingly to those five students.

He only looked at Judit to ask, "So do you plan to try again?" Judit just stared. He took that as assent and said, "You know, every pregnancy is unique, just like a snowflake." "That's what the midwife said," said Judit. He said, "She's right."

Then off she went, but not without getting her binder back. She crossed the pedestrian bridge across the highway, hugging the binder the way she had seen a patient in a room she passed hug a hard white pillow when he coughed. She didn't go back to her room. She phoned Hans from the lobby and said, "I'm going crazy."

"Come home," Hans said. Then, "I should have come along."

"I didn't want you to," Judit said. "No need for both of us to go crazy. Besides, isn't tonight the big audition? Where you step in?" That was the first of several times Hans would guest-conduct the Dresden orchestra.

"It was last night," His voice sounded very far away.

"So are you a master conductor?"

"Lamb, come home."

She did, although she had to pay for two nights in the hotel anyway. The report was mailed to her three months later, in an impressive-looking envelope, and when Judit looked back on that day in Leipzig, she couldn't remember why she'd booked a second night. It might have been that she had intended to see Anna Lehmann. She suspected that she'd hoped the doctor would discover a problem that required urgent and immediate attention, and that would explain everything.

8

Transcript: CONFIDENTIAL. Dresden 1952. [Note: the following was recorded in the office of the Prime Minister of Judenstaat, Leopold Stein, via hidden mic. Soviet Diplomatic Mission re: Trade.]

MOLOTOV: Impressive, Stein, the Parliament. You Jews amaze me.

STEIN: I hope we will continue to work together in harmony for years to come.

MOLOTOV: It is a hope we share. I have a proposition for you, Mr. Stein. How much is a Jew worth?

STEIN: [Inaudible.]

MOLOTOV: In our country, we have tried for many years to come to grips with the National Question. Comrade Stalin offered Jews a homeland in the Crimea. They rejected it. He gave them a home in Birobidjan. It proved to be full of traitors. Now we give you Germany and we still have a million of your people within Soviet borders. What do you say to that?

STEIN: They are welcome here.

MOLOTOV: How much will you give me for them?

STEIN: Surely they can arrange for their own transportation should they choose to come home.

MOLOTOV: So you agree. Germany is their home. They are not Soviets. They are essentially without loyalty and without scruples. There are plans to transport these Jews to Siberia. Troops stand at the ready. He [Stalin] need only say the word. Yet I am here to see if other arrangements are amenable.

STEIN: With all due respect, why do you speak of a financial transaction? With some encouragements, they'll emigrate. There is no need to send Jews to the ends of the earth and make another country for them.

MOLOTOV: Are you a literary man, Stein?

STEIN: [Inaudible.]

MOLOTOV: There is a story by our own Tolstoy called "How Much Land Does a Man Need?" It's a small masterpiece. A man is told he can have as much land as he can cover on horseback in a day, and he rides himself into exhaustion. In fact, he rides himself to death because he doesn't know his limits. In the end, the riddle has an answer. How much land does a man need? As much as it takes to bury him.

STEIN: Comrade, how is your wife?

[Note: Molotov had a Jewish wife with whom Stein corresponded. She had been arrested and executed after the war. A.L.]

MOLOTOV: [Inaudible.]

STEIN: And how are those young men, our officers in training? No one has heard from them in eighteen months. What is their status?

MOLOTOV: Stein, whose Jew are you? You're playing both sides. It's a dangerous game, and you can't win it.

STEIN: It's not a game. Children play games. We aren't children.

MOLOTOV: Think carefully, sir. I can speak for both myself and for others when I say that our patience is not infinite, and that, pragmatic as we are, we have firm principles.

STEIN: You need us. You can't admit it, but you need us. So does the West. Don't burn your bridges.

MOLOTOV: How much will you give us for our Jews, Mr. Stein?

STEIN: [Inaudible.]

MOLOTOV: The arrangement must be a gentlemen's agreement, and if you are to take action, you must do so without delay. We will expect an answer by the end of the week.

[END OF REEL. Transcript made available December 1987 for the National Museum of Judenstaat in preparation for that country's 40th Anniversary celebration.]

9

THEY just delivered that?" Judit addressed Sammy Gluck, who had watched her as she listened to the tape on an old-fashioned reel-to-reel machine they'd rigged up in the basement.

"It was delivered by parcel post, like an ordinary package. It's really amazing, Mrs. Klemmer." Gluck's face was red, and he was sweating so heavily, his glasses steamed. "The Soviets are releasing all kinds of stuff these days."

"And they just mailed it." Judit's voice was flat. "Parcel post."

"The thing is, we need visuals. So Oscar wants to know if you can come up with something."

"How on earth would I have footage of that conversation, Sammy?"

"Of course you wouldn't. But don't you have a picture of Molotov and Stein together? Or maybe Russian Jews in an old newsreel. We need it right away."

He just stood there swaying. Judit let him sway. Then she said, "You realize what Molotov was saying? Buy our Jews—or we'll deport them. This isn't Nazi Germany. It's Moscow—1953."

"I didn't study history in college," Sammy said. "I guess it must have been the same year Leopold Stein had that stroke. It doesn't sound like him, though, not like in the old newsreels. Maybe it's the tape."

"It was recorded in someone's basement a month ago."

"But it was sent parcel post," Sammy said helplessly. "By Professor Lehmann. I still have the receipt, Mrs. Klemmer. Look." He held up the slip of paper, and waved it around in a way that made Judit seasick. Or maybe she already felt that way. Her face was burning.

She leaned against the cabinet and tried to get her bearings. Lehmann would not send anything that hadn't been verified. Yet what she heard was a reactionary fantasy out of an American spy novel. It felt stagey, grotesque. It made no sense. It was a piece of a puzzle that felt deliberately manufactured. And if it were true? She heard herself say, "If that's the kind of thing they're looking for, I'm off the project, Sammy."

Sammy blinked. "You can't mean that."

"I mean it!" Judit said, and fiercely and abruptly, she did. "Take everything upstairs. Transfer it to video. Try to find that newsreel where Stein's hooked up on life support with that male nurse. From '53—same year: sixteen millimeter. Or there are photographs. You want explosive? That'll do just fine."

She pulled open a wide, heavy drawer and wrenched it from the cabinet. Then she opened up another, pulled and pulled, and when it would not come out, she stumbled, tried to right herself, and Sammy said, "Are you okay, Mrs. Klemmer?"

"You'll need to bring down the cart," Judit said. "The catalogue's all self-explanatory except for some junk you won't want anyway."

"I'll get you a glass of water," Sammy said, and with hesitation, turned to go. He really seemed concerned about her, and she felt sorry for him. Then, before he closed the door, he had to turn and say, "Can't you just take things on faith? You can't always know."

* * *

Take it on faith. You can't always know. If Judit could strangle sentences, she would have forcefully taken both of them in her hands and snapped their necks. She'd heard them forever. They were unanswerable, because the people who said them had their answers ready. The arrogance—the empty-headed arrogance of people who believe in videos or heparin injections or Shabbos candles or the State. She would not take a lie on faith, never. She believed in facts. Facts matter. You can verify, and with great effort, if you take into account what is discarded, you can find the truth. It's humbling work, but it's the work that makes us human. And sometimes, you get tired, you despair, because there seems to be no explanation. That's when it's tempting to surrender to something that feels a lot like death.

Yes, Hans was dead. The case was closed. That note had been in her pocket for nearly three months now. There wasn't much left of it. She took it out again.

They lied about the murder.

The ghost appeared by her side, smiling critically, not a sly smile, more melancholy.

Judit addressed that ghost. "Whose murder? Leo Stein's? Not yours."

When Sammy took the stuff upstairs, then he might find that unmarked reel of Stein and those Soviet soldiers; it would be out of her hands, into the Stasi's, and they would find the man who'd broken in, and arrest him for trespassing and a thousand other petty crimes. She probably had a fever, and she asked that ghost as though he knew:

"The Soviets—our liberators with the guns. The ones at the synagogue. What could Stein say to them? I should have turned the sound on."

The ghost drifted back without acknowledgment and left a cold wake. If only it had been warm, there'd be some justice. It could have come in from behind and leaned into her body the way Hans used to do when he came home from a concert and found her at her sewing machine. It would be after midnight. Even when she heard the door open, she wouldn't turn around. She would pretend to keep on sewing, waiting for what was about to happen. It was the sweetest of discoveries that habit has its own eroticism and can deepen.

Yes, once she had not been alone. She had been loved. Her life was full of tenderness and possibility. And now the ghost did just what she'd willed it to do. It came up from behind her. She could feel its cold breath in her ear.

"So you don't like that story?"

Judit's breath caught. It was her husband's voice. No question. It came out of the cold throat like the note of a bassoon. It broke her heart. Her legs went out from under her, but she was held upright by the ghost's arms, as its face moved towards her own, so close she could make out the texture of the light hair pushed back from the forehead, faint creases around the mouth, the little white patch of a cigarette burn on the chin that Hans had gotten as a boy in Leipzig. He was just a ghost. He couldn't hurt someone who was still alive. The eyelashes were long, the shrouded eyes grayer and colder than they should have been.

"You should avenge me."

She could feel an articulate hand move up through her loose hair and press against her skull.

Again, his voice: "Avenge me."

The ghost held out the other hand. It was the hand of Hans, long-fingered, flexible, the hand of a conductor. Was she supposed to take it? Where would it lead her? No, that was not the expectation. Judit passed the note to the ghost, who turned it over on the table. For the first time, Judit saw something was written on the other side:

Yenidze. 7th Floor.

It was the Chabad House.

Angels and Demons

1

THE Yenidze Cigarette Factory was named after a town in Thrace. As a girl, like every child in Dresden, Judit had been fascinated by the building. It wasn't far from Stein Square, and it came on you suddenly. You'd turn a corner, pass a railway bridge, and there it was: an exotic monster taking up a whole block, with a chimney disguised as a minaret, and an enormous dome. It had closed down even before the war, and it stood vacant, except for a restaurant. You'd go through a little gate that led to a special entrance with an elevator that went five flights up to the dome where, as Leonora said, a cup of cocoa cost twice as much as anywhere else. Most of the dome's stained glass was missing, but the waiters wore fezzes, and the little porthole windows transformed even the most ordinary view of Dresden into a fairy tale.

When Hans was appointed concertmaster of the Dresden Orchestra, and he and Judit were looking at apartments, she heard that some of the old factories around the Yenidze had been converted into luxury condominiums with new appliances and even private telephones, and a realtor showed them a place with a window that looked right out on the dome. In fact, if she'd been eating at the restaurant, she could have looked out from the porthole into her living room. The Yenidze had been restored, and someone had put a lot of money into the place. At night, the dome glowed like sugar-candy. When she worked late at the archive, and walked back across Stein Square, she could see it lit up in vibrant reds and blues and yellows. There was even scaffolding around the minaret.

Of course, the realtor had said nothing about Chabad. She knew her clients, and one look at Judit told her that the information would have been a deal-breaker, and it almost was. There was a certain kind of buyer who would have found Chabad charming with their Mitzvah Tanks and cheery Shabbos greetings. Judit was not that sort of buyer.

"How did they get the money to fix the place up?" Judit asked everyone she saw, the realtor, her co-workers, the oboe player who came to dinner after they moved into the apartment, even Hans himself. Then she answered her own question. "I'll tell you how they got the money. From us. Money that ought to go to roads or medical research goes straight into their pockets. Or worse yet, they get it from anti-Bundist donors from America who want to undermine the State."

Hans said, "Aren't you glad to see a light on in the dome?"

"You don't understand," said Judit, and so she talked to her mother, who did understand, and as the two of them went on and on about those people and the subsidies they're given by the government and their manipulative political power, Hans listened in wonder. Never had he seen Judit and her mother in such complete accord.

Maybe it was that same night that Leonora offered them her dining room table and insisted on finding an identical replacement for the broken leaf, and in the heat of solidarity, mother and daughter talked about whether they needed good china for entertaining, and if the new pieces from Meissen were cheaper if they came straight from the factory. Hans let that conversation go on without interruption, and only afterwards, when they were alone, did he say to Judit:

"I think she finally believes we're married. And a good thing too. Otherwise, we'd have to get Chabad to do a ceremony."

"Don't even joke about that," Judit said. "I know those people. They're predators. They move in if they see any sign of weakness."

"You know," Hans said, "they only have the power you give them, Lamb. And that appears to be considerable."

In the years since Hans's murder, Judit hadn't been back to their old neighborhood. She'd been afraid of what she'd find there, maybe afraid it hadn't changed at all. As it turned out, most of the renovated former factories had lapsed back into vacancy, and there was no one on the street. A wall between two empty lots was covered with the remnants of a mural of Leopold Stein at the helm of a yellow tractor, but his head was obscured by graffiti. Was that Yiddish? Could it be Cyrillic? She couldn't trust her own eyes. Most of the other walls were plastered with enormous pictures of Chabad's Rebbe: Schneerson's stern, white-bearded face and cunning eyes flashed below a black fedora. If their apartment was still standing, it would be full of black-hats and their children.

But this was just speculation. In the late winter afternoon, her old block looked so empty that maybe no one was there at all. Her body felt empty too, light, heavy, light again, like someone else's. Yes, that graffiti was Cyrillic. So were the fliers tacked onto utility poles. This was no Soviet army base. Why all the Russian? Well, why not? Why shouldn't she have to pass through a gauntlet of obscurity and draw on yet another alphabet she had to understand?

She didn't even see the white van until it pulled right up to her. A woman rolled down the window.

"Let me give you a ride."

Judit was freezing; her coat was practically pulled over her head. Still, she knew what this was about. She walked a little faster. The van followed at a crawl, and the low, pleasant, female voice trailed behind her.

"Would you deny me the pleasure of doing a favor for a fellow Jew?"

She must have pulled over then. Judit heard the clatter of high heels, and when they caught up with her, Judit turned around and said, "Not interested."

"In what?" the woman asked. She was unusually tall, and wore a warm, gray coat, and of course a wig like all their women, this one adorned by a yellow knitted beret with a green ornament that made it look like a hand-puppet. Her face was rosy with cold. "Not interested in a ride? Or in something else? Look, we're only offering the ride, Thursday night special, just for you. No lecture. No asking if my husband can say Kaddish for your grandparents. No chicken soup. Look, you're smiling already," she added, though Judit wasn't smiling. Then Judit sneezed, and the woman said, "*Gezuntheit.* Maybe you do need chicken soup."

"I don't need anything," Judit said. "It's just another block. I'm fine."

"But then you must be going to Chabad!" Now, the woman was absolutely glowing. "You probably don't know it, but a lot of people can't find the entrance on a weekday. You can walk right by it after dark. We only light the dome before Shabbos." Then, she pushed back the beret a little. She gave Judit a long look. "What do you know. Ginsberg. Don't you recognize your old Youth Leader?"

Now it was Judit's turn to stare. "Charlotte?" The face was rounder and less serious, but once Judit knew it, it couldn't be unknown. She could see signs of the girl that Charlotte had been, the eyebrows and substantial forehead, and the long neck, though most of that was covered by a scarf. Her wig was stiff and glossy but more or less the color of her old, black hair. Judit said, "My God, what are you doing with these people?"

"Living," said Charlotte. Then, in Yiddish, "*Some make a living and some make a life*. It's Chana Batya now, by the way. Last name's Rabinovitch. Judi, come on. Your nose is running. Why are we standing here like a couple of *schmendricks*? I've got a van full of groceries to put away, and I've got to start cooking Shabbos dinner. We're expecting a whole battalion tomorrow. Come home with me. Meet my husband and my children."

Judit tried to protest, but Charlotte made cunning use of her sonorous alto voice.

"It's coooold, Ginsberg. Get in the scaaaaareeeey Mitzvah Tank with the scaaaareeeey black-hat." She grabbed Judit's arm and pulled her into the van, and they drove around the corner to the Chabad House.

2

ACCORDING to Charlotte's husband, Mendel, Chabad house only had five floors. "Unless you count the dome. That would make six. But nobody would be there on a Thursday. We have a minyan in the lobby twice a day, and *Baruch Ha Shem,* on Fridays we light the dome just before Chana Batya and the girls light candles, and we daven there on Shabbos." He smiled at her right through his beard and gave her a warm, long look, magnified through his glasses. "Sit down. Please. My wife will bring you coffee."

Judit did sit, with reluctance, on a worn couch where two little girls were also sitting, a three-year-old who held a sippy cup, and a fragile-looking child in a pinafore who was propped against a pillow and was intently studying a sock she had just removed.

Charlotte picked up the sock-girl absentmindedly, and showed no sign of bringing Judit coffee. "Maybe she's going to be on the radio. They might be adding on a new floor for a studio. Ginsberg, would you believe it? There's a radio tower in the minaret, and as soon as they approve our application for bandwidth, our Rebbe will transmit his teachings all over the world. Every day, there's something new. Even since we moved here from Gorlitz, there's the women's dormitory on the fourth floor, and the theater. There's so much news. I know so much about you, and you don't know anything about me. That's not fair at all!"

"Chana Batya," Mendel said to her. "Calm down." His manner was a little like the old Charlotte's, solemn and slow. He pushed back his black fedora, which made him look wistful and beleaguered. Those tolerant brown eyes met Judit's own in a way that felt like a recruitment tactic. Wasn't he supposed to look away from women? Maybe Chabad men got special dispensation. He asked her, "Was she always like this?"

"No, actually," Judit said carefully. When she'd last seen Charlotte twenty years ago, she was studying at the Polytechnic, engrossed in some work too complicated to explain to someone Judit's age, but she'd spent one final summer at Archeology Camp out of what she'd called "a sense of duty." Judit could still hear those words. She had both admired and feared her, and assumed she'd either end up finding a cure for cancer or designing a deadly weapon.

The Rabinovich apartment had been completed just that year, with funding from a source in Montreal. Until then, the couple and their children had lived in Gorlitz and before that, Halle, moving wherever Rabbi Schneerson had told them they were needed, but never in such a place as this, where donors from North America and England had opened their pockets and their hearts to bring about the Messianic Age.

Charlotte went on. "It wasn't easy at first, but since Prime Minister Sokolov eased restrictions on foreign transactions, the money just keeps pouring in. And Judi, these people are so hungry for what we offer—especially the new arrivals from the Soviet Union. You didn't know? But it was in all the papers when the prime minister made that agreement with Gorbachev. Those Russian Jews, they suffered so much. Their souls are empty and we fill them. Did I tell you? Mendel came from Russia. He was one of the first, and he was born *frum* too, a regular Talmud Torah scholar, a prodigy, and speaks German like a native already. Then, just last year, he brought his mother. Wait till you meet her! What she's been through. Talk about stories to make your hair stand on end!" She interrupted herself. "I forgot to tell you. Do take off your shoes. House rule. You don't wear heels? Well, I have to make sure I'm as tall as my husband, or he won't respect me."

"I'm not staying," Judit said.

From another room came a high-pitched scream. Charlotte pivoted with the little girl in her arms and called out, "Dov! Let your sister work in peace." She turned to Judit and said, "Leah's cutting vegetables for tomorrow's soup, and that boy thinks he's helping but he shouldn't be anywhere near a knife. That girl's got a healthy set of lungs. And the one next to you's Rebecca. You look like she's about to bite you, Ginsberg. She's offering you her cup. Such a little hostess. The one I'm holding's Dahlia, my miracle child. Born under a kilo and on a breathing machine for six months. She still takes oxygen at night." Then Charlotte said, "What do you mean, you're not staying?"

"You say there's no seventh floor," Judit said. "I must not have the right address."

"Nonsense," said Charlotte.

Mendel, as though roused from a reverie, said, "Perhaps I can help. Do you have the address in writing?"

"Let's see it," Charlotte said.

Judit shook her head and shook it hard. It was difficult to remember what she'd hoped to find. Some kind of answer? These people had all the answers, sure, and now it was clear she'd walked into a trap. "I need to go, Charlotte," she said.

"I'm Chana Batya," Charlotte said. "Look, we're not holding you prisoner, but it's a cold night. At least take my coat. You can bring it back tomorrow when you come for Shabbos."

In a voice louder than Judit had intended, she said, "I'm not coming for Shabbos."

Charlotte stared at her. The sippy-cup girl stared at her. Dahlia, the miracle baby, turned up her dull blue eyes in her direction. A door swung open, and there was big-lunged Leah with her hair pulled back like Shaindel's, and behind her was a pudgy boy who must have been the brother. Then, like a pendulum, their full attention swung to Mendel.

Mendel folded his hands and addressed the room: "According to the Sages, if every Jew just once properly observed the Sabbath, the Messiah would immediately arrive."

Mendel's ponderous voice, his presence, was so exactly like the old Charlotte's that Judit wondered if she'd taught him how to do it. She said, "I have to work. I'm on a deadline."

Then she was off—out the door and in the foyer—trying to remember how to get back to the lobby. She'd left her duffle coat in the apartment, and the abstract sense of floating somewhere outside her body had returned. Face it, she was sick and feverish, had been light-headed for days or even weeks, and she was fully aware that it would be insane to get back outside that night. But even more insane was what she did next, what she had to do.

She had to get to the seventh floor, not because there'd be an answer waiting, but because if she left, she would not come back. To leave without walking a few more flights of stairs and seeing what was there—she couldn't do it. She knew it would not be Hans. It might be that pornographer, a bomb, a Loschwitz black-hat. Whatever was up there was still there, months after she'd received the invitation. She was half-aware of Charlotte calling after her repeatedly, and it was only when she'd started up the stairs in her stocking feet that Judit realized she'd not only left without her coat, but left her shoes behind.

Mendel had told the truth. The stairs went up five flights. She walked into a dark hallway, struggling to recollect the few times in her childhood that she'd been inside the restaurant. There'd been a spiral staircase to the dome—yes, from a lower level—and it could be reached by double-doors she could make out just ahead. She could feel the texture of the hallway rug through her stockinged feet. She gripped a central railing, and carefully pressed each foot on the tread of each step, slow enough to combat vertigo. Then, she reached a door she recognized, and opened it. The air expanded.

Her hand must have hit a switch. All at once, that dome filled with dazzling colors, swirling and jewel-toned. She stopped dead.

Someone else was there. Standing behind her was an old man wearing pajama bottoms and an undershirt. He held a bottle of something. His long, unshaven face was stained all over with the colors of the dome.

"So it's you knocking around here. I wondered when you'd show up." There was the high-pitched, too-loud voice.

Judit steeled herself and said, "Who are you?"

"What kind of question is that? You know who I am!"

She recognized him and felt vertigo return. "But you're in prison."

"Released for good behavior," Arno Durmersheimer said. Then he frowned. "Now you look like you're going to be sick. Nobody told you? Well, that's no surprise!" He reached for her arm, and she drew back, but he ignored it and tucked his own around her elbow. "You're freezing too. Where are your shoes? Do I have to carry you? No? A good thing! We got a climb. You just lean on me."

3

YOU took your sweet time," Durmersheimer said. "If you'd shown up next week, I might have been gone. Too bad. They're alright, these kind of black-hats. At least they speak German."

They'd reached the room above the dome by way of a pull-down ladder, and he'd set Judit up with a cup of hot rum, and filled his own glass. He sat at an odd angle because, he told Judit, he was deaf in one ear. It happened in '56, when he'd slipped back across the border after that business in Rathen. He kept a low profile—worked in demolition—was one of the crew that blew up everything that was in the way of the Protective Rampart. He'd blown up houses in Dessau, Gohrisch, Papstdorf, Cunnersdorf, Saxon towns and villages that weren't even on the map now. That's how he'd lost his hearing—all those explosives. He couldn't hear his own voice, half the time.

He made a point of saying that he wasn't much of a drinker but since he'd been out of jail, he found it helped him sleep. Granted, this place was so small that there wasn't much to do but sleep between their Sabbaths.

"These Chabad black-hats are alright. But they don't like me much. I turn on lights for them Saturdays, and they're not allowed to ask me or it breaks a law or something. Now listen, no offense, but how am I supposed to read their minds? I'm not a Jew."

Judit pretended to drink the rum and shifted her weight on the folding chair. To see this man she'd heard about so often, to see him in the flesh, leaning back in his chair and scratching himself through that undershirt, the poisonous absurdity of it all worked at her until she just said, "Do they know who you are?"

Durmersheimer frowned. "Of course they do."

"I don't know what you want from me. You think I'll forgive you?"

"For what? You can't believe that story. Face it, you wouldn't be here if you did."

"The bullet came from your gun," Judit said tonelessly.

"You read the police report? I'll bet you didn't. I haven't fired that gun in forty years!"

"They found the list on you—the collaborators."

"Collaborators? Right—that's what they said. We wanted Saxons you people listen to, names Jews know. The ones with family who died in '46. And he was the only one who was ready to speak out about the massacre."

This was all going too fast, the back-and-forth, the information that he seemed to think she knew. If she had a gun, she'd kill him, but she had no gun. The ladder to that crawl space was still hanging from a trapdoor. She could probably get past him if she took him by surprise. Then he leaned in and blocked out any chance. His whisper was like gravel.

"Look, I don't know who killed your husband, but if you ask me, it had to be a Soviet assassin, Moscow trained. And think about it—a Moscow-trained assassin in a balcony shoots your husband in the head and shuts up the other people on the list."

"What the hell are you talking about?" Judit said.

Durmersheimer said, "The massacre!" When she was silent, he

went on. "But aren't you here because you watched that movie? I know you can't see much from that distance, but you don't know how long I had to trade favors in that filthy Loschwitz ghetto to even find it! The Dresden massacre in '46. The Reds who killed his parents!"

"My husband didn't know how his parents died."

Durmersheimer poured himself another drink. "Sure he knew. But the dead can't testify. That's why they're dead. I saw that movie you made—the nice old lady talking about her Russian on the white horse. So-called liberation! It's a pack of lies. Your husband knew it. You've got to tell the story that your man didn't live to tell."

"Don't mix my husband into this load of shit!" That came from Judit with a force that shook her. Her hand trembled around that cup of rum that seemed to have emptied all by itself.

"Little girl," said Durmersheimer, "Red Russians killed your husband. If you don't believe me now, there's not too much I can do about it. Go home and try to find that evidence I left you. Bet it's missing."

Judit put down the cup and stared into it.

"Watch out," said Durmersheimer. His eyes narrowed. "And you keep away from Loschwitz. Everyone knows you there. Those Loschwitz people, they're no joke. They're not like us. Nothing matters to them. I hate the Reds with all my heart, but in the end, it's Loschwitz Jews and Cosmopolitans who own this country. Their hands are soaked in blood. I hate the Soviets with all my heart, but they won't last. It's Weiss who lasts. Yes, Stephen Weiss. There's a reason you look at me like that when I say his name."

Judit hadn't been aware of what her face was doing. The pressure of those weeks and hours that led her to this place had settled on her like dead weight, and she could only ask, "Could you turn down the heat?"

"But it's so cold, I can see my breath. Look." Durmersheimer blew out a trail of vapor.

"Then why am I so hot?"

"Because you're sick, I guess," said Durmersheimer. "Fuck. They'll blame me. Everyone's counting on you. You watch your back. You need protection, and I can't give it. Fuck," he said again, and then he guided Judit towards his bed.

Now she was horizontal. The overwhelming heat had formed a yellow penumbra around the metal bed-frame beyond her stockinged feet, and when Durmersheimer threw a thin blanket over her, it fell down in slow motion. She was powerless to stop it. Something else fluttered against her cheek.

"Do you read French?"

Not really, Judit said. Or did she think it? Durmersheimer must have left the room, and Judit moved her head and tried to block out the aggressive light that plastered itself to her forehead. There were three pages, clipped together:

Le Manifeste de Stefane Weiss

4

U*NE spectre hant l'Europe—la spectre de la catastrophe . . .*

Why had he left the light on? She'd had some French in college, but her head felt thick.

Oui, elle signifie, la catastrophe, une esthétique, une symétrie, et une unité.

Would it make any sense if she were in her archive or her dormitory? Those places felt distant now, like pages in a foreign language.

. . . Une réponse personnelle ne peut pas s'éloigner au delà de la vengeance.

It all came flooding back, a shouting match she'd once had with a fashionable lecturer in graduate school who'd shown slides of archeological parks and kept going on and on about the Jewish Narrative and the Saxon Narrative, and Saxon homes that were demolished to make room for excavations, as if half of them weren't fascist strongholds like the one in so-called Saxon Switzerland. He brought in French sources that supposedly proved that the Ashkenazi artifacts they'd excavated in those sites were all transported from Cologne. There was a family resemblance between the argument with that polished faker in his expensive sweater and what had come to pass between herself and the man who killed her husband.

Because of course he'd killed her husband. It was written on his face. And all the talk about Russians and atrocities was just evasion. . . . *au delà de la vengeance*. . . . Her husband's ghost had called for vengeance, and instead she'd let the man who killed him fill her with his rum, lay her in his bed, and blanket her with phrases that she didn't understand.

La catastrophe permet à les victimes la liberté definitive: l'abdication de la responsibilité . . .

How had he gotten this translation? Of course, she knew it existed, everyone knew after *Studies in the Mother Tongue* was shut down in 1967. The original manifesto was a rumor. But Weiss was real. In that discarded footage, she caught fleeting images of Weiss: lean, craven, eyes hard behind round glasses, head thrust determinedly forward, a vulture of a man.

How had Weiss been unmasked? There were a thousand reports: suitcases full of gold bullion discovered in his basement, surveillance cameras tracking his meetings with a fascist in a restaurant in Bavaria, leases from apartments in Spain, Syria, and Argentina, testimony from one of his apprentices who'd sworn a blood-oath to be loyal to no country but to offer himself to the highest bidder, and in those years, the highest bidder surely was the Soviet Union's enemy, America.

Judit had been born the same year Weiss had fled the country. There was a line of silence drawn across that year; 1951 was a hard year all around—martial music playing on the radio, neighbors looking over their shoulders at each other, all those half-finished constructions projects that had been funded by Americans, and Leopold Stein finding traitor after traitor in his own cabinet. Until the death of Stalin two years later, those prison trains full of Weiss's followers left station after station and crossed into the Soviet Union and from there, they went to the end of the world.

Une mémoire n'a aucun de pouvoir inhérent. Un monument convient et absorb la mémoire et la vengeance. Ainsi, l'état devient lui-même le monument. Mais, un monument à propos de quoi?

Monument. Absorbs memory and vengeance. What was the point of struggling with the words? Stein himself had said it many times. This country is our monument. And it was Weiss himself who raised the question. Judit had first seen it on one of those Yiddish *pashkevils* in 1968.

A monument to what?

It was a provocation. Everything in '68 had been a provocation. The miners' strike in Halle, the protests in Leipzig, the vote of no confidence in Anton Steinsaltz that had thrust his terrified opponent Klein into the position of prime minister. Steinsaltz had led the country for eight years, and Klein was so used to being the voice of the loyal opposition that once he had power, he lost his voice completely. He just stammered and watched what happened to the country, raising his hands in a gesture of surrender.

It began when the Judenstaat Defense Force was deployed across the border in Czechoslovakia. These boys rolled into Prague to suppress a coup. Their tanks were soon surrounded by fascists—that's what the radio said—the same scum who had herded Jews into Thereisenstadt. Photographs surfaced: stone-throwing thugs attacking JDF troops. Wearing their blue striped helmets with the yellow stars, those soldiers continued the brave work of the ghetto partisans, and, as before, they fought side by side with their Soviet brothers, completing the work of the Liberation.

Judit had been seventeen then. She'd kept an ear on the radio, fixated on the Youth Leader who'd been her boyfriend in Archeology Camp, and who'd been deployed six weeks before. She'd exchanged two letters with him since the summer's end, and now she felt sure he was somewhere on those miserable, cobblestoned streets, bloodied by the mob, fighting his way towards ancient synagogues the radio said were all on fire.

Leonora said, "I don't see why we're over there. It's not our problem."

Judit had been appalled. "Prague is right on our border. Do you want them to invade?"

"That's not the border I'm worried about," Leonora said. "Our boy should be at the Protective Rampart, keeping the Germans out. Let the Russians take care of their own business."

Those words were dangerous. And more and more, Judit heard that kind of language everywhere, waiting in line at the fabric store, along the river promenade where her youth group volunteered to prune the bushes, even at school among students whose older brothers were in the JDF. Since Judit could remember, the Judenstaat Defense Force was kind of a joke, with their badly fitting uniforms and Soviet rifles from the '40s. Maybe if those officers in training had returned from Moscow, or if the soldiers had something to do other than sit in their little watchtowers by the Protective Rampart, they would have been ready for Prague. But the young men—those hapless boys straight out of secondary school—to thrust them into Soviet-made tanks and turn them loose against civilians—

"They're not civilians," Judit insisted to anyone who made those claims. "They're Czech Nazis. They're fascists. Don't you listen to the radio?"

Still, even at seventeen, Judit knew that news came from a hundred other sources. There had always been a push and pull between those sources and the facts. How could anyone trust rumors? Yet people did trust rumors, maybe even listened to the badly blocked transmission from abroad, and those who understood English sometimes received a faint whiff of the BBC.

Another rumor: soldiers had deserted. They'd crossed the border on foot and were hiding all over Judenstaat. It could even be that the widow downstairs had a nephew sleeping in her husband's study, but it wasn't a good idea to talk about those things.

Sometimes, Judit would think she saw him, a tall young man, too tall for that tiny study. He'd smoke a cigarette on the fire escape late at night, not too far from Judit's window. She knew she ought to report him to the Stasi, and knew she would never report him to the Stasi, and this felt like the first conscious contradiction of her life. She'd watch the orange end of the cigarette, and the long shadow he threw, and be amazed at her own awareness of his vulnerability.

Maybe it was in October that the first *pashkevils* appeared. There were always a few of them scattered around the garment district, notices about this or that event only of interest to black-hats, but those were dense wall-posters full of religious obscurities. This one was in Yiddish too, but it was just one line long:

How do we know they're fascists?

There were dozens of them, plastered on the wall of the train stations in the Altstadt and the Neustadt, and on the sides of buildings, black block Hebrew letters, cheaply stenciled on a square of newsprint. Supposedly, no one could read that language anymore. Yet people slowed down when they saw the *pashkevils,* and if they were a certain age, they'd stop. They'd whisper something to a neighbor. The next day, there was a new one:

Are the synagogues really on fire?

They were everywhere you looked. By afternoon, they'd all been whitewashed, but the next morning found three times as many plastered in those same strategic places:

Are we Moscow's Court Jews?
Are we Moscow's Court Jews?
Are we Moscow's Court Jews?

And more were glued to the broad avenue by Parliament, the blackened sandstone façade of the Opera House, the National Museum. They were soon whitewashed or blackwashed, but someone replaced them even before sunset, dozens more, lined up in rows. At first, the messages were one line long. Then, students began to tell their parents that they'd seen longer *pashkevils* at the Dresden Polytechnic, whole paragraphs of Yiddish. Soon young people led their mothers and fathers to wall-posters with eyewitness dispatches from the soldiers in Prague. When those *pashkevils* were blackwashed, more were pasted over them.

Whitewashed, blackwashed, night after night, somehow more of them appeared on top of old ones every day until the day—Judit remembered—when a teacher at her school took her aside and said, "A group of us are meeting tonight, Judi. It's important." Judit spent the rest of the day wondering how she'd tell her parents that she had to go out after dark. Getting the two of them entangled felt at cross-purposes with everything else she was feeling. The teacher who'd spoken to her was her algebra instructor, and Judit was no particular favorite of hers, but the glamour of the invitation made her breathless.

In the end, she didn't ask her parents for permission. She just climbed out the window and down the fire escape—all the while hoping she'd startle the nephew in the middle of a cigarette—and walked to the designated place, an alley just off Bautzen Strasse.

The teacher was there. Five other students stood around her, most of whom Judit knew from her Bundist Youth Group. She held a paint-pot. A second pot of black paint was open at her feet, and the students all held brushes. She nodded towards Judit, neutrally, and gestured towards a brush already lying cross-wise over the mouth of the pot.

Of course, Judit picked up the brush and dipped it in black paint, but even as she erased each new *pashkevil,* she read it. This time, they were in German.

> **For twenty years, this country has labored under a master with a whip. What we produce is exported to the Soviets. What we consume is imported by the Soviets. The free press of our early years has all been broken. The artists of our early years have all been tamed.**
>
> **We have been told our country is a monument to those who perished in the Churban, and in that name, everything is permitted. Yet is it permitted to deceive ourselves?**
>
> **WE DEMAND a full investigation of the truth behind the order to suppress the uprising in Prague.**
>
> **WE DEMAND the truth behind the death of Leopold Stein.**
>
> **WE DEMAND the right to form independent unions and an end to press censorship.**
>
> **WE DEMAND nothing less than a full historical reckoning.**

That was the month when the television played endless loops of the children's show *Miss Heidi's House*, the one with the hand-puppets. Dresden suddenly felt provincial; history was taking place somewhere else. In railroad junctions, workers refused to load shipments of coal crossing Poland to the Soviet border. In Halle, the Stasi tracked down twenty deserters who'd been found hiding in a mineshaft, but the miners blocked their van; five miners were crushed in the fray. The University of Leipzig was shut down after a group of professors were arrested, and fifty more resigned in protest. There were rumors that every industry and college in Judenstaat had called a general strike.

Judit's secondary school was shut down, but not because of a strike. It was closed because there was no heat and only sporadic electricity. Leonora's great fear was that the Protective Rampart would be compromised, and Germans would invade. Rudolph spent a lot of time calming her down and telling her that Steinsaltz would never let that happen. In fact, that month, the country was under martial law for the first time since the '50s. Saxons were not allowed out of their homes. If there was no threat of treason, Leonora insisted, why would that be the case? Why would there be a curfew, and why would the radio keep playing that awful, slow version of Eisler's national anthem?

A week later, Judit's school would be re-opened. The electricity was on a generator, as they were understaffed at the plant, and coal was in short supply. Everyone wore a winter coat indoors. The algebra teacher was still there, though she never paid Judit any special attention. The physics teacher was gone. His class was assured that he hadn't been arrested. He'd simply taken a leave of absence to take care of his son who had just returned from Prague. Judit was never sure if the physics teacher came back; she never passed his old classroom, and by the time she graduated, no one talked about him anymore.

The soldiers would be home by the new year, and most of them had little to say about the events in Prague. There was talk of a victory parade along the Elbe in front of Parliament, and a rally in Stein Square, but somehow the weather was too cold, the tanks didn't have petrol, and on the whole, no one seemed anxious to get in a tank again.

Of course, it was clear that the period of upheaval was the work of American and German agents. All you had to do was look at those lists of demands and the signs the students held in Leipzig. Words like "free" and "open" were all code that any patriot could decipher. They were borrowed from U.S. counterparts who'd borrowed them from the French who'd borrowed them from Stephen Weiss.

Steinsaltz was the one who'd brought up Weiss. In 1968, Steinsaltz was still an imposing presence, with the grizzled face of the Warsaw Ghetto Fighter he had been. His hair was steel-gray, his suit impeccable.

"Comrades," he said to both the audience in Parliament and to the citizens who gathered around their radios and televisions in community centers and in private homes. "We have gone through a grave crisis. And it is no surprise that we've come out the other side with our principles and our borders intact. The Cosmopolitans have been defeated."

If it had been the '80s, there would have been several cameras, and those with televisions could watch members of Parliament rise as a body and applaud the man they'd voted out of office six months before. Back then, the single camera stayed on Steinsaltz. He paused to acknowledge the response with a lowered head. He checked his notes, and looked up through thick eyebrows until he could continue.

"It is not the first time we have faced such a crisis. In 1951, our founder Leopold Stein discovered that his own house was unsound, and he took measures to secure our future. Weiss and his followers had infected our young country so deeply that even now, we see their long, sinister shadow." Then he said, "There are times when ruthless cynicism calls for a ruthless response."

The television in the Ginsberg apartment went dark. The electricity had been going on and off all day, and Rudolph fiddled with the prongs on the plug. Neighbors had crowded into their living room, filling the couch and standing behind it, dismal and shivering in their coats. It was February, and everyone knew someone touched by what had happened. Most of the neighbors were old enough to remember the wave of arrests that had followed Weiss's exile in '51. Would the traitors go to Soviet prisons now? More likely, Leonora said, Steinsaltz would send them across the border to Poland where he'd gotten all those scars on his face, and he knew they would welcome Jews.

The television picture flashed back on and caught Steinsaltz clearing his throat. His face had darkened. He had clearly said a few things in the interim, and now he finished a sentence: "—must face this challenge with another challenge and guide our youth in such a way that they will answer their Cosmopolitan professors: I have roots here. How can we honor our workers and soldiers, enriching their Bundist education so they understand that they are the very foundation of the state?"

Leonora whispered to her husband, "What's he saying? I don't understand."

"He's pardoning them," Rudolph said.

Judit broke in. "Who? What do you mean?"

The others in the room whispered to each other, as though testing the acoustics. Rudolph did the same, as he said to Judit, "There won't be any more arrests. A general amnesty. There must be some change in policy. He must have been told."

"By who?" Judit asked, and she didn't lower her voice at all. Everyone looked at her and hushed her because Steinsaltz was still talking: about pensions for veterans and a new trade policy with Poland and Hungary, and also Switzerland and Finland, which had a particular interest in economic and cultural exchange.

Judit felt cross and went to bed. In a few years, she'd be in Leipzig, where vestiges of 1968 lingered: in a curfew at the dormitory and an initial prohibition against gatherings of more than five students anywhere on campus, in a JDF veteran who got into an argument with a girl who wore a T-shirt with a Czech flag on it, and especially in those empty offices, the doors all open, books tossed off the shelves and left there, though it wouldn't be too long before the university would hire replacements and the doors would close again. But that night, through the wall, Judit could only hear the sound of muffled, grown-up conversation, energetic argument. She knew that if she got up and went in, they'd stop talking, so she just lay there and listened to what she couldn't understand.

5

SHE was in a different room. That much was clear. Someone had taken off her clothes and put her in a nightgown. She'd been tucked into one of two twin beds. Her hair was stuck to the side of her face, and her skin felt clammy. The beds were pink. Her blanket was pink. The little nightlight on the wall was pink too, and through the pink walls came voices, and a clattering of dishes. There were no windows. She couldn't tell what time it was or how long she'd been sleeping.

With effort, Judit managed to kick the blankets off and sit up. That must have been when Charlotte heard her because the door opened right away, and there she was, looking sober and elegant in a long-sleeved black wool dress, same wig, but a lace cap now and a string of pearls. "Well," she said, "I didn't think you'd be up so soon. You were in quite a state."

"How did I get here?" Judit asked.

"You really can't remember? It was quite a production up there. Can you imagine, all the men coming up to the dome to daven, and then the Rebbe suddenly stops, and his eyes twinkle the way they always do, and he says, 'The Shabbos Bride has arrived early.'

He says it in Russian, of course, so the guests will understand. Then he looks right up at the trapdoor."

Judit squeezed her head in her hands like a big sponge. She must have been carried, and there must have been a struggle because everything ached, her joints, her neck, her shoulders, and especially her head. "I'd better go," she said.

"You're not going anywhere, young lady," Charlotte said cheerfully. "I tell you, the way you cursed, like the devil was in you, and when some of the lady guests—I took them over myself in the van—when they came out from behind the *mechitzah* to get you out of the room and help me get you down that ladder, once you're on solid ground they start chattering away in Russian and you almost knock them over. And the cursing! Poor ladies. They were from the neighborhood. It was their first time at Chabad." She laughed, and said, "I shouldn't laugh. So Rabbi Schneerson, he just stood there, facing you between these great big Russian ladies. Then he laughed too, right out loud. I guess it was either that or perform an exorcism."

Charlotte would have gone on and on, and Judit would have been relieved to have nothing more expected of her than to keep sitting with her legs tangled in the pink blanket she'd thrown off the bed.

Then Charlotte said, "Don't you want to see him?"

"See who?" Judit asked.

"The Rebbe. Rabbi Schneerson. He asked for you. He always has a big *tish* in the ballroom after we daven. It's so beautiful, Judit, all the children running around, and the guests, and those songs without words, beautiful, beautiful melodies from the first Lubovicher Rebbe hundreds of years ago. And he shares out little morsels of whatever's on his plate. You know, he gave me one when my Dahlia was in the prenatal unit and nobody thought she'd have a chance. And I ate it, and look what happened. A miracle."

"I'm not hungry," Judit said. She tried to pull the covers up again for emphasis, but felt resistance. Maybe they'd caught on something. Maybe Charlotte had stepped on them. Judit went on. "Listen, you're confusing me with someone else."

"You know, Rabbi Schneerson studied at the Sorbonne. In France," Charlotte added, to clarify. "He speaks a dozen languages. He's not like they are in Loschwitz, though he'd never say a word against them because they're all fellow Jews. Honestly, most people, they don't understand how open he is, and how he wants to reach out his hand to everyone."

"Look," Judit said, "I'm sorry I caused so much trouble. But honestly, just tell me where you put my stuff."

"I know why you're here," Charlotte said. "It was only a matter of time. After all, with everything you've been through, all your tragedies." Now she sat down on the other bed and faced Judit. Her face softened under the wig. "It's human nature, wanting to confront the man upstairs. But then you realize that's not the point. It's not the point of living. And it's not the point of all those tragedies. Honestly."

"Tragedies have no point," said Judit.

"You sound just like I did, when I first came," Charlotte said. "After I failed my exams and my father died so suddenly, I was just drifting. When I lit the Shabbos candles, they told me, just go through the motions and the rest will follow. I said it was dishonest. But face it, we can't know what's honest. And we can't judge. We have to stop being afraid of the dark."

Judit looked at Charlotte. "Don't tell me what I shouldn't be afraid of."

Then she lay back in bed and turned to face the wall. It was so easy that it was amazing that she hadn't done it as soon as Charlotte walked into the room.

* * *

There was always a time after she'd lost each of the girls when Judit would sit in her sewing room, and she'd be grateful that there were no clocks or windows. She'd find a length of dull blue cotton and a pattern that she'd gotten years before, and she would cut and sew and mess up all the seams, and have to pick the stitches out; there was never enough light, and she didn't care.

The third time they tried, she'd injected herself with heparin every morning, and on Thursdays, she arranged to leave work early to take the express to Leipzig for a sonogram that was performed by that technician with the gray hair and the gray smock who checked her progress week by week. At week sixteen, the pattern had repeated. Judit didn't wait it out. She took two days off to have a procedure under anesthetic. Maybe a month later, the doorbell rang. It was early evening. Judit had been sewing the same piece of cloth over and over again with an intensity that was so like her rhythm as a film editor that it felt like real work, like salvation. The stitches were so neat that they were almost invisible, and she couldn't explain why she didn't ignore the doorbell, but instead, got up, and when she opened the door, there was a woman in a wig who smiled across the threshold and handed Judit a little booklet of psalms.

"These bring comfort," the woman said. "After all, Ha Shem will give us nothing that we can't endure, as long as we know we're not alone."

"My God!" Judit shouted at Hans later that night. "Does Chabad have spies in the hospital?" He looked beleaguered. She suspected that he'd told them himself.

Then, one night, when they lay a distance apart in bed, Hans reached out to touch her. His hand moved through her nightgown, and slowly, against the protest of her spirit, she could feel her body rise to meet him, and then something broke in her, and she began to cry.

He didn't ask if he should stop, and she didn't pull away. She kept on sobbing, even as he touched her in the ways they knew, and she responded, and when she moved with him, she realized the period of mourning had an end, and they had reached it. Afterwards, Hans's long, familiar body lay against her own, breathing, letting out a faint and rhythmic snore, the way he always did after they made love. She wished he were awake. She wanted to talk, but she had no idea what she'd say. Mostly, she knew she had to go on living.

Hans was dead. Judit dreamed that the dome of the Yenidze was lit from within, full of floating islands, red, yellow, and blue. She dreamed of miracle babies with dull blue eyes, baby girls embedded in stained glass the way a fetus is embedded in the womb. She dreamed she was in her archive, and all the drawers were open. There was one drawer like a deep, long bed, and she climbed inside. Although she knew the archive's footage, reel by reel, the metal canisters under her feet and hands were unfamiliar. She rooted through the drawer, opening first one canister and then another, taking from her pocket Shaindel's plastic flashlight. The cells of the film glittered like leaves of gold. Imperfectly, she could observe the outlines of what she'd never seen before. If she pressed on, she could find films that had even more promise; they winked up from the depths. Yet she wasn't searching for something new. She was searching for something that was in her hand. How could she have held it for so long, for her whole life, and never thought to turn it over and see what was on the other side?

And now she turned over what she had been holding. She turned everything over. Reel after reel contained another side, mysterious and maddening, and under the cheap, faint bulb of Shaindel's flashlight, she could start to parse it out, an old-new thing that told a story part of her already knew. She lifted out each canister, took out what it contained, and flipped the old reel over, stock footage or discarded, and she saw the different story, faint but undeniable, and she may not like that story, but she could define its structure. And that was when she knew that the drawer she'd climbed into had been locked.

Someone had closed it. Someone had locked it with a lock of iron. A metal padlock snapped into place, and even as she'd fixated on what she saw, she had ignored what she had heard. She'd heard the drawer close and the key turn. Although she was deaf in one ear, she'd heard it all.

Not until now did she realize she was deaf in one ear. It had happened during the explosion when she fired the shot that killed her husband. Her hands were soaked in blood. There was nothing behind her now, not even the closed drawer. Did she have a choice? She had to move on. She must take that cheap flashlight, and she must shine it on everything she saw because it was all vividly important. She must move on because the drawer was locked behind her.

6

AND Judit dreamed she looked at reel after reel; they lied about the murder. She couldn't voice the nature of the lie, only that it was profound, and it was one of countless lies that threaded through her consciousness and met each other like a string of pearls. Some of the footage that she watched was half-familiar, the ruins of '46, those men with spades. But as she shined Shaindel's flashlight on those spades, they became translucent. What was clear became unclear. The rifles aimed right at the camera lens; they fired, and it shattered. Light merged front and back until there was no front and back at all.

And Stein, at the crater of the Great Synagogue of Dresden, his enormous head, those hands cradling his chin, it all had swollen to the proportions of a mountain or a monument. A monument to what? His mouth moved. Words were forming. It was the very frame that had fixed her attention when Durmersheimer left that note.

If only she was not deaf in one ear, she would know who killed her husband, but now those words came from a muddled past that showed both sides at once, and in the unforgiving beam of Shaindel's flashlight, flaws in the film stock, flaws in the bulb, the shadows of her fingers, it showed a deeper mystery.

There was too much she couldn't know. The truth lay outside of the parameters of her dream, in her own archive, where she retraced that film's precise location. Now she would wake up. In an hour, she'd be back there. She did not wake up.

"Will she wake up?"

"Don't get so close. She's probably contagious."

"Will she be sick all over my bed again?"

"Shhh. She can hear you. Can't you tell? Her eyes are moving under her eyelids."

They were leaning over her, three girls: the one—was it Leah?—with the long hair pulled back, a taller girl who'd clipped her hair to the side with a butterfly barrette, and Rebecca of the sippy-cup, two tiny hands on the side of that bed.

The barrette-girl asked, "Did we wake you up? I'll bet we woke you up."

"You were sleeping for a long time," Leah said. "You're in my bed."

"Leah! That's not right, saying that," said the barrette-girl.

"But it's a mitzvah that she's in my bed!" Then Leah turned around and shouted, "Momma!" with a force that broke the room to bits and caused little Rebecca to lose her grip on the mattress and stumble back in terror; then she also cried out, "Momma!" and the third girl, whose barrette implied some kind of girlish status, turned to Judit with a look of resignation or complicity. She was holding Judit's clothes.

"We washed them yesterday," she said. "The sweater shrank a little. Sorry."

The girl's name was Ruth. She was the oldest, but she was downstairs more than upstairs, helping staff the nursery school. She even slept down there on Shabbos. The oldest boy, Aaron, had left at dawn because he went to a yeshiva halfway across town, the most rigorous one in Dresden. "He takes after his father," Charlotte said. She explained all this to Judit over breakfast, a chaotic affair, with paper plates and plastic flatware and Leah and that boy—was it Dov?—each frying eggs in a separate pan, and tiny Dahlia scattering fistfuls of breakfast cereal from her highchair. "You're much better," Charlotte said to Judit. "I'll admit, we started to get worried when you slept through Shabbos, but Mendel checked with the Rebbe—you know he has a scientific background—and he said it was important for you to gather your strength for the task ahead."

"Is it Sunday?" Judit asked. She could hear the hesitation in her own voice.

"Monday," Charlotte said. "Leah, put on another egg for Mrs. Klemmer, no, two, and I think there must be some coffee left. Dov, pour her some. You know how to. Don't be scared. She's a nice lady. I knew her as a girl, and now she's a famous filmmaker."

While Dov very nervously poured her coffee from the heavy pot, Judit rested her hand on the warm, soft head of Rebecca and was about to ask for a full count of Charlotte's children when another little boy appeared in striped pajamas, leading a hard-looking old lady in a pink bathrobe.

"Bubba, we didn't think you'd join us!" Charlotte said, though it was clear the woman didn't understand a word of German. She added, "That's Mendel's mother. I told you about her." Charlotte pulled out a chair and anxiously addressed the woman in a whisper as she sat down and glared straight ahead under black eyebrows. Her white hair was clipped short. She said something in Russian without moving her lips.

Charlotte said, "Mendel's mother says she's been very anxious to meet you."

It was clear to Judit that the woman had no interest in her. That seemed only fair. Judit had heard about those Russian immigrants to Judenstaat, along with a lot of other things that had happened in the past four years, and none of it had seemed to matter much. Those lips kept emitting Russian to no one in particular as her grandchildren ate their eggs or toast or cereal, and after a while, Ruth brought her over a glass of tea. She raised that glass to her lips, and sputtered.

"It's still too hot for her," Charlotte said to Ruth, "but it's just the way she likes it, baby. Don't worry. She's really very grateful." Then, to Judit, "Mrs. Rabinovich has seen it all, the fascist massacres, hiding in the forest with her older brother and coming across dead bodies frozen in a lake, and it turned out one of them was her best friend. And this was all when the fascists invaded the Soviet Union during the war—terrible, terrible things. You know, she saw her own parents shot by the man they'd paid to hide them. It turned out he was in the pay of the fascists all along. I'll tell you, Judit, there's so much evil in the world."

By now, Mrs. Rabinovich had started on her tea, which she drank slowly. She smacked her lips, and certainly seemed to make no sense of what Charlotte was saying. She did survey the room and took in, without visible appreciation, all of her grandchildren wandering around with their plates or bowls.

Charlotte said, "If we didn't know that Ha Shem had a plan for us, we couldn't go on living."

Judit did not reply. She was dressed now, and if she could find her shoes and coat, there was no reason she had to stay. It couldn't have been Monday. That was some Chabad trick. There were no windows in the kitchen, and no clock at all in that apartment, but time didn't just lose its elasticity. She would have felt it pass. She pushed her chair back and got up.

Mrs. Rabinovich looked right at Judit and said, in perfect German, "The Russians killed my husband."

The words had been quite clear. Nevertheless, Judit said to Charlotte, "What did she just say?"

Charlotte shook her head. "Yes, isn't it shocking? After everything she'd been through. A terrible story. Terrible. Mendel was five years old when it happened. It was just after the war, a terrible time. It wasn't safe to be a Jew in Russia then, and there was no escape. No one talks about it. He was buried alive." Then she asked, "Do you understand Russian?"

It felt jarring, walking down those stairs and through the glass revolving door and out into the street. Judit was still unsteady on her feet, and she almost walked into a Mitzvah Tank parked in the driveway. The day was overcast. Getting out of that apartment, of course, was a true production, with the girls hanging on her and Charlotte buttoning the duffle coat to the top, insisting that she really ought to wait and get her strength back. There was a free bed in the women's dormitory. She should eat lunch. She could see Rabbi Schneerson afterwards. Mendel had met with him yesterday, and could easily arrange an appointment on short notice.

After Judit dislodged herself and found the exit, she was relieved, almost surprised, to find an ordinary street with a recognizable sidewalk and a familiar, if oppressive, railway bridge, and then she saw the bus to Stein Square pass; she had just missed it.

How long would it take to walk to the museum? Once she arrived, she knew just where she'd find the footage of Stein at the Great Synagogue, and there'd be audio. She knew it. There'd be audio and mystery and certainty. Of what? Soon she would know.

Then Judit did something acutely un-Judit-like. She hailed a taxi. The gesture felt expansive. She'd done so without being sure she had the cash to cover it, and when she awkwardly climbed in, she reached inside the pocket of her coat. That's when she found the envelope. There was a letter inside.

Dear Mrs. Klemmer,

We met only briefly, but I take the liberty to write you to let you know that our encounter has left a deep impression on me and on my family as well as on the whole of our community. Chana Batya informed me of your childhood friendship, and I can only take it as evidence of your loyalty to our people, Israel, that even in these confusing times, you have performed mitzvah after mitzvah telling our stories through the medium of film. Yesterday, I approached the Rebbe, and he is very aware of your work, which he has followed closely. Rabbi Schneerson's message to you, for which I am only an emissary, is this: Remember, always, you are a Jew. When miracles occur, you may laugh, like Mother Sarah, or you may weep, like Mother Rachel, but you are forbidden to despair.

Sincerely,

Mendel Rabinovitch

Folded inside was an American dollar bill. At least Judit assumed that it must be one. She'd never seen an actual dollar bill before. It was dull green, smaller than a Judenmark. She didn't know what it was worth these days. There wasn't time to calculate exchange rates. The taxi pulled up by the entrance of the National Museum, and Judit fished around for Judenmarks. It was morning, and she had work to do.

7

IT wasn't morning, though. It was past eleven. Judit glanced at the clock above the front desk as she passed and was surprised to find Mr. Rosenblatt rising in alarm and calling, "Wait! Mrs. Klemmer—Judit!" and abandoning his post to follow her. She kept going, right to the stairwell that led down to her archive, and she opened the door when she felt his hand on her arm.

She turned at last. The poor old man had her arm in a grip. "I know I'm late," she said. "And I know I missed a day. I should have called the office. But I'll make up for lost time even if I have to work all night."

"Judit," said Mr. Rosenblatt, "no one's allowed downstairs."

"That's ridiculous," Judit said. "What is this? Was Sammy in there? Did he touch my stuff?"

"You'd better check with Mr. Kornfeld," Mr. Rosenblatt said carefully.

Judit shook his hand off her arm with difficulty; he was stronger than he looked. She switched on the light and started down the stairwell, conscious that Mr. Rosenblatt had gone back to his station, and aware that he was phoning someone; she could hear his thin, anxious old-man's voice rising and falling. Then she saw the padlock.

It was clamped, crosswise, on the door, a padlock with a combination. She stood there. Then she shook it. She called up, "Mr. Rosenblatt! What's this about?" He didn't answer. Finally, she walked back to the lobby and saw that Mr. Rosenblatt was still on the phone, and he turned to Judit, cupping the receiver with his hand.

"They're waiting for you. Upstairs." His voice shook a little.

Had someone found out about the break-in three months ago? He did look spooked. Judit hoped that she hadn't inadvertently caused the poor man trouble. When she reached Kornfeld's office, his secretary said, "Gosh. I'm glad you're back, Judit. Everything here's been topsy-turvy. The new setup must have cost a fortune." That's how Judit found out that her footage had been moved to the Media Room.

That room, which Judit had always refused to enter, was in a newly restored atrium that had been boarded over until just last year. When the museum had been a palace, this must have been its greenhouse, walls of glass awash in light, and an expansive view of Stein Square. Several expensive-looking chairs faced each other across an oblong table where five dull-plastic monitors sat like burlap sacks. There was a lot of business underneath the table too, dials and switches, tiny flashing green lights. It was no surprise that Sammy Gluck was there to greet her, looking moist and holding both his hands out effusively, happy enough to burst.

"Welcome back!" he said. "Isn't this beautiful?" He switched on a screen, and there was the face of Leopold Stein as he looked in 1952, square-jawed and hostile. Sammy wiggled a dangling object on that table, and the eyes of Stein were suddenly all whites. Blue irises appeared. Then the whole face vanished, leaving a pair of angry blue eyes.

Judit said, "Sammy, this is an incredible waste of time and money. We're not here to play."

Someone spoke up from behind. "No. We're here to work." The accent was a strange one. Judit turned, and faced a well-dressed, slim blond woman in rectangular glasses who extended a hand and introduced herself. "Fredericka Schumaker from Berlin. Freddi. I take it you're the editor. I've been waiting on tenterhooks. I hear you're terrifying." She smiled. Her teeth were excellent. Judit took the hand because she wasn't sure what else to do with it.

"I guess you're the director," Judit said in a voice that sounded childish even to herself.

"Good guess," said Freddi. "Now sit down, kiddo. I laid out most of the storyboard even before I got here, and the interviews are almost done, but what we need's a feel to the thing, see? It needs a flow." Freddi leaned back in one of those chairs and crossed her expensive-looking legs. Her shoes had square toes, and thick high heels; her feet were enormous. "Sammy's already worked with some of the footage from downstairs."

To Judit's horror, across those screens ran film she'd pieced together—shots of rubble, construction sites from 1949—and what had been sunlight was now white and flattened, not a shadow visible. Then Judit realized he'd done something else to the footage. There were no people in it. Reading Judit's face, Sammy said, "Hey, I just cleaned it up a little, Mrs. Klemmer."

"Cleaned it up?"

"Better to start with an empty canvas," Sammy said. "Then we can add what we need later." He looked at Freddi for reassurance, but her face was unreadable. Somewhat deflated, he said, "Nothing that can't be undone. I mean, that's the whole point. Nothing's permanent."

Judit pulled one of those chairs from behind the table and sat glaring at them both. She had no intention of condoning this brand of mischief, but she couldn't take it seriously. Then it came back to her: what she had said to Sammy on Thursday in her delirium. Well, now she had recovered and she would let him know that it was all a misunderstanding. That the archive was padlocked, that this mad scientist's laboratory was functioning, that a Berliner marched in here on legs like a giraffe's and talked about a storyboard, none of it had anything to do with her work. Kornfeld would have some explaining to do, but in the end, it wasn't possible that any real damage could have been done in just four days.

The first thing Kornfeld said was, "We thought you were dead. A week and a half, no sign of you."

"I was just here Thursday," Judit said.

"No you weren't. And you weren't at your dormitory, or at your mother's." He looked shaken, and actually seemed more angry than relieved to find Judit sitting across from him. "That poor woman's called here twice a day."

"Oscar," Judit said, "I swear I don't know what you're talking about."

Kornfeld fell back into his chair and gave something between a growl and a sigh. He ran his hand over his forehead and face so that what little hair he had stood up, and then he said, "I was told to say you'd taken a vacation. It was simpler that way. Gluck worked night and day transferring the stuff to video before that German could take over completely. Where the hell were you, anyway?"

Judit felt sweat bead all over her body. "I need the combination."

"What combination?" Kornfeld asked. Then he said, "Oh. I see. Well, that's beyond my jurisdiction."

"What are you talking about?" Judit asked. "Whose jurisdiction is it?"

"Ministry of State Security," Kornfeld said. "Apparently, there was some funny business down there. But you wouldn't know anything about that, would you?" He looked at her hard, bluster gone from his face. "No, you didn't do a thing to compromise yourself. You haven't gone anywhere you shouldn't have gone. You've been as good as gold, Judit. And what they found down there had nothing to do with you at all."

Shaken, Judit wasn't sure what to answer. All she could imagine were the reels of footage, uncoiled and exposed, the images of Weiss she'd found all tangled on the floor, the viewer torn from the table, all in the blaze of the fluorescent light she'd turned on maybe two times in her ten years at the archive. And down there was that reel with Stein at the synagogue. And down there was the ghost.

Kornfeld dropped his voice. "Judit, what have you been doing? You know, you could've had my job."

"Why did you let them search?" Judit asked, feebly.

"I could ask you plenty of questions, of course," Kornfeld said. "Like where you've been for nearly two weeks. Mr. Rosenblatt's job is on the line. But we were tipped off, thank God. The bomb squad took a pair of wire cutters to it."

Judit felt so violated and raw that it took her a moment to realize the implications. "They found explosives?"

"Apparently," Kornfeld said. "Inside a video cassette. Plastics with a timer. You don't even have a cassette player down there. What if Sammy had taken it upstairs? They'd be scraping him off the ceiling of the Media Room, or no, there'd be no Media Room. We'd have a hole where it used to be. My God, Judit. All of this, and no one can find you." He lowered his voice in bewildered sympathy. "We're keeping it quiet, but they do expect a resignation. Just a short note, sweetheart. Don't give it too much thought. Just have it to me by the end of the day."

She was not about to resign. If she had to face the consequences, so be it, but she would see this through, and when she was questioned, she would tell the Stasi everything: Durmersheimer and the note left in the dark, the trips to Loschwitz, the pink nightlight at Chabad House, the husband who had been buried alive, all of it concocted to get her anniversary film out of her hands and get her out of the archive so the German could take over. With the force of that conviction, she strode out of Kornfeld's office, out of the museum, and into the winter sunshine. It was late afternoon now, a cold December Monday, though the date was still an open question. The clean, gray light implied a clarity of mind.

Her conviction was still burning when she caught a taxi to her dormitory. Flagging one down felt automatic. Once inside, she stared ahead, full of suspicions, and knew if she could just dredge through them she would find a logic and coherence.

When she arrived, the porter looked up from her magazine, impassive. "You have some messages."

She took them and sorted through. Five from her mother, three from Kornfeld. That Stasi agent—what was his name? Bondi. He hadn't called. That was his name, Joseph Bondi. She would have to call him herself. She walked to her room and was surprised to find it was just as she had left it. The small refrigerator, goose-necked lamp on the nightstand, the narrow bed with the square pillow, and beneath her bed, in its case, her sewing machine. No one had taken that sewing machine apart and searched for a hidden bomb. Then there was the desk. That was where she was supposed to write the letter of resignation. What she looked at now was the pile of cards from Joseph Bondi.

She lifted the topmost card and turned it over. Nothing was written on the back. She spread the other cards across the table, with their Stasi sword and shield, and flipped them over, one by one until they spread across the surface of the desk, rectangles of card-stock, some a little worn around the edges. This Bondi, he had stood by her bedside during those awful days after the murder, fielding phone calls in that old apartment. When she was strong enough to care, she hated, beyond words, the sight of his brown hat on the table.

This Bondi, he'd undressed her at night when she was still under sedation. He had sent her clothing to be laundered. And the day she'd moved to this dormitory, he had said he would look in on her once a month.

Who was Joseph Bondi? His suits had grown more expensive as time passed. He had less hair. The rest was speculation. She must have imagined the Yiddish she'd seen written on the back of his card a month ago. She picked up one of the cards and walked outside to a phone booth to place the call.

The Age of Reason

1

THE phone was answered by a woman who knew who Judit was, and didn't seem surprised to hear from her. "He can see you tomorrow afternoon."

"No. Today," Judit said.

"He's out of the office, but I'll page him," the woman said. Who was she to Bondi? Did she work a switchboard? Was there a location? The call could have been answered anywhere in Dresden, or in another city altogether.

"Tell him," Judit said, "that I'm prepared to cooperate completely. I'll be outside."

She put the phone back on the hook and turned around. She half-expected Bondi to be standing behind her, looking through the glass of the phone booth with that intensity and seriousness that might have a second meaning. But he wasn't there. She didn't know what to do with herself. She walked back to the dormitory entrance. A cold rain started falling. The air was raw, and she was trapped with no umbrella. She felt in her coat pocket. What if Charlotte had cleaned out the contents? No, it was there, that note from last October, wadded up, almost impossible to unfold. She should have handed it to Bondi the day she'd gotten it, but she had refused to let herself be used by him, so instead she had been used by everybody else.

The rain turned to sleet as she reviewed those meetings with him, from the night he'd stood in the apartment doorway in that hat until the recent afternoon when he'd taken her pulse with such terrible intimacy, to their last awkward encounter. He would assume she'd read what he had written on the back of his card and had dismissed it. He wouldn't show up. Not now.

Then, she saw a figure under an umbrella coming towards her, and her heart caught. She felt hot inside her clothes.

Bondi said, "There was no need to wait outside."

"Take me somewhere," Judit said.

He gestured her under the umbrella, and they walked in silence just long enough for Judit to be impressed by both his tact and the way his heavy coat gave off real heat. She didn't ask where they were going. There were a number of office complexes straight ahead, sleek and colorless as the rain and sky. They walked against a raw wind that logically should have turned his umbrella inside out, but it held steady. After a while, he guided her down a few steps through a passageway, closed that umbrella, and unfastened the first two buttons of his coat.

"We should sit down," he said. They were standing at the entrance of an employee cafeteria for an Austrian corporation. Lunch had ended hours before. A janitor ran an electric sweeper. Bondi led Judit to a round white table stained with coffee, and he pulled out a chair for her. Then he said, "There's another place. A room. But it's in Johannstadt. Closer to your museum. Some other time, if you'd prefer."

"Is it warmer?" Judit asked.

"Yes," said Bondi.

"Do I need to tell you what you already know?" It was impossible for Judit not to sound angry, even though she wasn't sure that she was angry anymore. "That's what happens next, isn't it?"

"Mrs. Klemmer," Bondi said, "what happens next?"

"You know I'm backed into a corner. And you must have a hand in it."

"A hand in it?" Bondi leaned towards her, and his voice dropped, though its diction was precise enough for it to be heard over the sweeper. "We've always kept a hands-off policy at your own insistence."

"Well somebody has their hands all over me," Judit said. Then, stupidly, she blushed. She said, "It's really cold in here," just to say something.

Of course, Bondi removed his coat and laid it across her shoulders. He wore a sweater under it, not a cheap one. She'd been right about the hair; it was thin on top and short around the ears. The coat smelled like expensive cologne.

She gave him the note. He got up from the table and walked towards the window where the light was better. He looked at the slip of paper with the same deductive focus that he'd turned on Judit, examining both front and back. Then, he took out a little notebook from his pocket and wrote something down with a pencil; he filled a page, flipped it over, and wrote more. Then, he walked back to her. "How long has this been in your possession?"

"Maybe three months," Judit said.

"More than three months? Less than three months?"

"Why does it matter?" Judit said. "I went to that address. He lured me there so he could stop the project—"

"Arno Durmersheimer doesn't want to stop the project," Bondi said. Now it was Judit's turn to be under that gaze. She could feel him watching and recording what his statement did to her face. "Of course, we have his handwriting on file."

"He lured me there. And Chabad black-hats locked me in a room for a week!"

"Chabad goes its own way," Bondi said. "Sometimes they're useful, but only by coincidence."

"Why don't you ask me how the videotape with the explosives got into the archive? It came from Loschwitz."

"Not my jurisdiction," Bondi said.

"Durmersheimer was in Loschwitz. Why don't you ask me what he had to say?"

"That doesn't interest us."

"He's an unrepentant fascist, an enemy of the Bund!"

"Mrs. Klemmer," Bondi began.

"And you people let him go!"

Bondi said, "Judit." At the sound of her given name, Judit stopped talking. Then Bondi said, "Arno Durmersheimer works for us."

Judit stood up. The coat dropped from her shoulders. The sound of the power-cleaning ceased, and all she could hear was her own raw breath expelling and contracting, the rain hitting the window, the buzz of the fluorescent lights.

Bondi said, "I'll get you a cup of soup."

"You planted those explosives and then tipped them off," Judit said, "to get me off the project."

Bondi paused for a moment before saying, "That's faulty logic. We want you on the project. Very much. There's important work to do."

"Then why is my archive locked?"

"Standard procedure." He turned around, picked his coat up off the floor, and set it on an empty chair. "The area has been cleared. The contents have been transferred or discarded. Now sit down."

Judit did not sit down. "If you want my help, get me back in there!"

Bondi shook his head. "That's not how it works. Those aren't the terms. First of all, if you cooperate, that means you're under our protection."

"I don't need protection," Judit said.

Bondi said, "You do. You've been mourning for almost four years. It's made you—"

"What? Unhealthy? Has it affected my complexion? Should I take a vacation? Should I drink more soup? You sound like my mother."

"It's made you into a child," Bondi said. He said it, and Judit wanted to strike him, but he did not back down. Rather, he set a hand on her shoulder to steady her, and said, more gently, "Your nose is running."

"I'm not a child," Judit said.

"I know," said Bondi.

"I don't need protection."

"You do," Bondi said. He handed her a handkerchief, and she took it. She didn't blow her nose, but she did wipe it, and also her eyes. "Judit, you do. You say you work best independently. Judit, no one works independently. You've put yourself in vulnerable situations that have led to consequences you did not intend, but they're real consequences. Frankly," he said, "you need protection from yourself. As things stand, you have no choice."

"I can't listen to language like that," Judit said.

"I thought you weren't a child," said Bondi. He made a move to brush the hair out of her eyes, and she flinched. He retreated, as though he were taming a fox. "Understand," he said, "that what I tell you will always be in your best interest. Arno Durmersheimer killed your husband."

"And I suppose he was working for you then," Judit said.

Bondi ignored the interruption. "He served his time. He is a bitter man, and drinks too much, and sometimes he gets confused, but he would no more try to stop this project than he would blow himself to pieces."

"What about those explosives?"

There was a pause. "That's still under investigation, and it's sensitive. At this time, as you are well aware, Loschwitz business is still officially beyond our jurisdiction. I must ask you to steer clear of it. We don't want you distracted or embroiled in any needless controversy. Your teeth are chattering."

"Don't get me soup."

"Then take my coat again," Bondi said. "If we're going to work together, you will need to face facts, and face them courageously. Maybe someone was a fascist yesterday. He's not today. Times change."

"Facts don't change with them," Judit said.

"That's right. And that brings me back to my earlier point. You have no choice. Facts don't change, and choices are illusions. If you're lucky—and you happen to be very, very lucky—you can have opportunities, but they're not the same as choices. You are obliged to take any opportunity that has social utility. You have the power to use your gifts for the greater good."

She could foresee the room in Johannstadt, closer to the museum, the warmer room. It would be up a flight of stairs, and there would be a single lamp on a night table and maybe a desk, a chair, a bed. They'd meet, and what would come to pass would be of a piece with Judit's promise of cooperation and submission. That promise and its consequences made her feel as though she'd stepped across a border. That afternoon, though, she believed something else would happen too. She said, "Mr. Bondi, maybe I don't have a choice. But if I do what you say, what do I get in return?"

"You serve justice," Bondi said.

"Which means?"

"Which means you use your considerable gifts to tell the truth."

"That Russians killed my husband," Judit said.

Bondi said, "Arno Durmersheimer killed your husband. As I said, he's a bitter man. But I believe he has reason to be. He's been used, just as we've all been used. Now we have a chance to tell the true story of our country."

Somehow, what Bondi said was not bombastic. The new material from Moscow would soon be followed by yet more tapes and footage, and the direction it was leading would change everything. If she resisted, what was she resisting? Was she still the willful Bundist girl who wanted time to stand still? The stories that she'd grown up with had been comforting, but she'd been vomiting up pieces of those stories for so long that there was nothing left. And what could fill those empty spaces? Empty spaces weakened you, and predators would scent that weakness, circle, and move in. She thought of Charlotte.

Still, Judit said, "I don't believe that Durmersheimer killed my husband."

"The case is closed," said Bondi.

"He has a different story. He said Hans was about to make a public statement about a Soviet massacre in Dresden."

Bondi said, "That is completely possible."

Judit said nothing. Bondi's face was impassive, and a heartbeat later, she burst out: "What massacre? When did it take place? Is there any proof?"

"That's your work, not mine," said Bondi.

Those words carried a promise. It would be her work. Even as she took in the implications of what Bondi said, she felt a bright thread of anticipation. She would have access to material that would make sense of things that everybody knew, and no one would acknowledge. A thought came to her with such force that she almost said it out loud. Someone could say it in the film she's making. For forty years, our country has been buried alive.

She thought those words, but what she said was this: "I don't believe my husband's case is closed. Where's the police report? If he was going to talk about a Soviet massacre, why would a Saxon try to stop him? Who put explosives in those tapes? If they're from Loschwitz, why would those people even care who killed my husband?"

The rain had stopped by now, and the janitor had long since

wiped down the rest of the tables in the cafeteria. Soon, the night shift would appear for supper. Bondi's overcoat weighed on Judit's shoulders. He gave her one of his long looks, but there was no calculation in it.

"I don't know," Bondi said. "If I knew, I'd tell you. But I also ask you, Judit, what would it serve?"

2

WHAT would it serve? She thought about it in the days and weeks that followed. If those questions had answers, it would serve justice. Justice would be served. These sentences had rhythms that she recognized: a Junior Bundist choral piece. And then she heard her own voice hectoring: justice for whom? A chain of facts was not the same as justice. An answer to a question served no one in isolation. Justice was the organizing principle of history.

And history fell right into her hands now, film stock transferred to video by five smart assistants overseen by Sammy Gluck in the Media Room overlooking Stein Square on rows of screens attached to big, gray boxes. Those screens projected images frame by frame, variants of Judit's footage for direct comparison, and Judit crossed from one screen to the other, referring to the storyboard. Then there was the new material from Anna Lehmann delivered by the couriers, young girls or boys on motorbikes who brought big, padded envelopes from who-knows-where: film canisters and also documents that verified their contents. The declassified material challenged Judit's dormant Russian, but she pored over it, fact-checked, and only afterwards passed on the film to Freddi Schumaker.

"This is brilliant stuff," Freddi said to Judit. She didn't come in often; most days, she moved back and forth across the border, conducting interviews. "Your old mentor's got friends in high places. Is she a holy terror?"

"No worse than I am," Judit said. She'd actually gotten to like Fredericka, who often feigned a charming intimidation. "She's got a bigger appetite, though. She looks like the Protective Rampart."

"Well then, I'll have to take her apart brick by brick," said Freddi. "I'm good at that." Then she said to Judit, "Good luck making sense of this office. It's a wreck. I'm glad we have you upstairs, kid. We need a little terror around here."

The tapes were in disarray, and Judit sorted through bins and found that Sammy had the sense to label the new videos with her old codes. She did attempt to look for the film that Sammy hadn't transferred, but although no one talked about the incident downstairs, her questions were met with evasion that implied she ought to let it go. The waste—the enormous waste—made Judit furious, but she had too much else to do.

If Oscar Kornfeld took issue with Judit's reappearance, he didn't show it. A month after he'd asked her to resign, he wandered into the Media Room, and such was her absorption that he was standing right behind her before she noticed him at all.

He said, "You need to sign off on this." He handed her a large manila envelope. She set it aside on the worktable, and several hours passed before she remembered the package, and scribbled her name in a corner without opening the thing or even giving any thought to the nature of her authority. Later, he ran into her in the hall and said, "So you're pleased with the proofs?"

Judit said, "Didn't Sammy hand them back to you?"

"Of course," Kornfeld said. Seeing no sign that Judit wanted to engage in further conversation, he melted off somewhere.

Hours themselves melted now. She no longer had to struggle to complete a puzzle. The pieces were laid out before her in Fredericka's notes, and she combined the interviews and footage into a coherent whole: "Singing Junior Bundists: 1960"; "Interview #21"; "Pastoral scene: Rathen." The yellow morning light, the white light of afternoon, and sometimes twilight itself passed over Judit and her screens. Such was her accumulated knowledge that once she'd established a filing system for the tapes, she knew just where to find the missing pieces.

At first, Gluck glued himself to Judit's side. The keyboard by the monitors was still moist from his fingers when he stepped back to watch her work. He had been clumsy; he erased too much, made everything too clean. He tried too hard. Now, only she was permitted to work with the new material, and he watched her translate Freddi's notes into visual form, waiting for her to throw him a question so he could pounce on it and tear it with his teeth and carry it around the room before returning it in some gross form. Once, he said, "You know, with pixels, you can increase the resolution, make it consistent, everything in focus."

Judit said, "That's no good."

"Well, then you're just reproducing a camera lens the way you've done it. The background and the foreground get lost."

"Right," Judit said, not really looking up from the two scenes she was interspersing, and therefore making Gluck go slightly crazy. He wanted acknowledgment; he wanted credit; he wanted, at the very least, to be needed, and after a while he admitted that he might as well stop pestering her and stick to the technical side of things.

Yet Sammy couldn't quite believe how quickly Judit mastered what she'd learned. She worked instinctively, often combining two tapes like a bartender muddling two kinds of spirits, mellowing the flat, contemporary interviews, creating continuity with footage decades old. Most days, she worked at an on-screen storyboard without audio, stopping at places only she could understand, and then she'd call in one of the assistants to take tapes back to Gluck for what he knew, frankly, was work a monkey could have done.

Gluck couldn't help but say, "Are you sure you didn't take a special tutorial last year? When we were at that conference?"

"What you don't understand," Judit said, "is that what I'm doing now is much easier than what I tried to do downstairs."

"So you finally admit it," Gluck said. He sounded giddy, but his face didn't show it. "All that time, you stuck to those old machines, and now look at you. We'll be done by early March for sure."

Then he too melted away, and it was only Judit, the videos, and piles of Freddi's notes. The only sound was the electric heater and the whine of the machines. If she looked up, she would be startled by her own reflection in the blackened windows—face drawn, eyes enormous, hair in her face. Once, she lost control of her hands. She rubbed them together for a while. Then she sat back and gave her eyes a rest. If she wasn't lucky, something would appear behind those eyes, and she'd have to rub them, hard.

It was after just such a night, knocked senseless, beyond exhausted, that she came to herself and realized she'd have to get some sleep. It must have been three in the morning. She tried to hail a taxi back to her dormitory, but the streets were deserted. As she wandered beyond Stein Square, the webbing of orange hazard tape around the new construction rattled and glowed like exotic grasses in the desert. Then she realized she'd reached the edge of Johannstadt, and was two blocks away from an address that Bondi had made her repeat several times when they last made contact. It was on a small street lined with Yiddish *pashkevils* trumpeting something about a birth or death that wasn't her concern. All she knew was that he'd told her that the door was never locked.

Up an uneven flight of stairs, she turned the doorknob, and walked into the small, warm room. There was that bed, a daybed covered with a striped synthetic bedspread. Maybe she was still under the spell of the screen, or the sight of herself reflected in the window. Maybe just as her hands and eyes stopped working, something else shut down. She lay on the bed and slept.

An hour passed, maybe two. She woke to find that she had been turned on her back and was in the process of being undressed. Her shoes were off, and her blouse unbuttoned. Someone was unfastening her skirt, and for a moment, she wondered if she'd be slipped into a modest nightgown, but those hands worked the skirt down her hips. They weren't women's hands. She kept her eyes closed. Maybe he'd stop there. Maybe he'd put a blanket over her. He paused at the elastic of her underwear. She was awake enough to know that if she moved one way or another, she could determine the direction. She held still. He slipped his hand inside.

The room was in a black-hat enclave, across the street from a school for girls, and above a kosher dairy restaurant. There was a picture of one of their Rebbes over the daybed, not Schneerson, another one, with a salt-and-pepper beard and a black skull-cap above tired-looking eyes. On the desk, there was a row of Yiddish books lined up between two bricks. It would be some time before Judit learned the full story of that room, just as it would take time to find out much about Bondi himself. He mentioned an ambitious father who pushed him to graduate from secondary school two years ahead of schedule. By 1975, he was a student at the academy, aged sixteen, sober and quiet. He had been hand-picked for special training before he turned twenty, and spent a year in Moscow, which he made clear had been an opportunity that "should have been given to someone else."

"What do you mean?" Judit asked him. It was hard to get Bondi to talk. It was hard to call him Joseph. Even after they'd made love, and his compact, beautiful body was naked on top of the striped bedspread, there was nothing vulnerable about Joseph Bondi. He would seldom answer a question like that in any way except:

"I mean just what I say. It was someone else's opportunity. As for me, I saw nothing wonderful about Moscow, and I heard nothing worth hearing there, except what is clear now and is not secret, that it's a dying city. I'm not a morbid man. Some men are. They would have appreciated Moscow in 1979."

He approached their lovemaking as he approached all things, with precision and sobriety, a quiet resignation. That might have been the only way that Judit could have entered the affair. It was like that doorbell at nine o'clock when she sat at her sewing machine and she knew. Even before she saw the man in the brown suit and hat, she knew. Maybe she even knew then that one day she would be in that bed with the man who'd made a widow of her.

"If you're not a morbid man," Judit asked Bondi, "why are you with me?"

He turned his head on the pillow, and pulled her towards him. "Are you warm enough?" Was that his answer? When Judit was with Hans, there were a thousand moments she could conjure when they were tangled into a single, breathing human being. Now she could feel her body against Bondi's, a few degrees cooler than his own, asserting a distinction.

"Have you ever been married?" Judit asked him.

Bondi said, "I'm married now."

"Of course you are," Judit said. "Where do you really live?"

After a pause, Bondi said, "You don't need to know that."

"Then don't tell me," said Judit. She could imagine the place well enough, an apartment in the Neustadt, though there'd also be a country house outside of Dresden, probably in Dolzchen, in one of the renovated villas. They were certainly childless, maybe saving to move to larger quarters when Bondi was promoted. Meanwhile, the wife worked, probably in a field that involves logic and precision, like bookkeeping. She would expect her husband to keep irregular hours. Something made Judit ask, "Are you on duty?"

Bondi gave her a sharp look. "What do you mean?"

Judit thought: I mean just what I say, but what she actually said was: "Does she think you're on duty now?"

"I don't know what she thinks," Bondi said.

Illogically, Judit did know what Bondi thought most of the time. It felt like a parlor trick, that she didn't even need to see his face to know what passed across it, sometimes impatience, most frequently deduction, and once in a while a conclusion reached that took the form of triumph or of joy.

She'd never felt that clarity with Hans. Their thoughts were too entangled. There was a loneliness to her hours with Bondi when her body was so satisfied and her mind so engaged and her soul so alienated from her circumstances. She didn't think he loved her either. Maybe he had, back when he wrote on that card. He didn't now.

She moved in with her mother. The apartment in the Altstadt had plenty of room, and given the pending demolition of the dormitory, her earlier resistance felt absurd. When she arrived with her suitcase and sewing machine, Leonora waited by the door.

"Judi, did you have any idea?"

"Of what?" Judit asked. Then, she looked past the entrance towards the six long wardrobe-sized boxes in the parlor. "Oh. They thought I ought to have some new things, you know, because I'm going to be a public person."

"Oh, sweetheart, why didn't you tell me? I was still in my nightgown when they came this morning, two wonderful men, and I was so embarrassed, I can't even tell you. They carried all this on their backs, right up the stairs, and all the neighbors opened their doors, and I didn't even know what to tell them. I wasn't even sure I had the right change for a tip."

"They aren't allowed to take tips," Judit said.

"Well they took it," Leonora said. "You really do need to tip people like that, no matter what anyone says. And they seemed to appreciate it."

So then, of course, Judit had to open all the boxes with her mother looking on and saying things like, "Heels aren't practical for a working woman," or "The skirt's too short—some women can carry it off but you don't have the right build, sweetheart," and "Of course, it'll all have to be dry-cleaned."

"I guess so," Judit said. She transferred the clothing to her old closet where her mother had kept everything that Judit had outgrown, from her baby clothes to her Junior Bundist uniform. Judit laid that strange, stale-smelling collection on her old bed without comment. Fortunately, the new clothes were packed on hangers or there wouldn't have been enough of them. Once Judit's closet was full, Leonora anxiously offered the one in the hallway, and then her own.

"So," Leonora began, almost bashfully, "what does that mean, a public person?"

"I think it has something to do with the film," Judit said.

"Will you be on television?"

"I hope not," Judit said.

"Don't be such a snob," said Leonora. "There are some wonderful things on television nowadays, very educational." By then, she'd finally made Judit sit in the kitchen and drink terrible coffee that she'd left on the burner in anticipation of her arrival. Judit did try to be a good sport. The kitchen, she suddenly realized, was small and grim, and through an archway, she could see the dining room without the table, just six chairs against the wall, each with a plastic cover on its pad, and further on, the living room where every window had a double-lace curtain and every cushion on a couch or chair was covered in plastic.

Judit felt moved to ask her mother, "Why do you keep plastic covers on the furniture?"

"What a question!" Leonora said. "Since Daddy died, I've always kept it covered so I don't have to bother cleaning it. You know that."

"Well take the covers off," Judit said. Then, "I mean, if you don't mind."

Speechless, Leonora sat, watching her daughter finish the coffee. Then she said, "Did the television people tell you I should? Will they film here too?"

"Maybe. I don't know," Judit said. When she came back twelve hours later, Leonora had been waiting up for her and had removed each slipcover, revealing crushed velveteen the color of mustard, and blue silk that appeared to glow in the dark. Judit had simply come to change her clothes, and she walked past this display without a word. It was two in the morning. Leonora followed her into the hallway.

"You can't go out now. It's not safe."

"There's a taxi outside," Judit said, and of course, Leonora had to run to the window to confirm this information. There it was, waiting. A light was on inside, and the driver was reading a newspaper. Then, Leonora couldn't say anything at all.

The television people never came to the apartment. They did film Judit at work, as part of a news broadcast. She'd had her hair and nails done and had shimmied into the same skirt that had struck Leonora as too short. As it was February, Lenora had insisted that she change out of the tweed blazer she'd chosen and instead put on a tawny-brown jacket and matching shoes. "Tweed is for autumn. Besides, these are better television colors," she'd said, and then she stopped speaking and watched in fascination as her daughter put on lipstick. "I never thought I'd see the day," Leonora said. "You never did a thing but wash your face." Then, with a different note in her voice: "Judi, is there something you want to tell me?"

"What should I tell you?" Judit asked, innocently enough.

"Are you seeing someone special?"

Judit blotted the lipstick, not very expertly, and slipped on those shoes. Her silence was an affirmation.

"I'm happy for you," Leonora said, though she didn't actually sound happy. In fact, when Judit told her she'd be moving back home, she'd been over the moon, but her exhilaration had drained away, leaving her with a daughter who was a stranger. Leonora watched that daughter's back, as she walked down the hall in high heels, and she called after her, "It's about time you moved on! It's past time, sweetheart!" By then, Judit had already gone.

An hour later, striding between monitors and followed by a camera, Judit spoke in the most general terms about the project, stating that the film would not reveal new information. There was no such thing as new information, Judit said. The facts had always been there. It was a matter of being capable of seeing what was right before their eyes. And what was the response she hoped the film would generate? She stopped, positioning herself in front of the Media Room's wall of glass, in her red-brown costume, against the landscape of Stein Square, and beyond it, the gleaming Bridge Between East and West, the gleaming Elbe. Her hair was shorter, feathered around her chin in a way that softened and obscured her face. She said, "I hope we recognize ourselves. That's all."

"You know," Sammy Gluck said to Judit one day, "you're bound to replace Kornfeld."

"Why would Kornfeld be replaced?" Judit asked.

"Well, you must know he's resigned."

"I didn't know," Judit said. She wanted very much to get back to her work, but Gluck was determined to complete this particular conversation. In a voice that was too loud, and with an air of knowing that it was too loud, he went on.

"He was pretty upset about the book. But you must have known that."

"What book?"

"You signed off on the proofs."

Judit tried to remember what this loud young man was talking about, and then she managed to say, "Well, didn't he want me to sign off on them?"

"You'd better talk to him about that," Gluck said, with some importance. He seemed to be aware that he was playing a game that was far more interesting than transferring film to video.

So Judit took the bait. She pushed herself out of her seat, and for the first time in three months, she walked to the administrative wing and the office she'd entered so many times before only to leave with so many varieties of frustration. She hadn't thought of Kornfeld since December and was surprised at the force of her reluctance to approach him now. His secretary wasn't there. His door was open.

Kornfeld's enormous desk was piled with odds and ends, old photographs, boxes full of reels of audiotape. He was actually on the floor, sorting through files on a low shelf, and he seemed genuinely surprised to see Judit standing there in her sleek trousers and heels. He got up with difficulty and said, "I suppose you're getting ready to move in."

"Why would I?" Judit asked. The response couldn't help but feel dismissive, as though she didn't want the room itself. In fact, she didn't. It wasn't a room where someone worked; it was a showplace. Kornfeld took the statement in that spirit. He walked right past Judit and closed the door.

"Fine," he said. "You get to decide what you want now. You get to decide what we all want. But maybe we're not buying what you're selling. We'll see."

"What are you talking about?" Judit asked. Her tone was mild; the pity she felt was real. Kornfeld, with his boxes of audiotape, with his little bald head and his suit-coat and cufflinks, he had been on his way out for years. But was that her fault?

"I'm talking about this," Kornfeld said. He pulled an enormous handsome volume from where it rested on his shelf and flipped it open. "This garbage. These Nazis. They're the new heroes?"

It was a photograph of a haggard man, dressed like a hunter. He was posed on a black and yellow sandstone cliff, shielding his eyes from the sun with the flat of his hand. Below: white type on black, a caption:

> **We stored weapons in the caves and attacked the Reds by night. The Soviet troop trains heading to Dresden all passed our camp, across the Elbe, in the Bastei cliffs near Rathen. Our proudest moment was the fire of '54. With nothing but an old grenade and a pint of kerosene, we forced a whole battalion to retreat.**

"Fascists," Kornfeld said, "sabotaging the work of liberation. I don't care what name they want to call it. It was liberation. The Soviet Union gave us our lives back. They liberated Auschwitz. They liberated Treblinka. They pushed those bastards out and gave us a country. The people I talk to, they know it's liberation."

"Oscar," Judit began, but he didn't let her say more.

"I don't even know why you bothered coming in here. What do you have to prove to somebody like me? When the book comes out, when the film comes out, though, there'll be hell to pay. People do remember, Judit. And not all of them are dead."

He was right. She shouldn't have bothered to come in here. What did she want? Some kind of blessing from that petty little man? Sure, it would make a lot of people angry: brutal descriptions of Soviet rapes and murders of Jews and Saxons both, interviews with partisans and their fight against the occupation. She also knew that she was telling the truth. Maybe Oscar Kornfeld couldn't see it, but his children would. Then she realized that she didn't know if Kornfeld had children.

"Well," Kornfeld said, "of course you're on board with this." He gave a bitter laugh. "After all, you married one of them."

3

Rough cut: Fortieth Anniversary Project. Working title: "Survival and Resistance" 28/02/88

[A Displaced Persons camp in Schmilka, 1946. The sky flat white, and hard lines of prefabricated barracks cut across the frame. Out of those huts, young men with bowls and cups for morning coffee. A banner by the coffee urn: "WE ARE HERE!" The frame freezes on a man with light hair and a hard jaw. The image dissolves into interview: a man of sixty, same jaw, lank, white hair. Caption identifies: "Samuel Fieffer, Survivor of Treblinka."]

> We were duped. [Fieffer shakes his head and runs a hand across his face.] We were told we bought this country with our martyrs' blood.

[More emblematic footage, young men in black and white montage, scrambling for those pairs of boots and dumping out those famous notes. Those notes are scattered in the dirt, and then a wind rises and blows them in the air through a gate where

Soviet troops stand guard. Two soldiers lean against a jeep. One of them pulls on a cigarette and laughs.]

> How were we supposed to know that we were still in prison, that we'd be in prison for another forty years? Nobody just hands you a country.

[Footage of Stalin, circa 1950, walking across a parade ground, doffing his cap and turning to speak to someone on his right.]

> What did he have in mind? Nothing's in writing. But there were some of us, even then, who'd heard things from the ones who'd seen what Stalin thought of Jews firsthand. Watch out, they said. That yellow star of yours, it's flying over the biggest concentration camp in Europe.

[Camera focuses on the iconic shot of Stripes and Star rippling in black and white. The images melt into washed- out color, and the camera pans back to a Judenstaat choir in their striped prison uniforms and red bandannas. Caption: "May 14th, 'Liberation' Day 1949." Eisler's national anthem blares, distorted by its punishing volume.]

> Let us plant, let us build
> Learn and create like never before
> And trusting in our strength
> A free generation is on the rise.

[A parade that same year, men and women in camp uniforms below banners marked: "Auschwitz," "Treblinka," "Dachau," "Belsen," carrying spades across their shoulders through the rubble of Dresden, followed by dignitaries in open cars. Suddenly, they are obscured by a deep shadow as a Soviet fighter plane passes overhead. Cut to interview: a lean, bald man with a ravaged face. Caption: "Lev Margolis, Applicant, Judenstaat Officer Corps." There is something wrong with his mouth, so that although he speaks German, subtitles are necessary.]

> We were told we would be the new officer corps. My comrades and I traveled to Moscow in 1950. You can imagine.

[Footage of jaunty men in leather jackets, heading towards an airplane. A propeller spins.]

> I was twenty-three. I'd fought in the Warsaw Ghetto uprising. I was so proud of myself and of our country. My whole life led me here. How could we know where we were really going?

[Mountain peaks, gray sand, round pits, and sound of wind. Caption: "Kolyma Mines, 1951." Miners working under heavy guard.]

> Now there were twenty of us, maybe, who made it through that first winter. I never even knew that Stalin died, just that some of the prisoners were pardoned, but not us. Us, they kept. We were buried alive. They took all of the fight out of me."

[Old film stock: five young men facing the camera, spades in their hands. One rolls up his sleeve to show the tattoo of a number, then another and another number is revealed. The camera pans in so close that the numbers dissolve into the flesh.]

> We could tell you things, you people in Judenstaat. We could tell you things your bones already know. Terror is terror.

[Rolling right over those words, a keening, and some cries in German. Stock-footage montage: army trucks with red stars, rolling down roads made more specific by a flash of the remains of Leipzig's Saint Thomas Church rising from the smoke. Fire in a field of barley. An open road with tank-treads through the mud and rain. A caption: "1946." Cut to photographs, a black and white portrait of a frail girl with black braids, sitting on a bench with a kitten. Cut to interview: tight close-up of a middle-aged woman, dark hair, tender-looking eyes. She is not identified.]

> I was on my way to school right here, when they found me—three of them. I told my father I'd fallen into a ditch and he scolded me and told me I needed to be careful. But my mother, she knew. She didn't say a word. After all, they were our liberators. [Pause.] It hurts me to come back here.

[Camera pulls back to reveal a second woman, an older, white-haired Saxon in a housedress. They are both standing in a barren field. She speaks.]

> It hurts me too.

[A caption appears: "German and Jewish survivors of Soviet sexual assault."]

> Our house was here. [The Saxon points to a stone foundation broken by weeds.] They took it over and moved us into the barn, my grandmother, mother, father, older sisters. They took her so often, and also my mother and my grandmother. The shame of it broke my father. Nobody talks about it.

[Grainy film stock, pastoral scene, an empty road, high grass. The two women talk together, the older woman limping slightly. She gestures towards a rock.]

> I left the baby on that stone. And then we burned the barn and took what we could carry into Brandenburg. Can I tell you what it means to come back to this place?

[Montage: silent figures standing in the street as Soviets tape signs to the door of a tavern, the door of a blacksmith's shop, silent figures watching the demolition of a church, passing by with bowed heads, a cloud, unnaturally low, over the ruins of Dresden. A voice in English begins, with simultaneous translation.]

> The Soviets had a plan.

[Interview: elegant old man sitting in a deck chair by what appears to be a bay; yachts float some distance off. Caption: "Lewis Richmond, U.S. Ambassador to Judenstaat, 1949. Professor Emeritus of International Studies, Amherst."]

> Their interest in Judenstaat was clear. In those years after the war, it would make all the sense in the world for this country to be—on paper—nonaligned, to be a so-called neutral zone the Soviet Union could exploit economically and politically. The analogy with Hong Kong and mainland China is quite instructive. But Judenstaat could serve as something even more pragmatic. Its actions would be legitimized by suffering, acting in its own name, but always in the interests of the Warsaw Pact. Of course, all of that fell apart by '53.

[More footage of expropriation, though now it is Jewish shops with signs in Yiddish. Soviet soldiers wrap a chain around the double-doors of a Dresden department store. Cut to a long prison train with Cyrillic lettering on its side, passing the Chemnitz station.]

> It wasn't just a matter of an anti-Semitic lunatic like Stalin. The problem goes far deeper. The fascists pursued policies that ultimately led to their destruction. The communists did the same. That your country has survived forty years and has—essentially—transcended its own history, that it has managed to overcome the terror and reached real stability and maturity, that is a true miracle. But of course, it was a country founded on resistance.

[Footage of schoolchildren wearing white blouses and red bandannas, circa 1960. They sing *The Song of the Ghetto Partisans*, in Yiddish. Subtitles are provided.]

> *Not with lead this song was written, but with blood.*
> *It wasn't warbled in the forest like a bird,*
> *but a people trapped between collapsing walls*
> *With weapons held in hand—they made this song!*

[Though the children still sing on-screen, the audio swells and shifts to German, a loud male voice, not tuneful.]

> Never say that we have reached the final road
> Though the lead-gray clouds conceal blue skies above
> That hour that we've longed for now draws near.
> Our steps proclaim like drumbeats: WE ARE HERE!

Our greatest stronghold was in those standstone cliffs, those bunkers outside Rathen that they flushed us out of back in '55. For years, we managed to sabotage the rail-lines between Prague and Dresden at least a few times a month.

[The speaker is revealed, a wizened man with cropped, rust-colored hair and bronze skin. Caption: "Arno Durmersheimer, Anti-Soviet Partisan."]

They killed my brother one night. He was standing right next to me. Red sniper got him. And Fieffer buried him.

[Black and white photograph of Fieffer, half-torn, but easy to identify. Durmersheimer holds it.]

He fought beside me. There were hundreds of us, Jews, Saxons, all together. Those Jews had seen firsthand what those butchers had done to their own brothers. [Voice breaks.] There was real friendship in those days. For me, they remain the most precious of my life.

[Camera pulls back, and a man obscured by shadow stumbles across short grass. Durmersheimer turns, and we hear his throat catch as he takes a step forward and cries out:]

My brother!

[It is Fieffer. The two men fall into each other's arms and weep.]

DURMERSHEIMER: That I would live to see this day.
FIEFFER: We have survived them! We have survived them!

[Voice rolls over this exchange, a voice with rich, warm intonation, though rough around the bass, implying age. It is a familiar voice.]

> You begin with nothing.

[Footage of the Displaced Persons camp in Schmilka, those young men reaching for pairs of boots lined up on benches.]

> From there germinates a need, to have a home. On any terms.

[Abrupt cut to a hospital room where an old man sits on the edge of a bed. He wears a gown unbuttoned just enough to show springing white tufts of hair, and his withered face looks like a balloon with half of the air pressed out. His eyes are vibrant, though, and he is the source of the voice that comes out of the concave throat, a voice that unmistakably identifies the man himself.]

> After forty years, you ask me, would I do it all again? That is like asking a man if he regrets having a son. The son has a life of his own, and maybe—who knows—redeems the father.

[Now a characteristic gesture, tracing a circle with his hands and then the bridge below his chin. His eyes roll up as though to follow a thought across the room.]

> Forgive the religious language. Sometimes you need to reach for that. As you well know.

4

HOW can that be?" Judit asked Bondi. "How can Stein still be alive?"

"He's surrounded by the most sophisticated medical team on earth," Bondi said. "Why wouldn't he be alive?"

"It doesn't seem physically possible," Judit said. She had just received the latest reel by courier, and had at once called Bondi. "I can't do this. I can't fabricate."

"Of course you can't. Neither can we," Bondi said. "Too much is at stake."

They were in their room above the dairy restaurant, both sitting on the daybed. It was midafternoon. Judit had been prepared to resign, but the physical proximity of Bondi and his clear sincerity made her feel seasick. "It could be an actor," she said, although she knew very well it was no actor. Then, "It could be an illusion. It could be an old image someone manipulated. I've seen Gluck do that a thousand times." Then, "It could be a ghost."

"You haven't eaten," Bondi said. "You haven't slept. You need to go back home and let your mother cook you something. Clear your head."

"I will not clear my head," Judit said. "This isn't what I signed on for."

"It's not a fabrication," Bondi said. The awful part was that Judit believed him. As though to seal the matter, he took her hand. "What do you want?"

"I want to meet him."

"How much do you want to meet him?" He put her hand somewhere else.

The game they were playing cut against the grain of her integrity, and also his. She wanted to cry or wanted to laugh. They passed an hour letting things take their course, and afterwards, she felt so spent and lost that she pulled herself up and said, "That didn't clear my head, Joseph. I don't think anything will clear my head."

He acknowledged what she said by lying on his back and closing his eyes. His profile was very beautiful, his face so peaceful that Judit envied him. He said, "You could do it, you know."

"Do what?"

"Meet Stein," Bondi said. "Why not? It could be arranged. But not before the film opens. Time is too short."

The documentary would premiere in three weeks at a special screening in Parliament. The press would be there, and of course Judit was invited. She'd already received the invitation, an envelope inside an envelope that her mother propped against a salt shaker on the kitchen table. The stock of the paper was so thick that it could almost stand by itself. Judit said to Bondi, "I'm not the only one who'll want to see him. Wouldn't anyone? Wouldn't you?"

Bondi shook his head. "An old man, a man who's been dying for thirty-five years, who doesn't know when to die, that doesn't interest me."

"It interests me," said Judit.

He rolled over and surprised her by kissing her. The kiss was a tender one. "You interest me," he said. He rolled back and closed his eyes. "We could take a trip after this is over. Surely, you've earned a vacation. I have time owed me. There's a spa. Mineral baths, that sort of thing. Bad Muskau. Right on the Polish border."

"Something to look forward to," said Judit.

"Don't sound so enthusiastic," Bondi said, and then he laughed. "No, really, I can make arrangements through my office. It'll be off-season, so it won't be too crowded. I'll lease a car. It's a very pretty drive." He added, "Why don't you invite your mother?"

"You're joking," Judit said. "I don't think I ever heard you tell a joke before."

"Maybe you have," said Bondi. "Maybe you just didn't get the joke."

"Maybe I didn't," Judit said. She gathered her things and dressed. "I do believe you, Joseph. What choice do I have? But if he's there—" She hesitated, and then added, "When I meet him, I want to ask him certain things directly. About the years after the war. And what happened when he went to Stalin's funeral. He's an important witness."

"That's up to you," Bondi said. "I hear he's more than ready to field questions. He's a lonely old man."

5

THESE days, Judit was never sure what time it was. There was something animal about her habits now, eating when she was hungry, sleeping when she felt the need, traveling to that room in Johannstadt when her body told her it was necessary. Most often, she arrived there first, but she never had to wait for long. She'd look out the window at the milling black-hat schoolgirls who would cross to buy an ice cream at the dairy restaurant. She'd doze on the bed, and sometimes flip through the shelf of Yiddish books—mostly devotional material, but also a few surprises like a volume of poetry by Peretz Markish, a tattered German-Yiddish dictionary, and a notebook where someone had practiced writing Hebrew characters in neat columns like a schoolboy. The man who ran the restaurant must have had a system for contacting Bondi because he'd be there soon enough and lay his own heavy coat next to her new cashmere one. Then he would undress her.

No one in the office commented on Judit's midday disappearances, not even Sammy Gluck, but when she returned by taxi one afternoon, Mr. Rosenblatt rushed towards her. He laid a hand on her arm.

"You're needed out back right away." He was out of breath. "There's a car—a driver's been waiting for two hours, a big Volvo."

"I'm not expecting anyone," Judit said. "I have work to do." Then she took another look at the poor man's face and said, "Well, what does he want?"

"They want to take you to lunch," said Mr. Rosenblatt. It was three o'clock.

"I've had lunch."

"Mrs. Klemmer. Judi. Just humor me," Mr. Rosenblatt said. "Go around the back. Then you'll understand." He pretty much dragged her to the side of the building, and there was the car he'd described, a black Volvo with tinted windows and a government license plate, sitting in the space intended for delivery trucks. Its motor was running, and its hazard lights were on. Mr. Rosenblatt whispered to her, "Two hours, it's been like that. Can you imagine the waste of fuel?" Judit broke away and approached, and as she did, the back window rolled silently down. She recognized a shape more than a face, but knew it was Professor Lehmann.

The identity was confirmed when Lehmann's voice emerged. "Well? Where were you, child? At playtime?"

From the depths, a bass voice, faintly recognizable. "She's a player? Good!"

The driver stepped out, and with blank-faced efficiency, opened the door for Judit. She looked back over her shoulder at Mr. Rosenblatt, who watched with awe and relief, and then she steeled herself and got inside. The interior was so smoky and chaotic that her first instinct was to get right out again.

Then she was drawn towards something all the more smoky, perfumed and damp. Anna Lehmann was giving her a grandmotherly kiss on the cheek. Judit pulled back and caught her breath.

The cabin of the car was enormous. Two long, plush seats faced each other, and a table in the center was covered with ashtrays, bowls of candy and their wrappers, and a lot of opened envelopes and scattered papers. Lehmann took up most of one seat, and once Judit recovered from that kiss, she addressed her.

"You clean up very well, dear," Lehmann said. "Good thing, too. You know, appearances do matter, in surprising ways." Lehmann drew her own hand to her breast, which was encased in a thick boiled-wool cloak secured by a pearl brooch. "I let Helena dress me these days." In case Judit hadn't followed, she said, "The prime minister, of course."

By now, the car was moving, but Judit felt compelled to say, "Professor, I have to get upstairs. The final cut is due next week, and I can't afford the time right now—"

"That didn't stop you earlier, young lady," Lehmann said. She pushed the clutter out of the way and reached for Judit's hand. "So," she said. "Relax. Work can always wait. When you're my age, you realize there's time enough in life for both business and pleasure."

"Where are we going?" Judit asked.

"Fish restaurant," the other passenger said, and then she realized he was next to her on the other end of the enormous seat, a very old man whose battered face was topped by an elaborate gray pompadour that looked shellacked. He was nattily dressed, and he balanced a cane between his knees. "Best restaurant in the country. Missed lunch hour, but that's no problem. They'll do something up specially. Don't worry about the wait, kid. Always plenty to talk about with Anna, as you know."

"You two haven't been introduced," Lehmann said. Judit realized who the man was and felt yet another impulse to jump out of the car. "Anton Steinsaltz, Judit Klemmer, née Ginsberg, editor of the anniversary documentary, and, I'm proud to say, my former student."

Steinsaltz grinned. His teeth were strong and yellow. His eyes looked young and crafty in his ancient face. "I'll bet you were the teacher's pet."

"Oh, stop it!" Lehmann said, and she reached across the table to give him a playful slap. Through the open window, Judit would see the familiar landmarks—the bridge, the Yenidze, the very outskirts of Dresden. She genuinely did have work to do, piles of it, and her body was still smarting and reverberating in all kinds of ways from her time with Bondi, which made her feel even more displaced and vulnerable. Worse, Steinsaltz seemed to smell the sex on her like catnip, and he leaned deliberately over her to roll the window up.

"More privacy," he said. "And of course, the glass is bulletproof."

"Oh, who'd shoot you, you old pussycat!" Professor Lehmann said.

Watching Anna Lehmann flirt with Anton Steinsaltz caused Judit pain, but she suppressed it. Judit asked her, "When did you get back from Moscow?"

"Gracious, child, weeks ago. Of course, I would have paid you a visit sooner, but Helena had other plans for me, you understand. I had to take a look at the proofs of that book. She's quite pedantic, really, wanted every source checked again and again so we could present full documentation. It was all terribly tedious. But it's a beautiful book, isn't it?"

"A historic document," Steinsaltz said, with some formality.

"The important thing," Lehmann said, "is that it's beautiful. And the film will be beautiful as well, both startling and beautiful. As I said, appearances do matter, Anton. That's why we have Ginsberg on the project." As though to forestall misinterpretation, she added, "I mean because you have a fantastic visual sense, dear. And yes, I know, it's Klemmer now, isn't it." She settled back into her seat, and the gray of her cloak melted into the upholstery. "Tragedy. Well that's beautiful too, tragedy, if you'll forgive my saying so. I think you will."

The fish restaurant turned out to be thirty kilometers north of the city, on the Elbe, a hideous flying saucer of a place that Judit suspected was chosen because no one would think to find them there, though when the Volvo pulled in, the door was immediately opened by a valet, who gave Judit a gloved hand and helped her out. Then the valet stood by as two men struggled with Lehmann before at last readying Steinsaltz for his wheelchair.

"Sorry for the floorshow," Steinsaltz said for Judit's benefit. "I think I've grown old, my dear."

Now that Judit knew the man was Steinsaltz, she was stunned that she hadn't recognized him instantly. He looked more or less the same since she had first seen him address the country on television when he'd been appointed prime minister in 1960, when she wondered why their leader was such an ugly man.

Once they'd finally gotten settled at a table, Steinsaltz had to urinate, and those same handlers reappeared and spirited him away. Judit's relief was evident. Lehmann smiled and said, "Dear, you'll have to get used to a few of those dinosaurs. They're almost extinct, mind you, but then, when you look at a swallow, it can claim a dinosaur as its ancestor."

Judit said, "It's hard to believe, even if it's true."

As soon as she said it, she felt foolish, until Lehmann passed her the basket of rolls and added, "You can see them all along the walkway now that they nest under the bridge again. Messy, but it makes for a better atmosphere on the whole. Take a roll. Take more than one. I want to ask you, how do you like what I've sent you from Moscow?"

Judit said, "It's hard to believe, even if it's true." Now, she didn't feel foolish. She felt giddy. Sitting across the deliberately rustic wooden table was Grandmother Professor without a doubt, lighting yet another cigarette and smiling through her smoke at her pet student. Even in this strange environment, Lehmann managed to create real intimacy. Judit knew she was being clever when she added, "My role seems to be making facts believable, at least as I understand it."

Lehmann buttered her own roll, and she drank a little of the white wine that the waiter offered. Then she leaned in closer. She still wore that strange over-dark lipstick, and maybe Prime Minister Sokolov dressed her now, but as she lapsed into her role as Grandmother Professor, even the new clothes turned into wallpaper from which her pale, broad face projected the old, wise cynicism. "Dear," she said, "I have to say something before Anton returns. I'm quite impressed with your work. I've followed it since you left Leipzig, as I'm sure you are aware. But I did take the liberty of looking at some of what you sent up to Oscar. And I noticed a certain fixation." She paused and dropped her voice. "I think you know what I mean."

"You mean Leopold Stein?" Judit said. "You knew he was alive all this time, didn't you?"

"That's hardly who I mean," Lehmann said. Then, with effort, she moved her chair closer until it actually touched Judit's, and said, "Now Stephen Weiss is not irrelevant. Far from it. No more than Birobidjan or Palestine or Uganda. In fact, he's fascinating. But you mustn't let yourself be pulled in. He holds a lesson for us, and as is the case with all failed experiments, the lesson is corrective."

Judit felt her skin against her blouse and jacket. She said, "None of that's in the film, Professor."

"Yet he still haunts you, doesn't he? Of course. Why not? He's in the air. It's a common error," Lehmann said, "to confuse cosmopolitanism with globalization. And this is a global age, my dear, as we both know. Weiss was no pragmatist."

Now, in a low voice, willing herself not to look over her shoulder, Judit asked, "What was Weiss then?"

"See? You want to know, don't you? It's really rather simple. Weiss was a mystic. All Cosmopolitans are mystics. They don't believe in global capital. They believe in something else."

"What do they believe in?" Judit asked under her breath, and Lehmann quickly replied:

"You should know. You married one, didn't you?" Then she added, "That new young man of yours might answer as well, I think. Goodness, what a fixation!" She actually laughed then, a strange sound Judit seldom heard, almost like indigestion. "I suppose you've read the manifesto. No? Perhaps it's time for me to send you a copy."

By then, Steinsaltz had reappeared, and the handlers moved him from his wheelchair to the table. He rubbed his hands together, and called the waiter to refill all three wineglasses. "Well, well," he said, and then he managed to transform his old man voice, briefly, into the familiar politician's trumpet that he'd blasted for nearly forty years. "We ought to toast the film's premiere, I know. But it's bigger than the film itself. I must say," Steinsaltz added, as he raised his glass in his right hand, "that it is moving beyond words to see, in the twilight of my life, a planting come to harvest."

"Anton," Lehmann said, "you're spilling wine all over yourself."

"So my hand's not steady," Steinsaltz said, and he rested his left hand against it. His face was flushed; a rash climbed up his neck, and for a moment, he said nothing. Then, he threw his glass of wine against the wall, and it shattered and sprayed glass and liquid all over the table.

Judit felt glass fly into the right side of her face, and when she brushed it off with a napkin, it left streaks of blood. The handlers rushed away to get whiskbrooms, and one of them gave a towel to Judit to mop up the wine on her lap and bread plate.

Lehmann shook her head and laughed. "Poor girl. She's gotten the worst of it. You shouldn't try to be so dramatic, Anton. It's not in your nature. Besides," she said, "it's not your work. It never was. I think you meant to drink to Leopold Stein, didn't you?"

Steinsaltz's face was completely red now. He was speechless with embarrassment, and it was only with effort that he managed to work his mouth around what he said next. "Of course. Who else?" But no one drank now. They were moved to a different table, easy enough as they were the restaurant's only party. Judit took her towel with her, and she could still feel glass splinters in her cheek. The cuts were shallow, though. If she washed carefully, by the time she got back to work, no one would notice.

6

JUDIT was the only member of the staff to get an invitation to the premiere screening, but she could select six guests. She realized, with some embarrassment, that aside from Gluck, she didn't know any of the assistants, and she asked Gluck to make the selections himself. He surprised her by refusing.

"I can't be your social director, Mrs. Klemmer," he said. "I have three other projects running now, freelance jobs. After all, that's paid work." That's when Judit realized that Sammy was still an intern.

"I'll pay you," Judit said, a little desperately. Gluck looked startled.

"How? Are you in charge of payroll now?" He shook his head. "No, if you're asking me if I'll go as your guest, of course I will. After all, I was the one who got this started. And if you wouldn't mind, I'd like to bring Patricia."

"Who's Patricia?" Judit couldn't help but ask.

"I did introduce her to you a few times. But I guess she's not too memorable. She's just my wife." Then, he must have felt embarrassed by his own rudeness because he lowered his voice. "Look, I guess a lot of us feel crummy about Oscar. But that's not your fault. It's just all the pressure riding on this makes me a little nuts, and sometimes a guy starts to feel like he has to take sides."

He was solemn, and Judit couldn't help but notice that he'd aged, these past few months. The bones of his face were more clearly defined. He looked almost handsome. She said, "I didn't know you got married, Sammy."

"We sent you an invitation, but maybe it went to your old address," Sammy said. "Besides, you've been pretty busy."

"You don't have to take sides," Judit said. "There are things that are true, and there are things that are false. How complicated can it be?"

Sammy looked at her. What he saw might have played with his own set of categories. He wanted to write her off as ambitious; she was not ambitious. He wanted to blame her for taking credit for his work; she desired no credit. Most of all, he wanted to tell her that everyone knew she was cooperating with the Stasi, and it would come back to haunt her. Judit watched all of this pass over Sammy's face. Then he said, "Say, didn't you want to get back into your old archive?"

It was Judit's turn to stare. "What are you talking about?"

"They opened it yesterday. It's a mess, I hear. Lots of stuff on the floor. They say they cleared everything out and sent it upstairs, but it sure doesn't sound that way."

"You mean it's open?"

"Didn't I just say that?" Sammy looked amused. "I didn't go in myself. Still has that yellow hazard tape everywhere. But you should check it out, Mrs. Klemmer. Maybe you'll find something really explosive down there. Who knows?"

For the rest of the afternoon, Judit wandered through the National Museum. She could have entered the archive more directly and bypassed the exhibitions, but something made her take the long way round. When she'd first started working there, she'd always visited those rooms she'd known from childhood. She hadn't done it for a while. A corridor led from the Media Room to the third floor of the museum exhibition wing: the Golden Age of Ashkenaz.

Worms, Mainz, Cologne, the three great centers in their medieval splendor, each had its room; fragments of prayer-houses, of ceremonial goblets, artifacts from more recent excavations, ornaments and tile work set in velvet, like precious stones. A diorama of a dance hall where a wedding took place, replicas of period instruments like lutes and tambourines, maps charting the routes of Jewish spice merchants both east and west, bags full of saffron, pepper, precious salves. Isaac of Navarone, Charlemagne's emissary, Isaac of Gans, Daniel Itzig, court Jews and bankers. Jacob of Franconia. These rooms had long been marked for renovation, and some of the panels were too faded to read. A sleepy female guard in a blue uniform stirred, looking up to wonder who this woman was who stepped quietly through the corridor in her high heels.

A room devoted to Moses Mendelssohn, who entered Brandenburg through the gate reserved for Jews and cattle, personal artifacts like the pocket watch he gave to his son-in-law, his china plates, portraits of his children, his translation of the Torah into German. A portrait of the man himself, whose homely, pale, clean-shaven face was dominated by benevolent brown eyes. Then onward through portraits of early heroes of the Bund, bearded socialists and trade unionists, the writer Peretz lit from below in a way that made his bushy mustache glitter, old publications under glass. No guard sat in that room. No one dusted. At one point, it went dark, and Judit had to fumble for a switch, only to discover that the light was movement-activated. She caught a glimpse of herself in the glass display. She was stunned as a rabbit, blinking at whatever was inside.

If she took the stairs down one flight, she'd reach the glass corridor that led to the Hall of the Churban. She couldn't count the times she'd been there as a girl, far more than the other exhibitions.

At first, she'd explored the artifacts and testimonies left by survivors, and when she'd followed the trail of her own martyred Elsa Neuman, she'd added her own impressions. Those rooms had been so dense with papers, photographs, shelves holding a spoon someone had used in hiding before capture, improvised cloth shoes that took a woman through a death-march she did not survive, a hair of a beloved son in a transparent package, it seemed impossible that more could be added or that anyone could pass through that dark place and climb out on the terrace. The very claustrophobia was the horror of it, and its real intention. Did anyone still take children there? Even when Judit was a child, it hadn't seemed a place where children ought to go.

Of course, there were exhibits like that everywhere in Judenstaat, and Judit knew from her own studies that they were deliberately homemade. In Dresden's own Churban Hall, Leonora's story was posted on the south-most wall; she'd written it in her ungrammatical and fearless German in 1951, five years after Liberation and the year Judit was born. Judit's father had laminated it to ensure a kind of permanence. As time went on, though, it would all decay, and yet this decay was more like a fermentation, turning what was there into something more volatile: the handwriting of the dead, the spoons of the dead, the crammed shelves full of suitcases of dead people, or survivors soon to die of other causes. Where did the dead travel? To their death.

It had been years since Judit had walked through that glass corridor to the first-floor, Churban wing of the museum. She'd concentrated on her own exhibits on Judenstaat's early history, on the far side of the terrace. Below it was her film archive. Such was the evolving nature of the Churban Hall that hundreds of items might have fallen off the shelves or been replaced with other artifacts or testimonies. She could only imagine what she'd find. She brushed her hair out of her eyes before she remembered that it was cut short now. She walked downstairs, through the glass entryway, and stopped.

The rooms were empty. Judit was so certain she was dreaming that she actually turned the light off and on again. There was nothing on the walls. She could still see places where things might have been, chipped paint, nail-holes. The floor had been swept recently. She walked through room after empty room, hardly knowing what she was doing, and she opened the door at the far end. Yellow hazard tape blocked the passage to the second-floor terrace, and the entrance to the permanent exhibition on the founding of Judenstaat.

Instantly, she was back upstairs in the Golden Age exhibit and she shook the guard who'd gone back to sleep. "What happened to the Churban Hall?"

The guard looked cross. "Closed for renovations."

"But I need to get through there."

The guard rolled her eyes. "Ma'am, the Churban Hall and the other permanent exhibit on the first floor are both closed until September. You'll have to go back the way you came, and take the elevator in the Administrative Wing. How did you even get in here?"

"I work here," Judit said.

"Well, if you work here, then you should know."

Judit knew many things at once, and felt many things at once, and just as the guard now doubted her authority, she doubted her own. She was in somebody else's clothing, with somebody else's haircut. The guard just shook her head, and picked up her newspaper, which had the following headline: "Sokolov Announces New Policy of Open Border."

"You're home early," Leonora said. She was washing the dish on which she'd eaten dinner. "I'll heat something up."

"Don't bother," Judit said. She threw her blazer on a chair, and opened the packed refrigerator. Without much thought, she dislodged an apple.

"Let me wash that," Leonora said, and Judit obediently handed her mother the apple, sat on a kitchen chair, and stared at nothing. "How about a nice piece of chicken?"

"Alright," said Judit. Her mother gave her a long look.

"Sweetheart," she said, "how are things at work?"

"Well, to be honest," Judit said, "I'm pretty much used up. I might sleep in tomorrow."

"Shouldn't you call and let someone know?"

"I don't even know who I'd call," Judit said.

Leonora handed Judit a plate with a cold chicken leg and some potato salad on it, and Judit took a bite out of the chicken leg and then a bite of the apple, holding one in each hand, her skirt hiked up well above her knees, her shoes half-kicked off, hanging from her toes. "Listen, I've been thinking," said Leonora. "I shouldn't go to the premiere. It's bound to be a late night, and if I need to leave before it's over, you'll have to figure out what to do with me."

Judit sat up. "Don't you want to go, Mom?"

"Well, to be honest, I just don't think I'm up to it." Leonora turned to the sink again, and squeezed out the sponge. "If it means enough to you, of course—"

"Don't you want to meet the prime minister?"

"I need to get up early for work," Leonora said. "It's a weeknight, after all, and there are people counting on me."

Judit didn't answer. She kept eating the apple and the chicken leg, turning each in her hands, biting into each in turn, and she didn't even notice when her mother placed a fork and knife and napkin on the table. Judit had made a purchase at the drugstore. It was in her purse. It wasn't so far to the bathroom, yet the distance through the hallway seemed impossible. That kitchen chair, with its hollow metal legs and plastic back, was like the cockpit of an airplane. If she got up, the world would tip and veer into free fall.

Leonora said, "Can I ask you something?"

"Sure," Judit said.

"Have things slowed down at work?"

"Actually, they have," said Judit. "I was thinking that maybe I'd take a vacation."

"Oh, that's nice," said Leonora. "That's wonderful news. And when will you go?"

"After the film premieres," she said. "I think, in June."

"Well, I'm asking you a long time in advance because I know how busy you are," Leonora said, "but I'm hoping this October you'll go to the cemetery with me to see Daddy."

"Sure," Judit said. She was eating the potato salad. Then, she added, "Just remind me when it's closer. I'll make sure I'm free."

"I appreciate that," said Leonora. She cleared the dish with the apple core and the chicken bone, and Judit at last forced herself to her feet. She knew already; what was the point? By now, she couldn't help but know that she was pregnant.

The Dybbuk

1

WHEN did you find out?" Bondi asked her. He must have been in the middle of some other project when she'd phoned. He sounded distant.

"I'm sorry I told you at all," Judit said, "but I figured you'd know when I went to the clinic to get rid of it." In fact, she'd taken the day off for just that purpose, though she would have been just as happy to stay in bed. Leonora had left for work before Judit had managed to make it to the kitchen, and she'd poured herself an orange drink that tasted like poison, dumped most of it in the sink, and threw on some of her old clothes because the apartment didn't have a private line and she couldn't walk to the phone booth in her bathrobe. She didn't have the clinic number, and her hand had dialed Bondi all by itself.

When she'd broken the news over the phone, he'd told her to wait, and she said, "Wait for what?"

"Wait until we talk."

"What's there to talk about?"

The silence on the other end of the phone thickened. By all rights, Judit should have hung up. Instead, she sowed that rich silence with memories, and tried to push herself to say what she was thinking, that the living sensation that she felt above her private parts was telling her a lie, that she would be seduced by that lie if she waited too long, and that when she made the appointment, she would tell him not to meet her there and hope that he would be there. That last piece, he might understand. Then Bondi said, "Turn around."

He was standing outside the phone booth in the sunshine. He had his old hat on, and a tan scarf, and he was holding a portable phone. They looked at each other through the glass. Below the brim of that hat, his eyes looked clear and bright. He opened the door of the booth and Judit fell right into him and let him hold her. He was strong enough to bear her weight, but she could tell that he was shaken.

When she let go, he said, "Don't do it."

"I'm going to lose it anyway," Judit said. "Why fool ourselves? Besides, what about your wife?"

"I'll leave her," Bondi said. There was something childish about the way he said it, and Judit was aware, maybe for the first time, that she was much older than Bondi.

She said, "I don't think I could take losing another one. I can't risk it. Don't ask me to."

"You won't lose this one," Bondi said. "Look at me, Judit. Not at the ground. At me," for she had been staring at the ground, trying to control herself. Now, they faced each other, and she forgot his age, his story, even forgot his name under the force of his conviction. "This one is different. We won't lose it. I promise you."

"How can you know?" Judit asked helplessly. "My body—"

"Your body is perfect," Bondi said.

He backed her into that same phone booth and arranged her against the glass. He took off his hat and put it on top of the telephone. Then, he hesitated.

"How does this work?" When she didn't answer right away, he clarified. "I don't want to hurt the baby."

"My God, Joseph," Judit said, "I love you." She started breathing hard, and tears ran down her cheeks. She was blushing. Bondi looked startled and awkward, very unlike himself, and she laughed and said, "I do love you." Then, she realized she had frightened him, so she pulled herself together and pressed against him. "Everything works. Everything is fine."

She did believe that everything was fine. And then she didn't. She cramped and bent at the waist, got up in the middle of the night and checked her underwear. She dropped an expensive camera on the floor. She went to the bathroom five times in a single afternoon. Fortunately, the film was edited and ready because many times, her hands stopped working now. She would turn them around and around at the wrists and then she'd think about the clinic and know Bondi would find out before she could so much as schedule a procedure. There was the abortionist in Loschwitz, but that was a rumor. That was a rumor and death was real. How could Bondi understand what it meant, to face this down?

Bondi hadn't been there when Judit sewed the same pattern over and over again afterwards. He hadn't seen the battles and the compromises and the hard-won resignation. Or had he? Hadn't he stood by her bed the weeks after the murder and watched the pieces of Judit's heart stitch themselves back together imperfectly? Those seams still showed. Maybe Bondi even loved those seams. Who knows? For years, he'd been the only constant in her life. And maybe now, there was another.

When Judit took off whole afternoons, she had expected someone to complain. No one did. Rather, they seemed to accept her absence, even welcome it, as the heavy machinery of the anniversary project went forward. All of her instincts told her to get out of the way. Sometimes, she was with Bondi, but most of the time, she walked and walked, just as she had before the age of taxi cabs and Media Rooms. She walked from Stein Square along the promenade and saw that, indeed, swallows once again dipped below the Bridge Between East and West, but she didn't stay to watch them. She didn't believe in those swallows. They were a product of someone's calculation, deliberately lured to reconstructed nests that an environmental artist designed on a computer. Or maybe it was just spring now, and the swallows knew it.

She crossed the bridge to the Neustadt, where construction on the bypass was complete, and a line of rational traffic signals eased her way across the road to her old dormitory. There were blue and white fliers plastered on the wall. "Future Site of Long-Term Corporate Solutions." A lot of dust had accumulated on the glass door, and when she cleared a little circle with her hand, she could make out the porter's desk, just barely, with its old-fashioned ink-blotter and the telephone that tenants couldn't use. If she had stayed, the porter would still sit behind the desk, the dormitory would be open; nothing would have changed. Her body wouldn't be a trap, following its own logic. It would not be owned by something else. She would be sad, but free.

If history was a machine and rolled its way interminably forward, people didn't matter. If they cross it, then they're crushed. They'd better ride on that machine or get out of the way. And even if they ride it, then they'd better watch their backs; they might think they were on the side of history, and end up with a bullet in the head.

"Hans," Judit said out loud. "Stop it. I have to trust him."

Yet it wasn't Hans. Hans lived in the archive. He'd given her instructions, and she'd failed him. She couldn't help it if he felt betrayed.

2

NOT long before Hans died, Judit had begun to look into adoption. Initially, she'd refused to believe rumors that there'd been a loosening of restrictions on applications to orphanages in Poland. In fact, she refused to believe she was interested at all. Then she surprised herself by walking into a social worker's office, and walking out again with a thick envelope full of fliers from international adoption programs, government foster-care agencies, and local children's homes. As she spread them on the table, she knew she was out of her depth. How could she evaluate these agencies? A brochure's production values? The copyediting? She tried not to look at pictures, but of course, she looked at pictures, and maybe that's when she realized that the hard, complicated thing she was feeling was hope.

Hans was home less frequently. Since he'd been appointed conductor, at least half of his schedule had nothing to do with music, and once the season began, he worked seven days a week. Left to herself, Judit pored over those brochures: photographs of dark-skinned children from Romania, from Poland, from Albania, probably gypsies. There was a Dresden orphanage that, from its wording, appeared to involve a home for wayward girls and to be affiliated with Chabad. She threw it in the trash. But time and time again, she would return to a brochure that described a hospital in Zeitz where young Saxon women would be offered special care throughout their pregnancies and know their children would be placed into a "loving home." The program was unique in that the girl herself would hand the infant over from the hospital bed.

One night, one of the few nights Hans was home for dinner, Judit tried to figure out a way to broach the subject. Hans was exhausted. The moment he'd come through the door, he'd slipped off his coat, thrown all his clothing on the bedroom floor, and emerged in pajama bottoms. She'd made a curry. He ate half of what was on his plate without looking up. It had been a struggle, the past few months, and for all the honor of his new position, Judit couldn't help but wish it could be undone. Some nights, he never seemed to sleep at all. She'd find him propped on the couch, surrounded by his music, scratching notes on a little pad. Maybe he wanted to be the one who fielded those late-night phone calls. The ones with no one on the other end.

Yet Hans had wanted to conduct the Dresden orchestra. It was the culmination of his life. He was doing the work he'd been born to do; that was clear even through the mask of his exhaustion. It was hard to ask more of him, but after a few glasses of wine, she did.

Hans said nothing for a moment. Then, "Lamb, I don't think you really know much about this."

Judit couldn't help but feel defensive. "I just started looking into it. I mean, there are so many ways to go."

"Like buying a car," Hans said.

Judit stared at Hans. He filled his wineglass again. Although the response seemed casual, surely he'd known the nature of what he'd just dismissed, and if he didn't know it, he could read Judit's face. He started to fill her glass too, but she put her hand over it and finally said, "You, of all people."

"You mean because I'm an orphan? Well, of course, no one ever bought me."

"That's not fair," said Judit. "That's not what this is about."

"Then what's it about?" Hans sat back and hooked his arms behind his head, the way he did when he was stating a conclusion. "I know the rhetoric. I grew up with it. Honestly, if you want to go that way, I'll go that way, but don't expect me to be enthusiastic."

That was the end of the conversation. Afterwards, Judit passed one of the hardest weeks of her life. For seven days, Hans rose from bed, looked over his sheet music, glanced up at her when she poured him coffee, and raised his hand, still working, when she said goodbye and left for the museum. He probably did speak to her; when she asked a question, certainly, he'd answer. During the night, he'd throw an arm or leg across her in the old way, and she'd lie still, as though a bird had landed and any movement would make it take flight. Then he'd wake up, and he would not be Hans. He would be someone who looked like Hans but didn't love her.

It might have been the seventh morning that Judit caught Hans by the arm as he was getting up to pour some coffee. She said, "I'm sorry."

"About what?" Hans asked. He knew, though, and maybe it had been hard for him too, because he sat back down and said, "If you really want it, I'll go along."

"Like you've been?" Judit asked.

"That's the best I can do."

"Then forget it," Judit said. She expelled those words like pellets. She couldn't take them back, and yes, she wanted to take them back because it was like a door closing. It was like shutting a door and locking it with her own hand. On the other side of that door was a life she had imagined for them, with its shape, substance, and meaning. She knew she ought to stop, but she went on. "It's so irrational. It feels wasteful, this home, and us, and no child. And if it's the only way—"

"We could try again," Hans said.

Judit said, "I'd lose it again. We both know it. That would break me. This is a way that wouldn't break me."

"Listen," Hans said, "a child we'd have together would be ours. A child we adopt would be someone else's. Even if he never knew his parents." What he said next was clearly difficult. "They know about my parents."

"What are you talking about?" Judit said.

"They showed me pictures. Of what happened to them. I'd heard about it, but I never knew the whole story. People expect things from me."

"What people? What do they expect?" Judit asked, and Hans just shook his head. It was hard for her to fathom such an act of needless cruelty, and it took her out of herself. She didn't press those questions, and he didn't answer. Instead, he took her hand.

Then he said, "Aren't I enough for you?"

3

BY April, the final cut of the documentary had long since left the office, and the staff who were not engaged in writing press releases played with computers and wandered the hallways, gossiping and marking time. Sokolov would give a speech after the television broadcast, and then the news came that the film would be televised simultaneously in Judenstaat and Germany. Freddi said, "You ought to come to my apartment and watch it, Judi."

"I can't just cross into Berlin like that," Judit said.

"Sure you can. It's just two hours away. I've got luxuries you people can't imagine—for example, my own telephone. What is it with you people and private telephones? I wanted one in my hotel room and the clerk looked like I'd asked for the impossible."

"I guess we have nothing to hide," Judit said.

It might have been then that Fredericka glanced outside and started walking towards the glass wall with the view of Stein Square. "Judi. Please come. What do you call those people, the ones with the hats and beards?"

In spite of herself, Judit joined her and looked down. The glass was soundproofed, but it vibrated with what was happening three stories below: the whole of Stein Square from the Elbe to Parliament literally packed with black-hats, yet more of them streaming in from the embankment, literally blackening the sideways and the streets.

"I'd film them, but isn't that against their law?" Freddi looked at Judit for guidance. "No? Maybe I will, then. It's quite a novelty for us, over on the other side." She ran to get her little video camera, and then asked, "Is it one of their festivals?"

"They're protesting," said Judit.

"But I thought they didn't get involved in politics. They just keep to themselves and pray. Isn't that right?"

In fact, it wasn't clear what the black-hats were doing. They might have been praying. Some sects had done it years ago, in the early battles for state-funded Yeshivas when their presence would postpone sessions of Parliament for hours or even days. This time, though, it seemed to be a united front: all kinds of hats, broad-brimmed, flat-crowned, high-crowned Chabad fedoras, black suits and caftans, wool and gabardine. Young men were climbing the sandstone pillars of Parliament, nimble as spiders, and suddenly, a Yiddish banner was unfurled, in clear Hebrew characters Judit could read a hundred yards away:

Finish what Hitler started

"Do you understand that jargon?" Freddi asked Judit.

Judit surprised both herself and Freddi by dodging the question. So did Sammy Gluck and another girl who'd joined them at the window who at the very least had enough Yiddish to understand *Hitler*. All were transfixed by the spectacle, by the sheer number of men who filled the streets and sidewalks and brought traffic to a halt. If police had been called in, there'd been no visible effect.

The phone in Kornfeld's office started ringing. No one had occupied that office for a month. It was just down the hall. Everyone looked at Judit. She stayed where she was, and on the fifth ring, Sammy Gluck ran off to answer it.

They could hear him even from a distance. "Who?" His voice sounded too high. "Well, do you think it's a good idea?" Then, he set the receiver down, walked back, and stood in the doorway. "There's one of them, wants to come upstairs." He looked at Judit.

"It's not up to me," Judit said.

"Who's it up to, then?" Sammy asked savagely. "She says she knows you."

Judit hesitated. Then she said, "I'll go meet her." Turning to the others, she added, "It's just a woman from Chabad."

Still, she admitted some anxiety as she walked towards the elevator. Nothing was less appealing than facing Charlotte in a state of panic, and with any luck, Charlotte would take one look at her and know that she was pregnant. The elevator door opened. It was Shaindel.

Shaindel tore down the hallway like she was on fire, pulling Judit with her and then suddenly, they were both in the Media Room surrounded by staff and their blinking screens. Shaindel's hair was out of her hair-band, wind-blown over a face fixed with terror. She'd lost one shoe and carried the other, leaving her in muddy stockinged feet.

Freddi asked, "Is that your niece?"

Sammy addressed her in Yiddish. "*Sit. You want a cookie?*"

But someone else said, "It wouldn't be kosher. Don't upset her." They brought her water in a paper cup, and she drank it. She didn't take her eyes off Judit, and finally, Judit had sense enough to shut the two of them in Kornfeld's office.

His desk was still there, and like the desk of the porter in her dormitory, it had an ink-blotter on it, and also that telephone, and a box of tissues. Judit pulled out Kornfeld's padded office chair, and Shaindel kept standing, shivering, holding that shoe and looking at Judit with her big, clear eyes. She whispered in Yiddish, "*Are you in charge?*"

Judit addressed her in German, hoping the shift to a rational language would calm her down. "You can stay here a little while. Then we'll find someone to take you home."

But Shaindel had forgotten her German completely. "*Are you in charge?*" she asked again, in crude Galician Yiddish. "*Is it my fault? I was the one who brought them. I didn't know they were bad.*"

Judit's hand went up to smooth Shaindel's hair, and Shaindel recoiled, but then she seemed to gather herself up again and suffered the affection. Judit asked, "*What are you talking about?*"

"*I thought they were what you wanted.*"

"*Are you talking about those video tapes?*" Judit asked. The question was unnecessary. This time, her voice was stronger, and she felt the hand that stroked Shaindel's hair rest on her neck, not very gently.

The girl burst into tears and said, "*I know there were naked people in them. I thought that's what you wanted. Now Uncle Moishe is in trouble. Don't send us all away because I did a bad thing, please. Have mercy on us.*"

"*So did you know what you were doing? What did you think would happen?*" Her own voice sounded strange to her, too harsh, and Shaindel wrenched herself away and backed into Kornfeld's desk. "*Shaindel, what are you people after?*"

She stopped asking questions. What was the point? She just let Shaindel sob into tissue after tissue. Her breasts hurt. Her bladder began to fill with urine. She moved to touch the girl again, and Shaindel gave a cry and said, "*Don't hurt me!*"

Someone knocked on the door. It was Mr. Rosenblatt himself, who'd come to retrieve Shaindel. Shaindel seemed glad to see him, and even took his hand. In turn, he put his cap on her head. She looked at Judit with terror and suspicion. He said to Judit, "She's been here almost every day, wanting to see you. I didn't have the heart to turn her away now, with all the trouble out there. You really ought to tell her that we don't let kids into the administrative offices unless they're relatives. She's not, is she?"

"Not what?" Judit asked.

"A relative. No? Well, she looks like you," he said, "or like you looked when you were her age. I still remember. You looked just like a little lamb, back then."

It wasn't until Judit returned to her mother's apartment that she learned what was behind the demonstrations. A copy of *A Home* lay open on the kitchen table: "Museum Bomber Arrested." Apparently, an investigation traced the explosives found in the archive to a Loschwitz location, and for the first time in Judenstaat's history, the case would not be handled by a rabbinic court. There was a photograph of Kravitz—untrimmed beard over his prison jumpsuit, velvet skull-cap on his head—a seedy, ignominious man whose shop was full of trigger-wires and timers and who faced arrest without resistance.

The arrest of Moses Kravitz took place early that same morning, and the scene when the police van parked in the heart of Loschwitz was apocalyptic. The van was overturned and set on fire, and the police shot in the air, but rather than dispersing, the mob poured down the street, and it was only when reinforcements arrived that they'd managed to plow right through a wall of men in caftans and put the suspect behind bars.

Well, it was about time, of course. Why should those people have a separate court and separate laws? The paper's editorial pressed the point and took it further. Isn't it about time to end the forty-year policy of subsidizing a community that didn't hold to common standards? Their schools produced paupers with no written knowledge of the national language. Their housing blocks were never up to code; the concrete foundations had been crumbling for years, and it was amazing that their children hadn't been electrocuted on the exposed wires that dangled from those ceilings.

Her mother heard her come in, and stood in her slippers and robe in the kitchen doorway. "Is it true, sweetheart?"

"Is what true?" Judit asked.

"That they're going to deport them all?" Leonora looked so fragile that Judit felt she ought to offer her a chair, but she shook her head. "I don't want to bother you. I try not to wait up for you anymore. But I just wanted to know. Is it true that there are trucks waiting at the border to take them to Siberia?"

"Where did you hear that?" Judit asked.

"Where I work," her mother said. "They're in a panic. Oh, it's terrible to see, the way they're overreacting and spreading rumors. The old ones in the home, they've all stopped eating. I had to force-feed one woman who actually struck me, Judi, right across the face, and they had to put her in restraints."

Leonora tended to keep to herself these days; she and Judit seldom crossed paths. She looked older than Judit had remembered, diminished, and the robe was too big for her. Her hazel eyes searched Judit's.

"That's crazy, Mom," Judit said. "They arrest one nut, and the black-hats get a persecution complex. He should be treated like everybody else."

"I know, I know," Leonora said. "But they don't see it that way. As far as they're concerned, they'll never be like everybody else."

"Go to bed, Mom," Judit said.

"Don't you agree? That they think they can't be like everybody else?"

"They're right," Judit said. "We can't be."

Leonora looked perplexed, and Judit herself wasn't sure what she just said and what she had confessed. She knew she owed her mother an explanation, but that would mean a longer night, and sharing a document she would prefer to keep to herself for a while. She suspected that her mother often went into her room, and thus, she'd placed it inside her old sewing machine, just below a panel where she kept spools of thread. Of course, it was Stephen Weiss's manifesto.

4

The Manifesto of Stephen Weiss

A specter is haunting Europe—the specter of genocide. The great powers struggle to exorcise this specter through solemn dedications, bad art, and rhetoric that is designed to drain the term of any specificity. Where is the nation that has not been decried as genocidal by its opponents? Where are the opponents who have not hurled the reproach of genocide against their adversaries?

Two things result from this state of affairs:

1. *Genocide has become a term for mass murder of a group on ideological grounds.*
2. *It is high time that we who were the objects of genocide should publish our views and meet these fairy tales with a manifesto that defines the meaning of the term and once and for all lays out a program of action for Churban survivors.*

I. The Meaning of Genocide

In earlier epochs, we find almost everywhere famine and bloodshed. As time went on, the opportunities for slaughter multi-

plied as death became the province not of random natural phenomena or personal vendettas, but of machinery and whole industrial armies. Today, conventional warfare no longer suffices. Given the first half of the twentieth century, the evidence is indisputable. The modern state is but a committee for managing murder.

Paradoxically, the modern state is an outgrowth of the Enlightenment, an ideology that privileges progress and abstraction. Beginning with the premise of man's goodness, Enlightenment philosophy assures that human action must be grounded in human reason. Forging ahead, vulgar ideologues insist all men are brothers. What they cannot acknowledge is that all men are, in equal measure, butchers, and that irrationality, along with reason, is our common currency.

Therefore, modern states fight in the name of reason, and battle the irrational. If they wipe out their enemies, surely all men will be brothers. Soldiers, indeed, are burnt sacrifices to this God of Reason. Yet these relations do not constitute genocide. Rather, the term will be defined as follows:

1. *Genocide is the attempted destruction of the Jews.*
2. *As survivors of genocide, we constitute a special class. The penumbra of our experience transforms not only us, but our relationships to other nations, in ways we shall delineate below.*

II. The Jewish Demon

We leave religious and ethnographic definitions to professionals in those disciplines, but insist that three elements distinguish Jews from what tradition might establish as Nations or Goyim.

In fact, Jews are the antithesis of Nations for the following reasons:

1. *We do not bow down.*
2. *We cross borders.*
3. *We remember.*

The first point can be confirmed both theologically and historically. Our ancient prohibition against idol-worship has had lasting power; we do not honor crowns or flags. The second point is central to our narrative; we thrive in no fixed place. Finally, if we are border-crossers, what we carry is our memories, both individual and collective.

Contrast this set of characteristics to the Nations. They are defined by their allegiances and by their borders. These loyalties can only be sustained by a compulsory amnesia. Otherwise, they would be so tangled in contradictory memories that they would not be able to bow down at all. It is fair to say that forgetting is a passport to the wider world. The Jews can only join the rank of nations if they learn to forget.

Yet we cannot forget. Our memories extend beyond the Churban. Because we do not bow down, we have no loyalty to a particular ideological idol of the age. We are the repository for the history of every border we have crossed. Therefore, how can we help but laugh at flags? We know they are just bits of colored cloth. We carry our contradictions and represent, in the deepest sense, what Nations fear.

III. The Jews and Genocide

In what relation does genocide stand to the Jews as a whole? Not all of us lived in countries under fascist domination, but if the fascists sought complete extermination of the Jews, perforce, all living Jews are survivors.

Yet here we come across a paradox: our continued survival is dependent on other Nations and on the implications of the Churban. When Nations see us, they see ghosts; thus, they have no choice but to respond with terror and revulsion, and the power of that response ensures a symbiotic, necessary partnership which will be explained below, and in more detail, in section IV.

Throughout the ages, Jews have inspired in Nations that same terror and revulsion. Whole libraries have been compiled by way of explanation: their ignorance of our customs, their belief in black magic, their association of Jews with an angry, unforgiving God-the-Father who castrates and kills His son. Yet in the end, it is our indelible identity as demons that ensures our lasting power.

In short, we Jews embody the irrational. Emperors, landlords, bishops, and petty tyrants have employed us as money-lenders, merchants, and tax collectors, and most classically, court Jews. Thus, they have shielded themselves from popular outrage while offering us a limited protection. This partnership extended even to the so-called Age of Reason. When nation-states wanted to invoke a demon, they turned to Jews, and gave us another name: Capitalism, Bolshevism, sexual deviance—anything that would provoke a restless, powerless population and keep them from turning against the nation-state that was the true object of their rage. Returning briefly to the ideology of the Enlightenment, we might speculate that one of the things that makes men brothers is their subterranean and visceral response to Jews.

Thus, the recent German fascist experiment in genocide was merely the expression, in complete terms, of an established dynamic. However, the distinguishing feature of German fascism was not the hatred of Jews generally, but the abolition of Jews altogether. In this, they came close to success. Yet like an overheated engine, the fascist machine spent its fuel in ways that guaranteed destruction. We are that fuel. We have survived them.

IV. Current Circumstances and Opportunities

At the time of this writing, survivors are dispersed throughout the globe, though we have gathered in increasing numbers in the zones of occupation here in Germany. It is clear that we can no longer serve as partners for conventional nation-states, with their flags, anthems, and armies.

The concentration of power in the United States and the Soviet Union has, to a great extent, made Nations obsolete. To be a Nation now is to have not only a common culture and landmass, but to establish a relationship with one of these two central powers. In our current landscape, no nation-state can exist unless it is, essentially, a colony.

For Americans, those colonies are a means to protect global capital. For the Soviet Union, the colonies are a means to secure borders against hostile forces and supply their own population with goods and services. In both cases, we survivors are offered an opportunity to renew and expand our historic role. We might accommodate both global capital and Soviet security by serving both interests.

We Jews will establish ourselves as a vanguard for both parties which, indeed, are only superficially in conflict. For the Soviets and the Americans, we will provide a center for world trade where resources can cross borders in both directions without calling either party's ideological principles into question. After all, we Jews are demons. Who expects demons to have principles?

We will certainly be met with revulsion and terror. That is our expectation. As survivors, we have suffered the ultimate catastrophe, all the more reason why we might deflect outrage. An irrational response from a survivor of genocide is expected, and credible. Thus, both the Soviet Union and the United States might use our irrationality to mask their own base actions.

On those terms, we will establish a haven where the following will be pretty much generally applicable:

1. *Refuge for all survivors.*
2. *Concentration of banks and headquarters of international industries.*
3. *Permanent occupation by both Soviet and American forces.*
4. *Collective ownership of the Churban and a claim to the unique nature of our genocide.*

You are horrified that we depend upon the same deep-set revulsion that inspired persecution and arguably led to genocide. Yet if we return to our own countries, certainly we return into similar conditions, and far less security. Fear of Jews is as deep-seated as fear of the dark.

Furthermore, who among us can claim a country? What is our history but a series of border-crossings, flag after irrelevant and foolish flag? The only banner for the Jews is the banner of memory. It is memory that defines us. It is memory that they fear.

As individual Churban survivors, we know that a personal response cannot move beyond vengeance. By uniting, we achieve breathtaking power. We use the very fear that we inspire to create a bridge between reason and terror, between the visible and invisible worlds. We ourselves become a monument.

A monument to what?

That is a question history will answer. Just as we believe that the very thing that makes men brothers also makes them butchers, we might also agree that the very thing that makes Jews hated makes us free. Consider where that freedom led such men as Marx, Freud, and Einstein, Jews who crossed into countries that no map could mark, and who returned to a landscape changed by their very crossing. The bridge they crossed transcends national utility. It is a bridge to the irrational, and to the future.

As survivors, we will never cease for a moment to instill in our fellow Jews the clearest possible recognition of the corruption of both East and West, and we openly declare our ends can only be attained by being hated as the cunning face of worldwide capital and the vanguard of Soviet oppression. Yet what shall we do with our freedom?

We promise this: we will refuse to hate ourselves. Let all who defy us tremble and recoil.

We have nothing to lose.

5

FREDERICKA was, as she put it, "pumped" for the premiere at Parliament that night. She confided to Judit that the director of the Conrad Wolf Academy was near retirement, and if she "performed up to standard," she'd not only fill his position but reinvent the institution as a true Center for German Media. "Watch. In a few years, we'll be the capital of Europe."

Judit said, "I'm not from Berlin, Freddi."

She shrugged. "Okay. But face it. We're leading parallel lives. We're even dressing alike." She gestured towards their shoes and stockings. "I like the patterned ones too. They're a little campy, a little racy, keep you from looking like a man in a skirt. You'll move right in and make this place world-class."

Judit looked at the stockings and wondered who'd chosen them. They looked like something a prostitute would wear. She said, "I haven't been asked to move in. I'm not sure I want to."

"You want some turtle in charge? Oh, no you don't!" Fredericka said. "The era of the turtles is behind us now. It's the year of the hare. Don't look like that. What? You want Gluck running the museum?"

"He's welcome to it," Judit said.

Freddi persisted. “It’s really essential that we help each other now. I mean, everything’s happening so fast. There are so many opportunities, and with your people pulling for you, with your connections abroad—”

“I don’t have connections abroad,” Judit said. Her tone was hostile.

“I don’t mean to imply anything,” said Fredericka. She seemed genuinely hurt. “I mean, with your people in Hollywood—”

“My father’s family lived in Dresden for over a hundred years. My mother was born in a village in southern Poland that I can’t even pronounce the name of.” Judit was overwhelmed with weariness. What she really wanted to do was ask Freddi about her own connections in Berlin, if she knew a private, inexpensive way to end a pregnancy, but such was the direction of the conversation that, instead, she said, “I’m sorry. I didn’t mean to sound that way.”

“Well, you do sound that way,” Freddi said. “And I don’t deserve it. I know you’re under a lot of pressure, but you’ll have to think differently now. Especially after the premiere. We’ll be working together one way or another.”

“Who else is on the panel?” Judit asked.

“Oh, your old professor, of course,” Freddi said, happy to change the subject. “And those two old partisans—Jewish and Saxon. Very dramatic stuff, really spectacular. Don’t change those stockings, sweetie,” she added. “They’re spectacular too.”

She didn’t change her stockings. But after that conversation, she felt determined to change something. She knew she ought to just go home and get some sleep, but since the film was finished, she’d had troubling dreams. She dreamed that she was buried alive, and burrowed out from underneath, and she emerged, soiled, naked, deeply embarrassed, and had the sensation that she’d given birth not to a baby but to herself, and in another country. She dreamed that there was something in the pocket of the duffle coat—the one she'd worn for years—and she couldn't remember where she'd put the coat or even why she'd worn it for so long, but she tossed everything else out of her closet, and only then remembered that she'd given that coat to a little girl in Loschwitz. Somehow, Judit had to find out what was in that pocket, which meant she had to find the girl who would take her to a room above a kosher butcher where the uncle screened footage of Stephen Weiss addressing mobs of furious survivors.

Her body was a trap, tightened by mechanisms past her understanding. Yes, Bondi could spring that trap, but then she was wide open, and sometimes, that was worse. The blocks around the dairy restaurant were slated for demolition. She'd seen the first signs a week ago, official yellow notices in German, and almost at once, enormous Yiddish *pashkevils,* and clusters of black-hats reading them. Angry neighbors packed the restaurant, and the volume of their Yiddish arguments carried through the floor into the room where Judit lay next to Bondi hours later. She was still wearing those stockings, though nothing else.

"Are you warm enough?" Bondi asked.

Judit said, "Sure," but when he pulled her against him, she felt warmer. "I wonder," she said, "if they're really going to knock down all their neighborhoods. I mean, where will they all go?"

"They have a history of resilience," Bondi said.

"I know. Like cockroaches. You sound like my mother." Judit laughed, though not happily. "You know, the other day, I tried to find that dollar I'd gotten from Chabad House. I think it's still in the pocket of my old coat, but I can't find that either. Will they knock the Chabad House down too? Or turn the dome back into a restaurant?" Without waiting for an answer, she said, "Maybe instead of all that stuff about the Soviets and the partisans, I should have made a film about the black-hats. They're the real survivors." She sat up and hugged her knees. "Joseph, how did you learn to write in Yiddish?"

Admittedly, the question seemed to come from nowhere. Bondi said, "It's not much of a trick. A lot of people do it." That's all he said, but now he knew she'd read his note.

Judit went on. "I got something by courier. It's all in Yiddish, and I'm having trouble getting through it. I thought maybe we could work on it together."

"Is it a new project?" Bondi asked.

"Maybe," Judit said. "It's Stephen Weiss's manifesto." It was only then that she returned Bondi's frankly exploratory look, and watched it deepen and hit something hard.

He said, "What about it?"

"It came from Anna Lehmann. She seemed to think it would interest you." Even as she said those words, Judit would have given a lot to take them back again, because Bondi got out of bed and picked up his discarded clothing. Still, helplessly, she kept on talking. "Joseph, listen, she couldn't mean anything by it." But now he was pulling on his boxer shorts and zipping his trousers. "What's the harm in reading it?" she asked him desperately. He turned his back before he answered.

"You trust her?"

"Shouldn't I?" Judit asked.

He said, "It's a hoax." Still with his back turned, he pulled his undershirt on, and Judit put her hands on his shoulders and felt them give a little. It was only with effort that he continued. "The manifesto's fabricated."

Then he turned around. When she saw his face, she had to say, "How do you know?"

Bondi sat on the daybed, in his trousers and undershirt, and Judit sat beside him, still wearing only those absurd stockings, yet he was the one who seemed disarmed. She was really cold now, and she pulled the synthetic bedspread over them both.

"Don't trust Lehmann," said Bondi. "She doesn't want what's best for you. This need of yours—to always know and know—she feeds it, Judit." He turned under the shelter of the bedspread. "My own mother was like that," he said. "She was the one who taught me to write Yiddish."

Judit said, "Joseph, you don't have to tell me a thing."

"I think I do," Bondi said. "Or Lehmann will tell you something half-true. My mother was an editor at that magazine, *The Book Peddler*. Her father was a Yiddish poet. She was very beautiful. I was twelve when she died. She killed herself somewhere in Russia. My father never forgave her, but I did. I suppose that's a character flaw."

"What is?" Judit asked.

"Forgiveness," said Bondi. "I don't make a cult of her, Judit. But she cared about this country and the Jewish people in ways that cynics like Lehmann can't imagine. They're opportunists. They can't understand a woman like my mother who really did believe that there was such a thing as justice."

Of course, that was the source of the Yiddish books in the apartment, secular writers from Warsaw and Vilna, the poet who won the Stalin Prize, the notebook with the alphabet in pencil, those carefully drawn Hebrew characters in handwriting that Judit had recognized at once, though even then she didn't know what to do with what she'd recognized. This room was Bondi's heart. He'd let her in, and now she couldn't help but ask, "Why did she do it, Joseph?"

"She found out what happened to her father," Bondi said. "It was after the magazine shut down. She had nothing to do with her time. She was under suspicion already. She crossed the border. I only found out what happened to her when I got to Moscow. She just kept digging and digging, Judit, and when you dig, what do you find? A corpse." His voice broke. "Her father disappeared in '51—sure—like so many others, and the government claimed he'd emigrated, crossed into Germany, that he wasn't a Bundist, he was a traitor, a Cosmopolitan like Stephen Weiss."

Judit said, "I still don't understand. What did she find out? What happened to him? How did he die?"

"Look, I'm not like you. I don't need to read the fine print. All I know is that I always thought I'd have to think one way and feel another. Now, our country is finally going in the right direction. After forty years, we can live normal lives. If we let ourselves. We can let ourselves." He pulled Judit down beside him and they lay back in bed. He lowered his head onto her stomach, just at the uterus, and the sensation was both erotic and clinical. "How far along now?"

"I'm not sure," Judit said. Then, "Maybe I don't want to know."

"That's a first." Bondi spoke right into her womb, and she knew she ought to laugh. Instead, a thickness welled in her throat. Did she mean it? Did she not want to know? No tests, no sonograms, no sessions with technicians? Could she let those weeks accumulate, let whatever happened take its course? If that was possible, if she could trust sensation, time would stretch out like open country she would enter with no map, and it would carry her along. It felt so possible, to mean just what she said. Bondi's cheek lay on her belly. He breathed softly. His eyes were closed, his mouth a little open, like a child's. She stroked his hair. What was it Hans had said to her mother all those years ago? When you don't know, you're free.

Judit's hand lingered on the vulnerable patch where Bondi's hair grew thin. She didn't want to know. Really? Where else could she draw that line? Could leaving well enough alone be a way of life? Maybe for someone else. Maybe for Bondi. From nowhere came a thought that hadn't crossed her mind in months. Who lied about the murder? Hans wasn't free. He had known something. Someone was afraid of what he knew.

A disembodied humming note reverberated in her uterus.

"I'm scared," she said. She said it so Bondi would look up. He did. Those candid eyes, the ones she could see right through, they reassured her that he was really there. It wasn't someone else.

Maybe five black-hats were outside when she emerged. They smoked and muttered in Yiddish, pointing to one of the *pashkevils.* Then one of them with a black beard and a high hat and a gold watch on his wrist gave Judit a look like a burning cigarette. In Yiddish, he asked, "*Are you a Jew?*"

Judit was in no mood for this. In that same language, she said, "*Go to hell.*"

"*You speak Yiddish like a German. Tell me,*" he said, "*do you fear God?*"

One of the other black-hats broke in and said something that stopped him short, and Judit knew she should just walk away and find a taxi, but instead, she said, "*I don't bow down.*"

That answer, from the tarted-up woman with the glowing hair, short skirt, and racy stockings was so unexpected that they didn't hear it. The headline on the *pashkevil* was about the deportation, but that wasn't what the black-hats were discussing. They were talking about their Rebbe's youngest son, a prodigy with mystic powers who predicted that on May 15th of that year, the Messiah would appear. In contrast, the eldest son was building a new Yeshiva in the heart of Loschwitz, and the Rebbe—may he live forever—sided with the eldest son, but it was likely that the prodigy and his followers would decamp to Poland because when the Messiah came the whole of Loschwitz would be swallowed by the earth.

Now Judit couldn't help it. She called out, in Yiddish, "*Who would notice?*"

The same black-bearded man with the high hat and the gold watch said, "*Do you know something, young lady? You're a slave.*"

"*You're the slave,*" Judit said.

"*Careful, careful,*" an older man said to the younger. "*What's the point? Just walk away from this.*"

"*I won't walk away from my own corner,*" said the black-hat. "*She speaks Yiddish like a German. She doesn't know she's a slave. She doesn't fear God. What does she fear?*"

"*Not you,*" said Judit.

"*Jews like her were the cause of the Churban,*" he said, not looking at Judit, "*and they will be again and again.*" He turned in her direction, worked something around in his mouth, and spat at her.

Judit stepped back. It was impossible to untangle anger and humiliation now. Why was she engaging with these people? The school across the street let out, and little girls who looked like Shaindel clustered in the doorway, whispering to each other. Bondi was upstairs, still, and he could hear them. Would he let this play itself out, or would he interfere in what she began to realize was not his business? No, it was someone else's business, that force that rose up in her with its own voice, and shouted in Yiddish: "*You parasites! You think that time stands still? It won't, and it will crush you!*"

They were already walking away, those men. They started for another corner, maybe for Poland, but she couldn't stop now, and the Yiddish wasn't the Yiddish of a German. It was rolling and Galician, a Yiddish that she never knew she had, and she called after them:

"*You'll all be crushed like vermin, and no one will even notice because time just doesn't stop, it rolls on over you and you're the slaves!*"

Now they were laughing. She trembled where she stood, and when a taxi passed by, she was so full of her own thoughts she didn't hail it. In a few hours, she'd be at the premiere, and whatever filled her now would fill her then and take her captive in a way that made her buckle at the knees. Maybe she was possessed. Maybe a dybbuk was inside her. A rabbi could perform an exorcism. Or an abortionist.

She stood in that luxuriant, oppressive sunlight. It was a lovely afternoon. There were a few hours before the premiere at Parliament. She knew what Shaindel would say. She had to go back into that archive. She had to ask that ghost what she should do, and show she was not afraid. She wasn't afraid, was she?

6

NO harm in it," said Mr. Rosenblatt. "But you be careful. There's still glass on the floor."

What harm she'd done was past repeating. Now Judit walked down the stairway she'd descended every day for ten years. There was the light switch just where it ought to be. There was the door, no padlock on it, but closed. The very familiarity pinched Judit's heart a little. She opened the door.

Mr. Rosenblatt was right. The place was a shambles. Glass plates had been wrenched from their viewing boxes and shattered on the floor; loose film was everywhere; a projector lay in pieces like a wounded dog. That was the first thing she noticed. The second was how small the room looked. It was hemmed in with drawers and drawers, most of which were open. The open ones all looked empty. There was the long, gunmetal gray worktable on the far wall, spotted with rust. Judit felt herself growing grayer and smaller as she took that room back in, and she ran her fingers over the cold handles of those drawers and walked slowly across the room to her old editing machine. She looked down. A wisp of celluloid was caught in its teeth.

Once, she'd known what to cut and what to keep. She waited

for a sign. Then, something tightly coiled began unwinding. She opened a closed drawer by the machine; it was empty. Had Kornfeld told the truth when he claimed everything had either been transferred or incinerated? Given this chaos, how could he be sure?

Then she heard a man breathing hoarsely.

She stood very still. "Who is it?"

No ghost. Ghosts never breathe. No, someone had been interrupted in the work of sorting through the wreckage. He rose, not easily, leveraging himself on an open drawer: Arno Durmersheimer.

He'd had a shave for the premiere and it made him look younger; so did the well-made jacket with all the buttons fastened. "I guess we got the same idea. Been here three times already," Durmersheimer said. "You find it yet?"

Scrubbed, relatively sober, Durmersheimer looked half-tamed. But not completely. Judit had edited those interviews, but this was something else: him, in the flesh again. His hands were full of tangled film he must have scooped off the floor.

She said, "Don't touch my stuff."

"Like I said, just cleaning up," Durmersheimer said, and now he was impatient. "They made a real mess. The way this place looks, anything could be here, and if it's still floating around, someone might take it the wrong way."

"You mean about the murder."

"I mean," Durmersheimer said, "I never should have left that movie. All I wanted was to set the record straight. What's done is done. An old man makes mistakes. I drank too much. I got confused."

Again, Judit said, "You mean about the murder."

A drawer slammed by the worktable.

Durmersheimer said, "That's not me."

Judit drew her hand over her mouth and looked back to that table. That's where the ghost of Hans should have been, with its long legs hanging and its arms braced, gangling and relaxed, an unwound bow-string, with its mouth turned up on one side and its baleful eyes.

"It's gone," Judit said. "He's gone."

Then she was weak with longing, and she couldn't get the words out. She would have given anything to see that ghost again, standing as he had in life, with a straight back and the stance of a conductor, conscious of his stature, but self-effacing in the way that secure people can be. But he wasn't there. He'd crossed the border. He'd taken memory with him. Now she felt her own eyes glitter, maybe balefully, and she straightened and stepped forward. Now she could see herself from the outside, her face emptied of everything, and she was staring into what Hans knew, the inexplicable, the uncut version, layer after layer of those stories piled like bodies in an open grave.

That's when she saw the reel. It was just where she had placed it in that dream she'd had a thousand years ago: camouflaged against the surface of the table.

"You're sick again," said Durmersheimer. "Oh, fuck. We don't need trouble." He was white as his dress shirt. He could have knocked her down, but some force seemed to hold him back, and he stood paralyzed as Judit reassembled the projector and switched on the audio.

She watched the footage. It was eight-millimeter, unmistakably the content she had seen before. But now the camera kept on going, from the moment Stein made that sweeping gesture with his hands. Even under these primitive circumstances, Judit could see enough and hear enough, and she didn't turn away, even as Durmersheimer kept repeating, "It's all a lie. It's a mistake. It doesn't matter. Turn off the damned machine!"

1946. A crater on the site of what was once the Great Synagogue of Dresden. A bearded Leopold Stein addresses a crowd of adolescents.

His big, working-class boxer's hands articulate a circle. Then, they turn upwards and cup his chin, an intimate gesture. He is about to address them, intimately, in Yiddish.

"*I make no promises. But there are some who can. I only know what we want. The fire returns. This is our monument. This is our prayer-house. No one can bring back the dead. I can only speak in their name for all of us today, tomorrow, throughout the generations. Bring them here, all the guilty ones. Six million Germans. We will blot out even their memory, and we will make them bleed.*"

7

HELENA Sokolov took Judit's hand in both of hers. Those hands were manicured and very small. She looked just like her photographs, though up close, her face was mapped with tiny wrinkles. "The woman of the hour," she said. "I can't believe we haven't met before."

To be in close proximity to Sokolov was a little like being in front of a radiation lamp. Judit managed to say, "I don't know."

"Somebody's been protecting you from me," Sokolov said, maybe slyly. "Well, get yourself a drink. And do make sure to circulate tonight. People need to know who you are." Then, lowering her voice, she added, "Keep this between us. In an hour, there will be two very special guests."

Judit nodded. She managed to back away and find a glass of mineral water. Everything tasted lousy now, but she had to have something in her hand; she had to look occupied. Durmersheimer was somewhere in the crowd, ready to disavow whatever happened. The small reel didn't quite fit in her evening purse, and it stuck out just enough to be conspicuous. At least one person said, "What's that? A new project?" and she answered, "I don't know." She said

"I don't know" so many times that evening that she began to wonder if there were any other words left in her.

Fortunately, she didn't have to say much of anything at all. Everyone present took Helena Sokolov's advice; they circulated. Judit stood with her glass and her purse like a stone in midstream. The only one who paid Judit the least attention was Sammy Gluck, who made much of a formal introduction to Patricia and was solicitous of Judit, bringing her a plate of herring on toast, and asking if she needed to get off her feet. Judit tried not to read too much into it, but it didn't help when Patricia said, "I love what you're wearing. I hope you don't mind me saying so, but that kind of blouse wouldn't have looked good on you before. Now, you fill it out."

"I don't know," Judit said, and then she hid her face in the glass of mineral water.

After a while, she searched for the bathroom. At least that's what she told herself. Really, she just wanted to be alone with the film. If she could review each frame in her head until the end, then she could consider actions and consequences. Could she slip it into the projector and force those present to confront what she had seen? And what would follow? An investigation? Of whom? A formal and pedantic voice framed these obvious questions, a whole string of them, and Judit managed to find a glass door that led to a veranda. The air was cool and damp. She sat on a bench with her purse in both hands like a little girl.

That was how Anna Lehmann found her. Certainly, Judit looked less polished than when Lehmann had last seen her, hair in her face, her blouse too tight around the chest. Lehmann had dressed up for the reception. Her massive body was encased in an embroidered tunic. As a result, she looked more than ever like a big couch turned upright and propped on heels. She wore eyeliner, lipstick, and rouge. The effect would have been comic if she hadn't been so monumental.

Judit was startled. "When did you get here?"

"Oh, I just arrived," Lehmann said. "Nobody shows up on time. Seven-thirty is more appropriate. When one has gone to enough of these receptions, one learns to maneuver in such a way that one needn't interact with other human beings. Unless," she added, "you have a preference for interacting with human beings. I thought not." She took out a cigarette and lit it.

"So tell me, how long did it take to dig that hole?" Judit asked. She'd been so certain that Lehmann would follow her train of thought that it took a while for her to realize that nothing in particular had passed across her old professor's face.

"In general, it doesn't take long, if one has a strong back and a willing spirit. Who knows what we'll dig up next? The thought exhausts me." She sank into the bench as though it were a divan and sucked on her cigarette. Smoke came out through her nose. "And off it goes into the marketplace of ideas. As though ideas were cabbages and one placed them next to other cabbages. Red, white, green, purple. In the end, it's just a cabbage."

"Professor," Judit said, "I'm talking about the synagogue."

"What do you mean, child?" Lehmann asked. Then, she glanced at Judit's purse and added sharply, "Somebody's been playing you for a fool." And finally, "You're not a fool. You check your sources. You won't go forward on the basis of rumor and fabrication."

It was a relief to talk to Lehmann, even as she smoked and made wry and dismissive comments. If Judit could describe what she had seen, surely Lehmann would know enough to confirm or deny, and as she outlined the contents, she could hear her own voice break. Lehmann nodded, and when Judit reached the point where Stein spoke to the crowd, she interrupted.

"You consider these materials important?"

"I think they will surprise some people," Judit said.

"I don't see why," said Lehmann. "Did they surprise you?"

"Yes," said Judit. "That Stein would say that. And it happened under his orders."

"Ginsberg," said Lehmann, "it's time we lost our illusions about how this state was founded. What was it Weiss wrote? The very thing that makes men brothers makes them butchers. Of course, Weiss didn't think that Jews were human beings at all. No. Jews are demons." She seemed about to laugh, but thought better of it.

Judit went on. "You knew about this."

"There's nothing to know," Lehmann said. "It was the only possible statement Leo could have made back then. And so he made it. And maybe," Lehmann said, adding the next words slowly, "it made him." She stubbed her cigarette out in a portable ashtray she kept in her purse.

After all, what is a founder? Who is the embodiment of the age? When Lehmann knew Stein in Berlin, he was young and full of life. One could not help but give way to his enormous appetite. He gobbled people up, even the trim, hard little beast that Lehmann had been back then, and she'd allowed herself to get caught between his big, white teeth. With time, that appetite had grown, and everyone and everything was gobbled up, but after the Churban, the nature of the beast—the nature of all beasts—had changed.

She'd been in Switzerland, working as a caretaker for an old blind lady, and after breakfast, she would read her ten pages of a novel by Émile Zola and ten pages of a novel by Thomas Mann. The lady's house overlooked the mountains, and Lehmann's bedroom was as big as the apartment she had fled in Heidelberg. Every afternoon, when she'd received her five newspapers and sat reading them on the deck while the lady napped, she'd taken her remorse and sharpened her wit against it until the remorse wore down and the wit could cut through steel. Such was her late girlhood, and she thought she'd hardened. She used the woman's large library to review her Latin and teach herself Greek, and sometimes she would walk to town to have coffee with the Russian expatriates—Whites of course—who tried to sleep with her. She perfected her Russian in those years, both spoken and written, and had her first affair with a woman, a former ballerina, but that wasn't what Judit wanted to know. That was another story.

What Judit wanted to know was about Stein. But why did Judit want to know about Stein? Why didn't she want to know about the ballerina who was a few years older than Lehmann, a free spirit whose father perished in the Russian Civil War? Why didn't Judit want to know about the other expatriates, awful middle-aged men, self-parodies with monocles and Tsarist medals? Why didn't she want to know about the blind lady? She was elderly and gentle, a dear family friend who happened to have a house where Anna could live safely and study in peace, and who had no children, and thus left her a portion of her estate when she died, the balance of which allowed her to spend the first few months after the war in London and Paris until she received a telegram. "Why travel? Work here. Indeed."

Lehmann received that telegram as she stood in a kimono in the hallway of a gorgeous hotel, with a cup of coffee in her hand. Her hair was very long then, the only time she'd ever worn it long. That "Indeed" got her smiling. Why not? What was she going to do in Paris aside from lounge around and play with a couple of ballerinas? "Indeed" for all practical purposes meant "In bed." With her current connections, it wasn't hard for Lehmann to book a ticket to Berlin and show her passport and documents, and before she could change her mind, she was standing in the rubble of Dresden, with dust and mud all over her expensive shoes, and a scrawny Jew leading her past Soviet barracks to a big, gray tent.

The tent was open. There was a desk inside, really a plank between two filing cabinets. She recognized Stein's back; it was a recognizable back, wide and meaty, and of course there was that famous hair. She could not remember now if she was the first to speak, or maybe say, "In fact." Such details were erased when the man turned around.

He had that beard. That was the first thing anyone noticed. But then she saw what was behind that beard, a mouth half-sunken, and eyes like lead. He got up and said, "I'm glad you came, Anna."

"My God," said Anna.

He gestured her over, and she'll admit that she approached him with hesitation. Then he kissed her on the mouth and told her to sit down. "You've come to work. Good. You'll get your fill of facts. I'll get you a secretary." When she started to speak again, he interrupted. "She'll be pretty. I have a girl in mind."

"What sort of facts?" she asked, although she already knew it was the wrong question. She was thrown by the way he looked at her, by the efficiency of the exchange, and by the chastity of that kiss.

Stein brushed the question aside and continued. "There are thousands—thousands in this place alone who will give you all the material you need. And don't be sparing. You'll use all your languages, including Hebrew. Then you'll translate and the secretary will write everything down, every description, every name, but in good, clear Russian, Anna. That's important."

Before Anna Lehmann could ask about the room that she'd been promised, before she could so much as leave her suitcase at the door, Leopold Stein rose from his seat and took her arm and told her to leave her suitcase in the tent. He had something to show her. His arm felt hard and cold. All of the flesh he'd worn so wonderfully as a young man had worn away. She noticed that he stank. But she'd come this far; she had come far enough to let him lead her across the mud and cold and the ridges of the tracks from tanks. This was in 1946.

He walked to the edge of a great pit. It was a quarter of a kilometer wide, and she couldn't see its bottom. He said, "Our people dug this. By hand. Imagine, Anna. They could barely lift their feet a month ago. But they did this by themselves, and in a week. In midwinter. That's what it means."

"What what means?" Lehmann asked him.

"The work you'll do," Stein said. He told her that men would be lining up, come daytime, and women too. She ought to get some sleep. He implied that she would share his bed that night, and although she'd traveled there for just that purpose, she wondered if it was in her interest to decline. Stein must have felt it. Perhaps that's why he said, "How strong is your stomach, Anna?"

"Strong enough," she replied, with some of the bravado that had brought her to him in the first place.

"Strong enough to fill that pit?"

"Indeed." Anna hardly knew what she was saying. He stood close to her now, enclosed her in his decomposing overcoat. She couldn't know what Stein knew. She hadn't been with those survivors and seen them return to life for the sole purpose of digging that pit because they knew it would be filled. And she couldn't know what her work would be for the next six months, through the spring, as she took down names and descriptions of Germans and turned those descriptions over to the Soviets, who rounded them up and shipped them to Dresden. No, not six million. But enough to fill that pit and others across liberated territory. Each of those Germans had a history, and based on the testimony of the Jews who named them, those Germans would be shot in the head and thrown into the pit.

"Don't say you're surprised," said Lehmann. "You've heard much worse. Seen worse. You've documented this century, and now we're near the end of it. Imagine that."

Judit said, "There are documents."

"There are always documents, somewhere," Lehmann said. "These are probably in Moscow. After all, we didn't fire a shot. Perhaps if we'd been in Palestine, we'd be the agents of our own salvation, and we would have had guns of our own. But that is just speculation. No, all we did was dig, my dear. Just tell the truth and dig. Is that a crime?"

Outside, the twilight had turned into evening. By now, the hall inside was packed with journalists, with dignitaries, with waiters bearing little plates of crackers and caviar. The very flow of history ran through that brilliant hallway, and on the veranda, Lehmann lit another cigarette and adjusted herself on the bench. The look she gave Judit was no challenge, simply an assessment.

"Well, it's bound to come out eventually. Everything does. With the way things are headed, every file will be open within the next five years, and there will be so much to read—so much—that people will have to choose what to remember. But now? Think hard, dear. All things have their proper time and place." Lehmann gave a grunt and pushed herself to her feet. "Speaking of which, we should go back inside."

Judit said, "Durmersheimer knows."

"I'm sure a lot of people know," Lehmann said. "How is that knowledge useful to them? You never ask yourself that question. You've got a self-destructive streak, Ginsberg. And you always get yourself into hot water. That's when cabbages begin to stink, isn't it? When they're in hot water? When they start to cook?"

Then, even through the walls, they heard applause explode. One surprise guest had arrived. It was Mikhail Gorbachev, flown in for the private screening, and later there would be talk that he shouldn't have come, that he'd taken things too far, and that he would pay for it later. Judit and Anna Lehmann both missed the spectacle of Gorbachev kissing Helena Sokolov, first on both cheeks and then on the mouth, and though the second guest had been delayed, the lights flashed on and off three times. The film would begin shortly.

Yet Judit persisted. "My husband is dead because he knew about this."

"About what? The Soviet atrocities against the Saxons? They're the subject of the film we're about to see. About those lost souls who lined up at my tent and told me horror stories? You've catalogued those stories too. So did those lost souls kill your husband? Did I kill him? Who is your quarrel with, Ginsberg?"

"Somebody killed him. Because he won't forget."

"So is your quarrel with memory?"

"I can't forget," Judit said helplessly. "I can't forget him."

"And so you avenge him. Just as Stein avenged the dead. And so did I. You know," said Lehmann, "the dead can only say one thing: Avenge me. It's a motif. It's as reliable as death itself, my dear." She looked, critically, at the end of her cigarette. "What you might ask yourself is this: What do the living say?"

8

From Helena Sokolov's Anniversary Address Televised immediately after the screening of the documentary: "We Have Survived Them," May 14th, 1988.

> Tonight, we have watched an extraordinary film. What is extraordinary about this film? I will say first that it is frank, and that it is courageous, and that it is of the moment. It is the embodiment of the extraordinary times in which we live. Forty years after our founding, businesses from around the world flock to our country and pour their resources into our economy. We see the results in the towers rising throughout the nation, in our new roads, new rail lines, new industries. And we will continue to grow. I have said time and time again that when a girl like me can stand before this body and tell the truth, everything is possible.
>
> Forty years after our founding, two girls like me have found each other. Each has suffered a tragedy. The first, we all know. Judit Klemmer was a young bride when she lost her husband, whose life was cut short as he

raised his baton over the Dresden Orchestra on this very day four years ago. His legacy of tolerance lives on through the work you saw tonight. The second story is no less compelling. Fredericka Shumaker was six months old when she was abandoned on the Brandenburg border in 1953. She was raised in Germany, but as you saw tonight, she found her way back to our country, and what she found here has made you reconsider everything you've known about our early years and everything you thought about the future.

Judenstaat is forty years old today. We've lived through challenging times. We have moved from an uneasy infancy to childhood to adulthood, and against all odds, have built ourselves a state that has surpassed the expectations of our founders. We have survived. But we are more than a nation of survivors. And I will say it now: it is not enough for a nation to survive. A nation must live.

A nation must live and a nation must grow. A nation must look towards the future and not be hemmed in by the expectations of the past. A nation must accept that living things cannot stand still. And I say to you today that the people of Germany and the people of Judenstaat have at last reached the age of reason.

Tonight, as I sat between the president of the United States and the leader of the Soviet Union, I thought, as I often do, of Leopold Stein. He himself said to me, quite recently, "Helena, I'd give anything to be sitting in that room with you." I said, "But Leo, you'll be there." He knew what I meant, and then he made his hands into that arc, that bridge, the way he does, the gesture that we all know, and the old man began to cry. He said, "Helena, I don't want to leave them with walls. That was never our way. It's time to build more bridges."

What could I say to that? To sit beside that man and hear his words, I felt an awesome responsibility. I say to you: we are ready to build more bridges. I say to you, we are ready to tear down walls. Tear down that wall—between East and West! Tear down that wall—between two peoples whose histories are intertwined. What is Germany? What is Judenstaat? We are one people! We live in one world! We must move on together!

And when we move on, when we cross the bridge our legacy has constructed, we leave nothing behind. We carry all of who we are into that future. And what a future it will be, where there are no closed doors, no shadows, no dark corners! The two women who made this film have shown us the way. Walk with them now, into the sunlight.

The Border

1

BAD Muskau was two hours northeast of Dresden. Bondi had described the place in detail, a holiday camp and spa dating from well before the war, with mud and thermal treatments, formal English-style gardens, and a lovely little river that crossed the Polish border. What with its amenities, Judit was surprised she'd never heard of it before, and that was a good sign. It was unlikely to be overrun with tourists.

The date had been long set, and in the havoc of the month that followed the screening, Judit had been overwhelmed with press conferences and public interviews, and they brought up strong, unpleasant memories. As had been the case four years before, she'd sleepwalked through those days, abstracted from her circumstances. Fredericka did the talking. The woman who arranged the microphone on Judit's lapel commented on her complexion. "You barely need foundation, Mrs. Klemmer." Judit responded with a nod that might have seemed serene, but actually was a way of shaking off exhaustion.

Her life was past impossible. There was no escape now, not even to the room in Johannstadt; with the black-hat demonstrations, meeting there was out of the question. Judit began to realize how much those afternoons with Bondi meant. They had been the only real thing in her life. Now, unmoored, she found herself in taxicabs and limousines, and her own self seeped away. By the time she came back to her mother's apartment, there was nothing left.

Yet her mother needed Judit's attention now. The night after the documentary was broadcast and Sokolov made her speech, Leonora confronted her in the kitchen and said, "Judi, I don't understand."

"Mom, don't ask me questions. I'm just a technician," Judit said. "That's all."

"But does she mean it? About the border?" Leonora looked as though she hadn't been outside all day. She wasn't alone. Something had happened. It was like a dog-whistle that only people of a certain age could hear. As Leonora stood in the kitchen in her robe and slippers, she seemed to have become all eyes. She was as she had been in the photograph taken with her husband, just after the war, a lemur meant to cling, but now she only had Judit. "The wall can't just disappear," she said. "It's the only thing keeping them out."

"They can't be kept out," Judit said, withholding many other things she could say, and the statement perplexed her mother to the degree that she couldn't hear it.

"I'm all for free trade. You know that. I have such admiration for the prime minister, and it was so moving when she talked about Leo Stein. Who could have known that he was still alive? Is he really alive, Judit? How can that be?" Then, "How can he agree with this? That's what I don't understand."

"Mom, get some sleep," Judit said.

"The Russians," Leonora said, "the fascists, we have so many enemies, and isn't that all the more reason to secure our borders? Don't you agree?"

What Leonora wanted now was more than confirmation. She wanted real engagement. She wanted her daughter argumentative, ready to give her trouble, and the only trouble Judit had to offer was too big for that old-fashioned kitchen. It was too big for her circumstances. It was also too big for the evening purse where she still stowed it—the film. She'd shoved that purse to the back of her closet in the bedroom, and when she managed to wrench herself out of her mother's grip, she still lost sleep.

She hadn't screened it again. It ran, maybe, seven minutes. Could she get it to a sympathetic party in Germany? Probably. What were those borders now? More systematically, she wanted confirmation, to get her hands on documents that Lehmann had assured her would be public. Would that mean traveling to the Soviet Union on her own? Would it be safe? During those wild nights of speculation, on the narrow bed she'd slept on as a child, she could pretend that she was free.

She wasn't free. Her clothing never fit now. Although her nausea didn't interfere with the breakfasts that her mother dutifully prepared, Leonora did notice something. She said, "A mother knows, sweetheart. You're run ragged. Can't you take a little break? Didn't you say you were going on vacation after this was over?"

Then, Judit did remember, and she said, "That's right. I am."

She waited for Bondi on a bench by the embankment, and only then did she admit how much she wanted this, to really get away. It was eleven on a Monday morning, and the Elbe was calm; swallows flew under the white suspension bridge and nested there, and warm June sunshine opened buds on ornamental bushes planted in new tubs. She hadn't seen him for so long that waiting itself felt sexual. Her trousers couldn't fasten all the way now. She wore a light blouse over them, but was still conscious of the warm few inches of skin swelling through that open zipper. A two-seat convertible pulled up, with Bondi at the wheel.

"That can't really belong to you," Judit said. The car was navy blue, and wildly conspicuous. Bondi wore sunglasses, and his coat was thrown across the passenger seat, leaving him looking boyish and stiff in shirt-sleeves.

"You don't like it?" Bondi asked, almost shyly.

"I like it very much," said Judit. "Maybe I just like laughing at you for a change. It feels good."

"It's a Jaguar. I'm almost its first driver. That's what the man who leased it to me said. I like things that run well."

The car did run well, and it moved out of Dresden onto the highway with so little effort that the highway seemed to move instead, and the very expense of that car, with its leather seats and fancy tape deck, made them both a little giddy. Judit said, "I wish you'd brought along some tapes. Do you like music?"

"Oh, you wouldn't like my music," Bondi said.

"How do you know?"

"Well, you must like serious stuff, after all."

"What do you like, Joseph?" Judit asked. She ran a hand across his neck, daring him to veer a little. "Not serious stuff?"

Bondi cleared his throat. "Do that again."

She did it again, and he took her hand and moved it to his pants.

"Your fly's undone," he said. "I could see it when I pulled up."

"That's your fault," Judit said.

He said, "Say that again." Then, when they couldn't stand it anymore, they just pulled off the highway. They kept the top down. Afterwards, Judit arranged herself back in the passenger seat and asked, "What music do you like?"

"If you must know," Bondi said, "I like Queen."

Judit asked, "What's that?" When Bondi told her, she said, "I thought only homosexuals liked that group."

"Apparently not," Bondi said, and they both laughed. The road grew more mountainous and pleasant, as late morning turned to full, bright afternoon. She allowed herself the luxury of putting on his coat and smelling him, forgetting what she knew and where she was going.

* * *

The spa was enormous, a complex of old mansions, villas, and formal gardens, and once they had arrived, they had to navigate their way through architecture that reflected every period from prewar imperial to the Bauhaus rigor of the early '50s. The biggest structure, with an arching entrance, led to a lobby flooded with sunlight. It seemed like the sort of place that would be popular for group excursions, but it looked abandoned, maybe because it was early in the season. The tennis nets had all been taken down, and the fountains were dry. Still, it was easy enough to imagine a busload of workers from Zeitz spilling into a dining hall, and Judit couldn't stand the thought of having to see anyone but Bondi. "We're not part of some package tour, are we?" Judit asked.

"No," Bondi said. "No package."

"I've never been to a spa before. What do you do here?"

"Relax," Bondi said.

"I can't imagine you relaxing," Judit said. She tried to keep up the hectoring and teasing because once they'd actually arrived at the facility, and Bondi was in the process of checking in, the illusion began to fray. The woman behind the desk wore a gray uniform, and took out a big logbook of a register with only the first page filled. Judit looked through a second set of glass doors, and something about the hallway felt familiar. Bondi wrote down their names, and picked up both of their bags, and when he approached her, she said, "What is this place, Joseph?"

"What does it look like?" Bondi asked.

"The hallway makes me think of my old dormitory," Judit said, just to say something.

"Then it should bring back fond memories," said Bondi. She followed him down the hall, which was wider than the one back in her dormitory, and then she remembered: the dormitory tiles were green and white, not black and white. There was only one kind of place where she'd seen that checkered pattern. The elevator was enormous, and opened from both ends. Something about its dimensions made Judit forget what side they'd entered from. She fought vertigo, and when they reached their room, the door was open. That's when Judit asked, "Is this a hospital?"

"It's a spa," Bondi said. "They have all kinds of treatments here. Some of them are therapeutic. I suppose it's a kind of hospital." The statement was unnecessary. There was nothing in the room except a small press-wood cabinet, a rolling rack for blood transfusions, and a narrow bed on wheels. Bondi put down the bags and closed the door. "You wanted this."

"I did?"

"To see him, Judit." Now, he gave a nervous half-smile.

"So he's here?"

"Of course he's here," Bondi said. "It's all been arranged. They're expecting us today. He's in good spirits, apparently. He's had a few visitors since that documentary premiered. I should say," he added, "that not all of those visitors come away with a positive impression."

"That's not surprising," said Judit. Thus, she acknowledged, at last, the visit's purpose. It was not a holiday. It was something else altogether, planned back in another lifetime, and she wondered if she could ask Bondi to cancel the appointment. Frankly, she didn't know what she would say to Stein, and couldn't remember what she'd planned to ask him. Could she back down? Probably not. At best, she would brazen the visit out and just move on. She said to Bondi, "Afterwards, let's see if you can get us a real room."

Bondi said, "I like this one. Lie down. Next to me. On the bed."

"It's awfully narrow," Judit said, but she did manage to lie next to him. He rearranged himself and unfastened the rest of her zipper, resting his cheek against her belly. "You won't hear anything, Joseph," Judit said. "Believe me, it's too soon."

"How do you know? I have remarkable abilities in that direction. I hear everything."

"And what do you hear?"

"A heartbeat."

"That's my own heart," Judit said, "or yours."

"I hear her say, *Momma, don't work so hard.*" Bondi spoke Yiddish.

Judit giggled. His cheek tickled, and the Yiddish couldn't help but sound a little comical. "How do you know it's a she?"

Bondi continued. "*Stop working, Momma, just for a while. Take a vacation. And throw the film away.*"

Judit sat up. Bondi was sitting too, right across from her, and he was no longer the boy in the convertible. He was a serious man who had his coat on, and he looked at her with clarity and authority. He continued in Yiddish.

"*Throw it away. Let it be. Please, Judit, it will do no good.*"

Judit said, "What film?" Almost before the words were out of her mouth, she asked, "Who told you?"

"Everyone knows," Bondi said. The shift to German seemed to cause him effort, as though he were struggling to keep the situation at arm's length. "You aren't discreet. You can't be. It's not your nature. And the timing couldn't be worse. Please tell me you have it here."

"I have it here," Judit said.

"Good," said Bondi. "Give it to me."

"I need to think, Joseph. It's not that simple. You can't understand. I have a responsibility—"

"Yes you do," said Bondi. "To our child."

Judit rolled over. The room had a wide window, and the view was magnificent, a stretch of meadow leading to woodlands hazy with buds and pinks. She laid a hand on her belly, just where Bondi had placed his cheek, and did imagine she felt something, though it was far too early. "Maybe after I talk to him," she said.

"He has nothing to do with it," said Bondi. "Why bother an old man who's been dying for thirty-five years, who's already dead?

So Soviet soldiers shot a lot of Germans in the head. That's what they always do. The Red Army were savages, and if you think Stein could give orders to men like that, you're just naïve."

"How could you even know?" Judit asked. Then she understood. Of course Bondi knew. He'd known for years, just as Lehmann had known. There must be thousands of people who knew, and they let history move on. Maybe they dismissed it, or maybe they forgot. Or did they? A generation of survivors lined up at that tent in Dresden. Did her own parents line up at that tent in Dresden? Did Rudolph Ginsberg dig the grave of Hans's parents? The Russians killed them, but her father dug their grave. Would she betray her own father? Would Hans avenge his parents? Would he step forward with the evidence? Who'd stop him? She could not move. She couldn't name what she was feeling, even as Bondi folded her into his arms.

"Sometimes I think that none of this is real to you," Bondi said. "Not me, not the baby. You're not living in the present. If I could only make you know how meaningless, how stupid it is to bring up that old stuff again."

"This is why my husband's dead," Judit said.

The words were buried in Bondi's coat. He was right. None of it was real to her, neither his arms, nor the citrus smell of his cologne, nor whatever had or hadn't been developing inside her since March. Nothing was real but what had happened in the Opera House four years ago.

But no. Bondi was real. He'd been there too. The muscles through that coat were hard, and there was something else she could feel against his thigh. Old grief gave way to instinct and she rubbed herself against it. He pulled back abruptly. It was a gun.

"Are you on duty?" Judit asked.

They looked at each other for a long time without speaking, and what passed between them was acknowledgment.

Then someone knocked. It was the orderly, who announced that the patient was ready to receive visitors.

2

JUDIT hadn't been sure what to expect. In the documentary, Stein had been sitting up, looking right at the camera, lean, but also wiry and vigorous. What she saw now was a figure arranged on a hospital bed, with a leonine head propped on several pillows. His eyes were closed, his wild hair translucent. Bags of fluid and blood-filled tubes extended from both wrists, and his arms were wrapped around a hard, white cushion. His male nurse sat him a little higher, as Judit and Bondi approached.

"Please, he shouldn't strain himself," Judit whispered.

Stein heard her. "No. No. It's good for me." And now, Judit was startled; as in the film, that voice remained rich, warm and strong in ways that seemed impossible. Then Stein opened his eyes. They were his own, hooded and liquid, in that ruin of a face. He added, "It's really been an honor, meeting so many young people these past few weeks."

She knew that what he said required some response, and Bondi gave it. "The honor is ours, sir."

"You know," Stein said, "you all surprise me. So formal. Sir. In our day, only martinets used that word. Are you a martinet, young man?"

Bondi blushed hard. Stein seemed to make him anxious, and Judit admitted that the old man's gaze unnerved her too. Already, she was struggling to remember what had brought her here. The questions she'd so carefully constructed months before felt like packages she'd left somewhere.

She did remember one thing. "Anna Lehmann sends regards."

"Who?" Then something seemed to open up, and he smiled quite warmly. "Anna's still alive? That's something, isn't it. Remember me to her. Who would have thought we'd live this long? We're a couple of old monuments, aren't we?" The words took the wind out of him, and he grabbed the cushion hard and coughed a few rich monumental coughs. He spat into a cup the nurse brought over. That nurse was the same one Judit had seen beside Stein in those countless blurry photographs, ageless and muscular, though his crew cut was a little threadbare.

Bondi was at Judit's elbow. "We shouldn't stay long. It's obviously not a good day."

Stein broke in. "Son, you don't know what a bad day is."

The nurse concurred. "This is one of Mr. Stein's good days. He's pleased that you've come. I can tell."

"So you know Anna. You're the historian. You're the one who made that movie with the German girl." He wiped his mouth with a shaking hand. "I don't suppose she'll come."

"You don't like Germans, do you?" Judit asked, cautiously.

"Young lady, I am a German," Stein said. "A historian should know better. All Jews are Germans to the bone, not like those fascists. That's the whole point of the project."

And one by one, all of Judit's questions came back to her, the questions she had compiled so carefully after they'd screened the rough cut of the documentary. What had happened in Moscow? Had he, in fact, been in a coma? Who had arranged for him to be transferred to this facility? How was it kept a secret? All of this had felt pressing and important once, but now it felt irrelevant. Who needs yet more evidence that Soviets were brutal occupiers and that Stein, the visionary, had survived them?

"So," Stein said, "let's see it."

"See what?" Judit asked. She had lost track of where she was.

Bondi broke in. "Surely you've already watched it, Mr. Stein."

Stein laughed. That made him cough again. "Of course I have, young man. What an idea! But not with the girl who made it. I suppose," Stein said, "she wants to tell me everything she left on the cutting room floor." He said to the nurse, "You remembered the projector?"

"Of course I did," the nurse said. "But it's an old one. I'm not sure it'll work."

"Then bring it in," said Stein. "We'll have to see for ourselves."

While they were waiting, Bondi drew Judit aside and whispered, "What do you think will happen when he sees that gift you brought him?"

"I don't know," said Judit.

"What if he has another stroke? What if it kills him?"

"What does that matter to you?" Judit asked.

She raised her voice in a way that drew the attention of the nurse, who said, "Mr. Stein requests that he and the filmmaker have a little privacy. That is, if you don't mind."

"What if I mind?" Bondi said.

His tone was frankly confrontational, and the nurse was surprised. Then he assessed the situation, and addressed Bondi as a Stasi colleague. "The old man gets his way. He can't do much these days, but at least he can look."

Bondi said to Judit, "Come back to the room."

"Afterwards," said Judit. "I'll be there afterwards."

"That's too late," Bondi said.

* * *

She didn't know what he meant. She also wasn't sure what the nurse meant until both men had gone, and Judit set up the projector and took the canister out of her bag. Stein watched and she could feel his liquid eyes all over her. The quality of his attention was so profoundly sexual that it didn't seem connected to the wreck in bed. It was hard to thread the film into that antique projector, to check the light. The machine worked, but it made an awful sound and smelled like something burning.

Stein said, "Sit by me, honey. So you can tell me what you see."

Judit did, on the edge of the mattress, and she watched Stein rather than the film, and gradually, he must have known it wasn't what he'd expected because he turned towards the projection on the wall. His arms tightened around the pillow, and he leaned forward. That was when Judit said, "I see a pit. I can't see its bottom. It's on the site of the Great Synagogue of Dresden, the one left as an open field. White things are falling into the pit, one at a time."

"We couldn't shoot the film close up," Stein said. "Too risky." He sounded thoughtful, as though he were talking to himself. After a few minutes, he cupped his chin, a gesture so embedded in his iconography that Judit lost track of the room and the projection as the screen-Stein cupped that same chin through a growth of beard.

"I see you with young people," Judit said. "Survivors. You're speaking Yiddish."

"The mother tongue," Stein said.

The rest of the film passed before them both in heavy silence. Judit hadn't realized that Stein had taken her hand until she felt his fingers tighten. The celluloid flapped in the old projector, and Judit made a move to switch it off and turn the light back on, but Stein wouldn't let go of her hand.

"That takes me back," he said.

Some quality had gone out of his voice. Judit couldn't make out the contours of his face now; it was as though his features had lost focus. It felt like a retreat, and Judit couldn't help but let her anger show. "That's what you have to say?"

"I wish I were young again." Stein stroked her hand, even as he held it, and he said, "Those days can't come back. It all felt clear, didn't it, the way forward."

"To make them bleed," said Judit.

"Back then, it was the time and place. We weren't angels and we weren't demons. We were men. We were flesh and blood, and now," said Stein, half in a whisper, "now we're all machines." He released Judit's hand and raised his loose-fleshed, thin white arms, extending tubes that ran up to clear bags hooked on a gurney. "There's a machine that keeps my heart beating and a machine that helps me breathe and a machine that takes away my bad blood and replaces it with good blood. I think that young man you brought here came to kill me. I know the type. He's an assassin." He lay back on the bed and closed his eyes. The liver spots on those arms looked all the darker in the strange, pale light of the projector. He whispered, "Maybe you could save him the trouble, do me a favor, pull the tubes out yourself."

"I want to make this information public," Judit said.

"Sure. Go ahead. *Goyim* kill *goyim* and they blame the Jews. It's who we are."

"As Stephen Weiss would say," Judit ventured, and then she thought she saw a ghost of a smile pass across Stein's face.

"Ah, Weiss. Well, he said a lot of things."

"He said we don't bow down."

"Ah, yes. He did say that. He's wrong. That's not how we live," Stein said. "That's how we die. Always, we must be on the side of life, of reason, and we must be human and we must be loved. Isn't that true? Don't we need to be loved?"

The voice that Judit heard no longer seemed to be coming from Stein at all, but from another place, a place he built a bridge to. It held a familiar note that she was loath to recognize. It was a dead voice, disembodied. The figure stretched back on that bed had nothing to do with what came out of it.

"That's what's left. I'm just a man. And I remember what a man remembers. Then, you reach the end, and you take ownership. You own up."

Judit addressed that man as best she could, though she felt her own voice straining against a current. "I want to take the film across the border. Maybe someone there will know what to do with it."

"Maybe. And then they'll mark the place where it happened. That's a way to lose a memory. Make a memorial. Make it somebody else's business. He was right there, wasn't he, our friend Weiss. Is he really dead, Anna? Out there in the *galut?* In Argentina?"

Long ago, Stein had released Judit's hand, and as she came back to herself, she realized that she was sitting in the dark. The only sounds were what she'd previously disregarded: the pulsing machines, the motor of the old projector, and the small, hoarse breathing that might just as likely have been coming from her as from the figure on the bed. Although the conversation had come to an end, she stayed there for a while. Then, she got up, rewound the film, placed it back in the metal canister, and switched off the projector. It was almost a shock to find the door still there, and a bright, alien corridor that led into the open.

3

IT wasn't easy to find the way back to her room. Without a guide, she walked down the wrong hallway, passing open doors and beds with no one in them. Of course, the whole wing was unoccupied. How could it be otherwise? The spa existed only to house Stein. It would be instructive to reproduce the chain of circumstances, from the supposed stroke in Moscow to the elaborate creation of a prison staffed with medical professionals, and finally to the reason why he had been kept alive at all. Yet that was not her task. Rather, she thought about the view from the window of her room. Could she find that river and bridge, and Poland? She'd have a week.

But she'd have to buy time. Bondi would never let her out of his sight. She knew that now. What if she just gave him what he wanted? It was no great loss. After all, the footage meant nothing on its own. She would need witnesses who would come forward, who could confirm events, not Stein, but others she might find if she crossed Poland and made it into Russia, if she gathered transcripts and authentic documents, the canister of film would be irrelevant. Finding all of this would be lonely work. Still, it would be her work, again.

She would have to be careful, though. Even as she knew this, something in her beat it back. She didn't want to be careful. She wanted to be honest. By the time she finally ran into a young man in scrubs, she said, "I'm lost," and the man recognized her and politely led her back to her room. Bondi had already unpacked both suitcases and sat on the bed, looking grim. Outside, the meadow and the woods were blue with twilight.

"You're angry," Judit said.

"No," said Bondi. "Just disappointed."

"Here," Judit said. "Just like I promised." She handed him the canister, and he took it without a word. She added, "You know, he thinks you're here to kill him."

"What's the point?" Bondi said, still not looking at her. There was an edge to his voice. Then, "I ordered us dinner. They serve it here in the room."

"It's a beautiful evening. Can't we take a walk?"

"You need to start eating regular meals," Bondi said.

"You're at least five years younger than me, Joseph. Stop pretending to be my father. I don't like it."

She did eat the food that was brought by that same young man in scrubs, her first full dinner in what felt like half a lifetime, salad and bread and chicken and green beans, apple strudel with vanilla ice cream, all rolled in on a table and served with a wine that made Judit just drunk enough to wish life were less complicated. Bondi thawed a little. She told him about Steinsaltz smashing that glass, and he said, "That sounds like him. The man's a brute."

"Are you a brute?" Judit asked carefully.

"No, I'm not," said Bondi.

"You are in bed," Judit said. Then she wished she hadn't said it because it implied that other things would happen, and set up an expectation she suspected neither could fulfill.

That was the case. After the orderly removed the table, they shared that narrow bed, and what she'd said was half a wish and half a curse. How clear is the border between the world in bed and out of bed? What if that border opens unawares and everything her body tells her becomes just as true as what her spirit knows? She was afraid of Bondi now. No, even if she hadn't accurately named who this man was to her, she'd always been afraid. Since the death of Hans, bringing her whole self forward to cross the border of that fear was what love had become for her. That was life after death, what she could face, but there were some things she couldn't face and couldn't name or they would become true. Bondi and Judit both lay naked under the thin hospital blanket. His back gave off familiar acid heat, and Judit knew that if she reached out to him, he'd respond, and if he reached out to her, she'd respond, but neither moved.

At some point, Judit must have fallen asleep. When she woke up, it was well past daybreak. Bondi stood over her, already dressed.

"I've scheduled something for this morning."

She blinked sleep out of her eyes. "Joseph, I think I should just go home."

"I've scheduled something," Bondi said again. "Since we're here." His face looked strange, tight around the mouth and eyes. She felt groggy and irritable, and then she looked past him.

She was in a different room. That much was clear. And what she'd thought was sunlight was a long fluorescent lamp above her head. A black monitor hung on a gurney, and beyond that, a gray curtain separated Judit from the door. "Was there something in the food?" Judit asked, and then she couldn't speak at all, because the curtain parted.

The technician's neat gray hair was arranged in a perfect dome. Her uniform was covered by a gray tunic, and she looked at Judit without recognition. She said, "So it's a high-risk pregnancy? Sixteen weeks along?"

"That's what we need to find out," Bondi said. "Whether we need to terminate."

"Well, it's high time we took a look," said the technician, and from a tube, she squeezed a length of gel on Judit's stomach, and reached for her device.

Judit found her voice. "I can't take a look, Joseph. Don't let her. You have the film already. What do you want from me?"

Bondi exchanged a glance with the technician, and by then, Judit knew she'd been strapped to the table. She craned her neck and closed her eyes but she could feel the dull pressure, and heard the static, and as the device moved off in its own direction, she pulled at the restraints and arched her back and cried with all her strength:

"I won't do anything to hurt her! I don't want to know!"

Judenstaat

THE cemetery was on the outskirts of Dresden. Because both Leonora and Judit had planned the outing well in advance, they had coordinated schedules, allowing for a late-morning trip and lunch in a café across from the gate. Leonora had gotten the day off from work, and was pleased and surprised that Judit didn't need to be reminded.

But her daughter was far more thoughtful these days. She kept—what was the term?—banker's hours. The amazing thing was that in spite of her new prominent position as director of the National Museum, Judit seemed to have more time for little things. She'd help with grocery shopping. She'd watch television with her in the evenings. On Sundays, she'd even do laundry, though Leonora always had to make sure she separated the more delicate fabrics.

"You'd think, all those beautiful things you have, you'd take better care of them," she said, although most of that clothing gathered dust now. She also said, "I wish you'd cut your hair again. It looked so nice, that short style."

"It didn't grow out well," Judit said, and that was true. It sprang out in all directions, and the highlights looked cheap and ragged.

She took to tying it back with a rubber band. When Leonora got the nerve to bring up the question of the man who'd been in her life, Judit had shrugged and said, "He didn't grow out well either."

Leonora felt close enough to Judit to ask, "What does that mean?"

And she felt close enough to reply, "Mom, he was married."

"Then good riddance to him," Leonora said, feeling daring and proud, especially considering the little gift he'd left her daughter with, and when the October *yartzeit* approached, she said, "Are you sure you're up to making the trip?"

"I'm looking forward to it," Judit said. She seemed to mean it. She even dressed up, for her mother's sake, in one of the skirts she had let out so it would fit under a loose T-shirt and nice blazer. "Will this do, Mom?" she asked.

"You look lovely, Judi," Leonora said. "But are you sure they won't miss you at work?"

"They've had enough notice," Judit said.

"Well, they miss me," said Leonora. "I had to practically threaten to quit to get today off." In fact, just as Judit seemed to have more time in her hands, Leonora had less; the people in that neighborhood were completely out of control now, half of them demanding copies of their family immigration records to claim land or property in Poland, and the other half barricading themselves into housing blocks. She almost wished the nursing home would hurry up and close, but now she had to bear up under all the complaints and find a way to appease them. But there was no appeasing black-hats. That was old news. She said to Judit, "Isn't that right? That there's no way to appease them?"

"Sure," said Judit. Well, they could protest now, but when the capital was moved to Berlin, see how far they'd get. Leonora asked Judit if that would stop their complaining, and again, Judit said, "Sure."

"I hear they're going to bring back the trams," Leonora said as they boarded the bus that went along the Elbe. Leonora always felt nostalgic when she took that route because it was the same route as the first tram-line that was unveiled in '49, the year that she and Rudi moved into their apartment. Of course, these trams would be brand-new, manufactured in Hamburg, but she hoped they'd still have those little bells, and the machines that made a satisfying crunch when you validated a ticket. Maybe they'd bring back the tourist train, too. She still remembered how the children competed to be engineers who wore those little visors, and held up the green or red signals to make the steam trains stop or go or change direction. They ought to run that train up the Elbe to the new National Park of Saxon and Jewish Heroism. Wouldn't the tourists appreciate it? An old-fashioned, Judenstaat coal-powered steam train, run by children, to a beautiful park in Saxon Switzerland?

"You may be right," Judit said. Leonora hadn't even been aware she'd spoken out loud. But she asked Judit:

"Can't you do something about it? In your position?"

Judit laughed, though not unkindly. "Mom, what exactly is my position? You know what I do? I sit behind a desk and watch things fly across it. Sometimes, I'm supposed to catch them with my pen and sign them."

"You don't read what you sign?"

"Don't sound so shocked. I'll be honest with you. There's just too much to read. My eyes can't take it."

"You should wear glasses," Leonora said helpfully. She didn't want to sound judgmental, but it was always good policy to know what you were signing. That was the trouble with people these days, especially politicians who just forged ahead without a clear idea of what was around the corner. Well, they say the future is an undiscovered country, but as for her, she'd just as soon not go there without some certainty that it would be better than the past.

Last June, when they televised Leopold Stein's funeral, the foreign dignitaries crowded into Parliament, representatives from

Europe, America, Asia, Africa. That was something, seeing those Africans in their robes, so dignified. It made her think about how all the world knew who Stein was and what he represented. There was a leader—lived long enough to own up to his mistakes. Who'd do that now? Most politicians, they just hope their mistakes will become last week's news.

Well anyway, Judit did look happy, and it wasn't true about her eyes. She'd always had perfect vision, just like her father. She could see a thimble in a treetop. Then, following that train of thought, Leonora said, "It's good to see you sewing again, sweetheart."

"It passes the time," said Judit. "And when you got me that fabric, what was I supposed to do with it? Hang it out the window?"

Leonora had thought hard before she'd given it to Judit, a soft cotton blend with little yellow ducks in a row. Was it too forward? Well, what could a mother do, under those circumstances? Maybe she should have waited until afterwards, when she would know that everything was fine, but frankly, it had meant something to her to buy it, especially when she found the old fabric store where she and Judit used to shop together, the one with the embroidered butterflies in the window. It wasn't easy to spot, embedded between a video rental store and a fancy bakery, almost invisible if you didn't look carefully. The lady recognized her and asked, "Where's your daughter?" When Leonora chose the fabric, she said, "That's very popular, especially if people aren't sure." She'd meant sure if it would be a boy or girl, of course. Then, she said, "*Mazel tov,*" and for at least a moment, Leonora had allowed herself the unambiguous *naches* that was the right of any woman with a grandchild on the way.

The bus was at the cemetery gate now. Leonora and her daughter disembarked. It was just as she'd remembered it, the ironwork over the entrance, the wide, swept sidewalk, and of course the old Saxon ladies selling clumps of violets. Judit bought three.

"That's too many," Leonora said. "Besides, they're out of season. They won't even have a scent."

"Yes they do. Smell," Judit said. She offered Leonora a bunch, and she waved them away.

"They'll smell like somebody's refrigerator." She pushed ahead. "I hope I can find it. I always get so confused once I get here. Better you should have gotten a map than violets."

"We have all day," said Judit. She arranged the wet bunches of violets in the crook of her arm, and with her free hand, guided her mother towards the end of the cemetery where Rudolph Ginsberg was buried.

Of course, there were cemeteries in Dresden proper, the old Jewish cemetery in the Altstadt, and the new Jewish cemetery in the Neustadt, but they both were full long before Leonora and Rudolph even thought about purchasing a plot. This one had been established just after the war, so the lettering on some of the headstones was as likely to be in Yiddish as in German. There was even Cyrillic on a few of them; Red Army soldiers had sometimes been laid to rest here at the request of their families.

Looking at those Russian stones now, and at their condition, Leonora couldn't help but say, "Will they dig them up now, do you think?"

Judit didn't answer. She looked past her mother. "I see Daddy over there. Isn't that him?"

"You've got a younger head than your mother. That's him alright," she said. They both headed cross-wise towards the little bush that the cemetery had replanted at her request, to the rust and white marker that read: "Rudolph Ginsberg, 1919–1970" and the six-pointed star marking him as a camp survivor. Some of the stones contained the numbers of tattoos, a fashion in the '50s and '60s. Lenora couldn't help but say, "Judi, do you think they'll still put stars on markers?"

"Why wouldn't they?" Judit asked, somewhat sharply.

"Should I have one on my marker?" Leonora asked. "Honestly, what do you think?"

"I think that's up to you," Judit said. She seemed to grow thoughtful, and she and Leonora took their time, in silence, digging through dead leaves for stones to place on Rudolph Ginsberg's grave. After a while, Judit said, "Remember those drawers?"

"What drawers?" Leonora asked, blushing, but then she realized that she and her daughter were thinking about two different things.

"The ones at the Hygiene Museum," Judit said. "They were full of objects children swallowed, rocks, thumbtacks, that sort of stuff. He always said that the children who swallowed them had died long ago, but all those rocks and things were still around."

"That's awful. It must have scared you to death," Leonora said, but the memory warmed her. If he could be there now, standing with them and looking at his own grave, what would he say? One thing was certain; she would not be lonely. He would confuse her, would confound her, would say things no one in his right mind ought to say, but those very things would make each day a new one.

Judit began to walk away, and Leonora called, "You're not going to leave the violets?"

"Oh, I forgot," said Judit. "I guess they can die here too."

It was so like something Rudi would have said that Leonora couldn't help it. She laughed. What would her husband have made of the daughter who so resembled him? But then again, what would he make of this new world? What kind of country will their grandchild know? Rudi would want to protect that child and so would she, but now there was no safe place.

There was no safe place anywhere on earth. She had been foolish. After she'd gotten married, she'd let down her guard. Then Rudi died. Three years later, Judit brought that boy home, and Leonora knew. She'd seen it in his face, just like a vision, that he was more than just himself; he was a sign of something terrible, a forerunner of what was to come, and now that world was here. Yet if she was really honest with herself, she had to say that she had let even Hans disarm her. She'd seen light in Judit's face when she looked at him, and then, after those tragedies, she'd seen the way that young man had stood by her. Never would Hans have left Judit in this condition. Never in a million years.

And now, as was her way, Leonora didn't speak her mind, not really, but she did say something. "Judi, how can you stand it?"

"Stand what?" Judit asked. It was a reasonable question.

"These open borders. Knowing the monster who killed him is free as a bird. It isn't right. We both know it."

Judit was still holding those violets, maybe because she had forgotten to put them down, or maybe because she just liked holding them. Who knows? She used them as an excuse to hide her face, and her mother sensed she'd hit a nerve. When she lowered them, her eyes were wet. She said, "Sometimes, things aren't right."

"So we make them right," said Leonora.

"Well, that would be a different line of work," Judit said. She smiled a little. "Mom, I've always said, I'm just a technician. I piece things together and let other people figure out what it all means. And anyway, it wouldn't have mattered to Hans. One of the first things he said to me was that he didn't believe in justice." She laid a hand on Rudi's marker, lowered herself down with some difficulty, and placed the violets there.

"But Judi, sweetheart," Leonora said, "he couldn't have meant it. Of course Hans believed in justice. Everyone believes in justice. Honestly, what else is there to believe in?" She moved to help her daughter to her feet.

And Judit answered, "I believe in ghosts."

HISTORICAL TIMELINE

Over the last few decades, the history of Judenstaat has become, shall we say, disputed territory. The timeline that follows, taken from materials approved by the National Archives in Dresden in 1987, might serve as a foundation for some readers.

1908–1938: Birth of Leopold Stein in Munich. Theoretical and practical basis of Jewish state in Germany established through Stein's travels through his homeland and interaction with Jews throughout Central and Eastern Europe. Alliance with Socialist Labor Bund in Poland and Lithuania. Rise of fascism in Germany.

1945: Liberation of Germany and its conquered territories by Allied forces. Stein meets in Yalta with Roosevelt, Churchill, and Stalin and gains informal approval of plan to establish Jewish homeland on territory of Saxony bordering Germany, Poland, and Czechoslovakia.

April 4, 1948: The nation of Judenstaat established.

1948–1950: Occupation of Judenstaat by Soviet liberators, and loans for rebuilding of capital in Dresden and other major urban centers financed by the United States.

1949: Population transfer of Saxon-German fascist sympathizers across the Brandenburg border to Germany. In-gathering of Jews from Displaced Persons camps in Germany, and neighboring Central and Eastern European countries, most notably Chasidim and other strictly religious Jews. Small Saxon minority remains.

1950: Against opposition from Yiddishists, German declared national language of Judenstaat.

1951: Stein's advisor, Stephan Weiss, unmasked as U.S. agent and flees the country. American businesses barred from Judenstaat. Campaign against Cosmopolitanism begins, coordinated by the Ministry of State Security.

1952: New Parliament completed on site of the old Cathedral in Dresden. Bundists voted into power by an overwhelming majority.

1953: Stein suffers stroke on the flight back from Joseph Stalin's funeral. Successors cultivate closer ties with the Soviet Union. Factories and businesses expropriated. Further emigration of Saxon population into Germany.

1953–1956: Saxon fascists based in villages and hillsides attack civilians throughout Judenstaat, staging night raids in major cities. Area along Czechoslovak border, formerly known as Saxon Switzerland, a base for terror attacks on Dresden.

1956: Fascist cells are broken through a network of informers coordinated through the State Security Police. Leaders are deported or imprisoned. In response to reports of weapons funneled from Germany, the Brandenburg border sealed and the Protective Rampart constructed.

1957–1967: Period of relative stability. Growth of Bundist Youth Movement, Bundist culture, discovery of important archeological evidence of Jewish settlement in Saxony.

1968: Judenstaat Defense Force joins Soviet army to defeat fascist uprising in neighboring Czechoslovakia. Reactionary and Cosmopolitan elements in Judenstaat initiate misinformation campaign that leads to domestic upheaval. Universities closed; coal miners strike; general curfew. Ringleaders apprehended and order restored.

1968–1980: New policy of liberalization opens trade with the West.

1983: Helena Sokolov of the Neustadt Party elected prime minister. Judenstaat gains status as a base for banking and trade.

1987: Country prepares for Fortieth Anniversary celebration.

ACKNOWLEDGMENTS

Six months before this novel's publication, we lost David Hartwell. It pains me to know that the book will enter the world without him.

The author would like to thank *Judenstaat*'s earliest readers, including Joseph Kenyon, who navigated through an impossibly rough draft, and other members of the Community College of Philadelphia Prose Writer's Group who gave crucial advice on early chapters. The novel was revised during a sabbatical from that same college during residencies at the Edward Albee Barn, I-Park, and Yaddo, and enriched by travel and research made possible by a grant from the National Endowment for the Arts. I spent a month at the Vilnius Yiddish Institute, where ex officio director and gadfly Dovid Katz struggled to honor complicated history in a country that would sooner sanitize its past; his highly unofficial tour of the Jewish partisan camp with ghetto fighter Fania Brantsovsky had a tremendous impact on this novel. Matthew Lyons's knowledge of German as well as leftist and Zionist history helped raise questions about the implications of this thought experiment, and S. L. Wisenberg, Gail Hochman, and Ethan Nosowsky's advice sharpened the book considerably until—as I put it later—"*Judenstaat* had a plot."

There is no way I can ever express the depth of my gratitude to Terry Bisson, who was the first person in the world of publishing who seemed to understand what I was doing and then helped me find others, including Hartwell and his assistant, Jennifer Gunnels, at Tor Books. A number of family members read *Judenstaat* in manuscript, and my mother, Laikee Zelitch, is not only a marvelous proofreader but also the model for Judit's mother, Leonora; she knows and doesn't mind, and it's about time I thanked her properly for being a model in so many other ways. Then, of course, there's my husband, Doug, my secret weapon, my sparring partner, and my great love, who puts up with my obsessions and cleans up after me as best he can, but understands that I can't ever throw anything away. *Welch Glück!*